THE FIREBRAND

The
FIREBRAND

by

GEORGE CHALLIS

HARPER & BROTHERS PUBLISHERS

NEW YORK

THE FIREBRAND

THE FIREBRAND

CHAPTER

1

LUIGI FALCONE at fifty-five had lost some hair from his head and some speed from his foot, but his shoulders were as strong and his hands almost as quick as in those days when he had been famous with spear and sword. Now, stepping back with a wide gesture of both sword and small target, he cried out, "Tizzo, you are asleep! Wake up! Wake up!"

Tizzo, given the name of Firebrand because his hair was flame red and his eyes were flame blue, looked up at the blue Italian sky and then through the vista of the trees toward Perugia which in the far distance threw up its towers like thin arms.

"Well, the day is warm," said Tizzo, and yawned.

But Tizzo himself was not warm. All the exercise of wielding the target and the long, heavy sword had hardly brought a moisture to his forehead or caused him to take a single deep breath, partly because he had been stepping through the fencing practice so carelessly and partly because—though he was neither tall nor heavy—he was muscled as supple and smooth as a cat.

"The day is warm but *you* are not warm, Tizzo!" exclaimed Falcone. "God has given you nothing but a pleasant sort of laughter. You lack two inches of six feet. I could button you almost twice inside of one of my jackets. Nothing but skill can make up for the lack of weight in your hand; and here I am giving you my time, teaching you my finest strokes, and yet you sleep through the work! If you could touch me twice with the point or once with the edge, I'd give you whatever you ask."

Tizzo stopped yawning and laughed that pleasant laughter which had commended him to the eye of rich Falcone fifteen years before when Luigi rode through the street of the little village. Through a swirl of fighting, scrambling lads he had heard screaming and laughter. The screaming came from a lad who had been cornered against a wall. The laughter came from a red-headed youngster who was pommeling the bigger boy.

So Falcone, stopping the fight, asked questions. The sound of that laughter had reminded him of his own childless years and empty, great house on the hill. To most Italians red hair and blue eyes would not have been attractive, but Falcone was one who always chose the unusual. That was why he had taken Tizzo home with him. The boy had no other name. Mother and father were unknown. He had simply grown up in the streets like a young wolf running along with many others of the same un-mothered kind; they were the brood of war which was scattered up and down Italy.

He had been a page, a valet, and then like the rightful son of the house of Falcone he had been educated with all care. Falcone, turning from war to the adventures of the study and the golden mines of Greek literature which were dazzling the wits of the learned throughout the Western world, had Tizzo trained in the same tongues which he himself had mastered. He was very fond of the slender youth, but that fire which had flamed in the lad when he ran wild through the streets of the village had grown dim. What he did was done well, without effort, without enthusiasm. And the big, headlong nature of Falcone was disgusted by that casual response, that ceaseless indifference.

Now, however, that old shimmer of flame blue glanced in the eyes of Tizzo as it had not shone for years.

"Shall I have the rest of the day to go where I wish and do what I please?" he asked. "If I touch you twice with the point or once with the edge, shall I have that gift?"

Falcone stared.

"What would you do with so many hours?" he asked. "You

[2]

could not travel as far as Perugia in that time. What would you do?"

Tizzo shrugged his shoulders.

"But you shall have what you please and a horse to take you on the way," said Falcone, "*if* you touch me—edge or point—a single time!"

Tizzo laughed and threw the target from his arm. "What? Are you giving up before you begin?" demanded Falcone.

"Why should I have that weight in my hand?" asked Tizzo. "Now—on your guard—"

And he came gliding at Falcone.

In that day of fencing, when men were set to ward off or deliver tremendous thrusts or sweeping cuts that might cleave through plate armor, there was generally a forward posture of the body, both arms thrust a little out. This caused stiffness and slowness, but it braced a man against every shock. It was in this manner that Falcone stood, scowling out of his years of long experience, at that flame-headed lad who came in erect and swift and delicately poised, like a dancer.

Falcone feinted with the point and then made a long sweeping cut which if it had landed, in spite of the blunted edge of the sword, certainly might have broken bones.

But the sword whirred through the empty air. Tizzo had vanished from its path. No, he was there again in flesh and laughter on the right. Falcone, growling deeply in his throat, made a sudden attack. Strokes downright and sidewise, dangerous little upcuts, darting thrusts he showered at Tizzo.

Sometimes a mere touch of steel against steel made the ponderous stroke of Falcone glance past its target, a hair's breadth from head or body. Sometimes a twist of the body, a short, lightning pass of the feet deceived the sword. Falcone, sweat streaming down his face, attacked that laughing shadow with redoubled might and in the midst of his attack felt a suddenly light pressure against his breast. He could hardly be sure for an instant. Then he realized that Tizzo had stepped in and out, moving his whole body more swiftly than most men could move the hand.

It was a touch, to be sure—with the point and exactly above the heart!

[3]

Luigi Falcone drew back a little and leaned on his blade.

"Quick! Neat! A pretty stroke! And worth not a straw against a man in armor."

"In every armor there are joints, crevices," said Tizzo. "Where is there armor through which a wasp cannot sting, somewhere? And where a wasp can sting the point of a sword can follow!"

"So?" said Falcone, through his teeth. He was very angry. He had a dim suspicion that for years, perhaps, this pupil of his had been playing idly through their fencing bouts. "Now, try again—"

He fell on guard. There would be no rash carelessness, now. His skill, his honor, almost his good name were involved in keeping that shadow dancer from touching him with the sword again. Well and warily, with buckler and ready sword, he watched the attack of Tizzo.

It was a simple thing. There was no apparent device as Tizzo walked straight in toward danger. But just as he stepped into reaching distance his sword—and his body behind it—flickered to this side and to that. A ray of sunlight flashed into the eyes of Falcone. Something cold touched him lightly in the center of the forehead. And Tizzo stood laughing at a little distance again.

Falcone wiped his forehead and looked at his hand as though the touch of the sword point must have left a stain of blood. His hand was clean, but his heart was more enraged.

"Have you been making a fool of me?" he shouted. "Have you been able to do this for years—and yet you have let me sweat and labor and scold? Have you been playing with me like a child? Take your horse and go. And stay as long as you please! Do you hear? As long as you please! I shall not miss you while you are away. Cold blood never yet made a gentle knight!"

He had a glimpse of Tizzo standing stiff and straight with the look of one who has been wounded deeply, near to the life.

But the anger of Falcone endured for a long time. It made him stride up and down through his room, glowering out the window, stamping as he turned in the corner. Now and again he knit his great hands together and groaned out with a wordless voice.

And every moment his rage increased.

He had rescued a nameless child from the streets. He had poured out upon the rearing of the youngster all that a man

[4]

could give to his own son. And in return the indolent rascal had chosen to laugh up his sleeve at his foster father!

Falcone shouted aloud. A servant, panting with fear and haste, jumped through the doorway.

"Tizzo! Bring him to me! On the run!" cried Falcone.

The broad face of the servant squinted with a malicious satisfaction. He was gone at once, and Falcone continued his striding with his rage hardening, growing colder, more deadly, every moment.

It was some time before the servant returned again, this time sweating with more than fear. He had been running far.

"He is not in his room," reported the man. "He is not at the stables or practicing in the field at the ring with his lance. He has not even been near his favorite hawk all day. He was not with the woodmen, learning to swing their heavy axes—a strange amusement for a gentleman! I ran to the stream but he was not there fishing. I asked everywhere. He has not been seen since he was fencing in the garden—"

Falcone, raising his hand, silenced this speech, and the fellow disappeared. Then he went to the room of Tizzo to see for himself.

The big hound rose from the casement where it was lying, snarled at the intruder, and crossed to the high-built bed as though it chose to guard this point most of all. Falcone, even in his anger, could not help remembering that Tizzo could make all things love him, men or beasts, when he chose. But how seldom he chose! The old master huntsman loved Tizzo like a son; so did one or two of the peasants, particularly those woodsmen who had taught him the mastery of their own craft in wielding the ax; but the majority of the servants and the dependents hated his indifference and his jests, so often cruel.

Falcone saw on the table in the center of the room—piled at either end with the books of Tizzo's study—a scroll of cheap parchment on which beautiful fresh writing appeared.

In the swift, easy, beautiful smooth writing of Tizzo, he read,

Messer Luigi, my more than father, benefactor, kindest of protectors, it is true that I have no name except the one that I found in the street. And yet I feel that my blood is not cold—

[5]

Falcone, lifting his head, remembered that he had used this phrase. He drew a breath and continued.

—and I have determined to take the permission which you gave me in your anger today. I am going out into the world. I think this afternoon I may be close to an opportunity which will take me away—in a very humble service. I shall stay in that service and try to find a chance to prove that my blood is as high as that of an honest man. If my birth is not gentle, at least I hope to show that my blood is not cold.

The wine and the meat of your charity are in themselves enough to make me more than a cold clod. If I cannot show that gentle fare has made me gentle, may I die in a ditch and be buried in the bellies of dogs.

Kind Messer Luigi, noble Messer Luigi, my heart is yearning, as I write this, to come and fling myself at your feet and beg you to forgive me. If I laughed as I fenced with you, it was not that I was sure of beating you but only because that laughter will come sometimes out of my throat even against my will.

Is there a laughing devil in me that is my master?

But if I came to beg your forgiveness, you would permit me to stay because of your gentleness. And I must not stay. I must go out to prove that I am a man.

Perhaps I shall even find a name.

I shall return with honor or I shall die not worthy of your remembering. But every day you will be in my thoughts.

Farewell. May God make my prayers strong to send you happiness. Prayers are all I can give.

From a heart that weeps with pain, farewell!

Tizzo

There were, in fact, a number of small blots on the parchment. Falcone examined them until his eyes grew dim and the spots blurred. Then he lifted his head.

It seemed to him that silence was flowing upon him through the chambers of his house.

CHAPTER

2

AT THE village wineshop, which was also the tavern, a number of ragged fellows were gathered, talking softly. They turned when they saw one in the doublet and hose and the long, pointed shoes of a gentleman enter the door; and they rose to show a decent respect to a superior. He waved them to sit again and came down the steps to the low room with his sword jingling faintly beside him.

Now that he was well inside the room and the sunlight did not dazzle the eyes of the others, they recognized Tizzo.

They remembered him from the old days, as keen as a knife for every mischief. They remembered that he had been one of them —less than one of them—a nameless urchin on the street, a nothing. Chance had lifted him up into the hall of the great, the rich Luigi Falcone. And therefore the villagers hated him willingly and he looked on them, always, with that flame-blue eye which no man could read, or with that laughter which made both men and women uneasy, because they could never understand what it might mean.

Now he walked up to the shopkeeper, saying: "Giovanni, has that stranger, the Englishman, found a manservant that pleases him? One that is good enough with a sword?"

Giovanni shook his head.

"He put them to fight one another. There were some bad cuts and bruises and Mateo, the son of Grifone, is cut through the

[7]

arm almost to the bone. But the Englishman sits there in the back room and laughs and calls them fools!"

"Give me a cup of wine, Giovanni."

"The red?"

"No. The Orvieto. Red wine in the middle of a hot day like this would boil a man's brains."

He picked up the wine cup which Giovanni filled and was about to empty it when he remembered himself, felt in the small purse attached to his belt, and then replaced the wine on the counter.

"I have no money with me," he said. "I cannot take the wine."

"Mother of Heaven!" exclaimed Giovanni. "Take the wine! Take the shop along with it, if you wish! Do you think I am such a fool that I cannot trust you and my master, Signore Falcone?"

"I have left his house," said Tizzo, lifting his head suddenly. "And you may as well know that I'm not returning to it. The noble Messer Luigi now has nothing to do with my comings and goings—or the state of my purse!"

He flushed a little as he said this, and saw his words strike a silence through the room. Some of the men began to leer with a wide, open-mouthed joy. Others seemed turned to stone with astonishment. But on the whole it was plain that they were pleased. Even Giovanni grinned suddenly but tried to cover his smile by thrusting out the cup of wine.

"Here! Take this!" he said. "You have been a good patron. This is a small gift but it comes from my heart."

"Thank you, Giovanni," said Tizzo. "But charity would poison that wine for me. Go tell the Englishman that I have come to try for the place."

"You?" cried Giovanni. "To become a servant?"

"I've been a master," said Tizzo, "and therefore I ought to make a good servant. Tell the Englishman that I am here."

"There is no use in that," said Giovanni. "The truth is that he rails at lads with red hair. You know that Marco, the son of the charcoal burner? He threw a stool at the head of Marco and drove him out of the room; and he began a tremendous cursing when he saw that fine fellow, Guido, simply because his hair was red, also."

"Is the Englishman this way?" asked Tizzo. "I'll go in and announce myself!"

Before he could be stopped, he had stepped straight back into the rear room which was the kitchen, and by far the largest chamber in the tavern. At the fire, the cook was turning a spit loaded with small birds and larding them anxiously. A steam of cookery mingled with smoke through the rafters of the room; and at a table near the window sat the Englishman.

Tizzo, looking at him, felt as though he had crossed swords with a master in the mere exchange of glances. He saw a tall man, dressed gaily enough to make a court figure. His short jacket was so belted around the waist that the skirts of the blue stuff flared out; his hose was plum colored, his shirtsleeves—those of the jacket stopped at the elbow—were red, and his jacket was laced with yellow. But this young and violent clashing of colors was of no importance. What mattered were the powerful shoulders, the deep chest, and the iron-gray hair of the stranger. In spite of the gray he could not have been much past forty; his look was half cruel, half carelessly wild. Just now he was pointing with the half consumed leg of a roast chicken toward the spit and warning the cook not to let the tidbits come too close to the flame. He broke off these orders to glance at Tizzo.

"Sir," said Tizzo, "are you Henry, baron of Melrose?"

"I am," answered the baron. "And who are you, my friend?"

"You have sent out word," said Tizzo, "that you want to find in this village a servant twenty-two years old and able to use a sword. I have come to ask for the place."

"You?" murmured the baron, surveying the fine clothes of Tizzo with a quick glance.

"I have come to ask for the place," said Tizzo.

"Well, you have asked," said the baron.

He began to eat the roast chicken again as though he had finished the interview.

"And what is my answer?" asked Tizzo.

"Redheads are all fools," said the baron. "In a time of trouble they run the wrong way. They have their brains in their feet. Get out!"

Tizzo began to laugh. He was helpless to keep back the musical

[9]

flowing of his mirth, and yet he was far from being amused. The Englishman stared at him.

"I came to serve you for pay," said Tizzo. "But I'll remain to slice off your ears for no reward at all. Just for the pleasure, my lord."

My lord, still staring, pushed back the bench on which he was sitting and started up. He caught a three-legged stool in a powerful hand.

"Get out!" shouted the baron. "Get out or I'll brain you—if there are any brains in a redheaded fool."

The sword of Tizzo came out of its sheath. It made a sound like the spitting of a cat.

"If you throw the stool," he said, "I'll cut your throat as well as your ears."

And he began to laugh once more. The sound of this laughter seemed to enchant the Englishman.

"Can it be?" he said. "Is this the truth?"

He cast the stool suddenly to one side and, leaning, drew his own sword from the belt and scabbard that lay nearby.

"My lords—my masters—" stammered the cook.

"Look, Tonio," said Tizzo. "You have carved a good deal for other people. Why don't you stand quietly and watch them carving for themselves?"

"And why not?" asked Tonio, blinking and nodding suddenly. He opened his mouth and swallowed not air but a delightful idea. "I suppose the blood of gentlemen will scrub off the floor as easily as the blood of chickens or red beef. So lay on and I'll cheer you."

"What is your name?" asked the baron.

"Tizzo."

"They call you the Firebrand, do they? But what is your real name?"

"If you get any more answers from me, you'll have to earn them," said Tizzo. "Tonio, bolt the doors!"

The cook, his eyes gleaming, ran in haste to bar the doors leading to the guest room and also to the rear yard of the tavern. Then he climbed up and sat on a stool which he placed on a table. He clapped his hands together and called out: "Begin, masters! Begin, gentlemen! Begin, my lords! My God, what a happiness it is! I have sweated to entertain the gentry and now they sweat to entertain me!"

"It will end as soon as it begins," said the Englishman, grinning suddenly at the joy of the cook. "But—I haven't any real pleasure in drawing your blood, Tizzo. I have a pair of blunted swords; and I'd as soon beat you with the dull edge of one of them."

"My lord," said Tizzo, "I am not a miser. I'll give my blood as freely as any tapster ever gave wine—if you are man enough to draw it!"

The Englishman, narrowing his eyes, drew a dagger to fill his left hand. "Ready, then," he said. "Where is your buckler or dagger or whatever you will in your left hand?"

"My sword is enough," said Tizzo. "Come on!"

And he fairly ran at the baron. The other, unwilling to have an advantage, instantly threw the dagger away; the sword blades clashed together, and by the first touch Tizzo knew he was engaged with a master.

He was accustomed to the beautifully precise, finished swordsmanship of Luigi Falcone, formed in the finest schools of Italy and Spain; he knew the rigid guards and heavy counters and strong attacks of Falcone; but in the Englishman he seemed to be confronting all the schools of fencing in the world. His own fencing was a marvel of delicacy of touch and he counted inches of safety where other men wanted to have feet; but the Englishman had almost as fine a hand and eye as his own, with that same subtlety in the engagement of the sword blade, as though the steel were possessed of the nerves and wisdom of the naked hand.

Moreover, the Baron Melrose was swift in all his movements, with a stride like the leap of a panther; and yet he seemed slow and clumsy compared with the lightning craft of Tizzo. The whole room was aflash and aglitter with the swordplay. The noise of the stamping and the crashing of steel caused Giovanni and others to beat on the door; but the cook bellowed out that there was a game here staged for his own entertainment, only. The cook, in an ecstasy, stood up on his table and shouted applause. With his fat hand he carved and thrust at the empty air. He grunted and puffed in sympathy with the failing strength of the Englishman—who now was coming to a stand, turning warily to meet the constant attacks of Tizzo; and again the cook was pretending to laugh like Tizzo himself as that youth like a dance of wildfire flashed here and there.

And then, feinting for the head but changing for the body suddenly, Tizzo drove the point of his sword fairly home against the target. The keen blade should have riven right through the body of Melrose. Instead, by the grace of the finest chance, it lodged against the broad, heavy buckle of his belt. Even so, the force of the lunge was enough to make the big man grunt and bend over.

But instead of retreating after this terrible instant of danger, he rushed out in a furious attack.

"Now! Now! Now!" he kept crying.

With edge and point he showered death at Tizzo, but all those bright flashes were touched away and seemed to glide like rain from a rock around the head and body of Tizzo. And still he was laughing, breathlessly, joyfully, as though he loved this danger more than wine.

"Protect yourself, Tizzo!" cried the cook. "Well done! Well moved, cat; well charged, lion! But now, now—"

For Tizzo was meeting the furious attack with an even more furious countermovement; and the Englishman gave slowly back before it.

"Now, Englishman—now, Tizzo!" shouted the cook. "Well struck! Well done! Oh, God, I am the happiest cook in the world! Ha—"

He shouted at this moment because the combat had ended suddenly. The Englishman, hard-pressed, with a desperate blue gleam in his eyes—very like the same flame-blue which was in the eyes of Tizzo—made at last a strange upward stroke which looked clumsy because it was unorthodox; but it was delivered with the speed of a cat's paw and it was, at the same instant, a parry, and a counterthrust. It knocked the weapon of Tizzo away and, for a hundredth part of a second, the point of the baron was directly in front of Tizzo's breast.

But the thrust did not drive home.

[12]

Tizzo, leaping away on guard, was ready to continue the fight; but then, by degrees, he realized what had happened.

"You could have cut my throat!" he said.

And he lowered his weapon and stood panting, leaning on the hilt of his sword.

"I would give," said Tizzo, "ten years of my life to learn that stroke."

The baron tossed his own blade away. It fell with a crash on the table. And now he held out his right hand.

"That stroke," said he, "is worth ten years of any life—but I was almost a dead man half a dozen times before I had a chance to use it! Give me your hand, Tizzo. You are not my servant, but if you choose to ride with me, you are my friend!"

Tizzo gripped the hand. The grasp that clutched his fingers was like hard iron.

"But," said the baron, "you have only come here as a jest—you are the son of a gentleman. Not my service—not even my friendship is what you desire. It was only to measure my sword that you came, and by the Lord, you've done it. Except for the trick, I was a beaten man. And—listen to me—I have faced Turkish scimitars and the wild Hungarian sabers. I have met the stamping, prancing Spaniards who make fencing a philosophy, and the quick little Frenchmen, and cursing Teutons—but I've never faced your master. In what school did you learn? Sit down! Take wine with me! Cook, unbolt the door and give wine to everyone in the shop. Broach a keg. Set it out in the street. Let the village drink itself red and drunk. Do you hear?

"Put all your sausages and bread and cheese on the tables in the taproom. If there is any music to be found in this place, let it play. I shall pay for everything with a glad heart and a happy hand, because today I have found a man!"

The cook, unbarring the door, began to shout orders; uproar commenced to spread through the little town; presently all the air was sour with the smell of the good red wine of the last vintage. But young Tizzo sat at the table with the baron hearing nothing, tasting nothing, for all his soul was staring into the future as he heard the big man speak.

CHAPTER

3

THEY had not been long at the table when a strange little path of silence cut through the increasing uproar of the taproom, and tall Luigi Falcone came striding into the kitchen. When he saw his portégé, he threw up a hand in happy salutation.

"Now I have found you, Tizzo!" he said. "My dear son, come home with me. Yes, and bring your friend with you. I read your message, and I've been the unhappiest man in Italy."

Tizzo introduced the two; they bowed to one another gravely. There was a great contrast between the immense dignity, the thoughtful and cultured face of Falcone, and the half handsome, half wild look of this man out of the savage North.

"It would be a happiness," said the Englishman, "to go any-where with my new friend, Tizzo. But this moment I am leaving the village. I must continue a journey. And we have been agree-ing to make the trip together."

Falcone sighed and shook his head.

"Tizzo cannot go," he said. "All that his heart desires waits for him here—Tizzo, you cannot turn your back on it."

Tizzo stood buried in silence which seemed to alarm Falcone, for he begged Melrose to excuse him and stepped aside for a moment with the younger man.

"It is always true," said Falcone. "We never know our hap-piness until it is endangered. When I found that you had gone, the house was empty. I read your letter and thought I found your honest heart in it. Tizzo, you came to me as a servant; you became my protégé; now go back with me and be my son. I mean it. There are no blood relations who stand close to me. I have far more wealth than I have ever showed to you. It is not with money that I wish to tempt you, Tizzo. If I thought you could be bought, I would despise and disown you. But I have kept you too closely to your books. Even Greek should be a servant and not a master when a youth has reached a certain age. And now when you return—I have been painting this picture while I hunted for you—you will enter a new life. Yonder is Perugia. I have friends in that city who will welcome you. You shall have your journeys to Rome to see the great life there. You shall enter the world as a gentleman should do."

Tizzo had started to break out into grateful speech, when the Englishman said, calmly but loudly, "My friends, I have heard what Messer Luigi has to say. It is my right to be heard also."

"My lord," said Falcone, "I have a right of many years over this young gentleman."

"Messer Luigi," said the Englishman, "I have a still greater right."

"A greater right?" exclaimed Falcone.

"We have pledged our right hands together," said the baron.

"A handshake—" began Falcone.

"In my country," answered the Englishman, "it is as binding as a holy oath sworn on a fragment of the true cross. We have pledged ourselves to one another; and he owes me ten years of his life."

"In the name of God," said Falcone, "how could this be? What have you seen in such a complete stranger, Tizzo?"

"I have seen—" said Tizzo. He paused and added: "I have seen the way down a beautiful road—by the light of his sword."

"But this means nothing," said Falcone. "These are only words. Have you given a solemn promise?"

"I have given a solemn promise," said Tizzo, glancing down at his right hand.

"I shall release you from it," said the baron suddenly.

"Ha!" said Falcone. "That is a very gentle offer. Do you hear, Tizzo?"

"I release him from it," said the Englishman, "but still I have something to offer him. Messer Luigi, it happens that I also am a

[15]

man without a son who bears my name. Like you, I understand certain things about loneliness. We do not need to talk about this any more.

"But I should like to match what I have to offer against what you propose to give him."

"Ah?" said Falcone. "Let us hear."

"You offer him," said the Englishman, "an old affection, wealth, an excellent name, a great house, many powerful friends. Am I right?"

"I offer him all of those things," agreed the Italian.

"As for me," said the baron, "the home of my fathers is a blackened heap of stones; my kin and my friends are dead at the hands of our enemies in my country; my wealth is the gold that I carry in this purse and the sword in my scabbard."

"Well?" asked Falcone.

"In spite of that," said the Englishman, "I have something to offer—to a redheaded man."

Tizzo started a little and glanced sharply at the baron.

Melrose went on: "I offer you, Tizzo, danger, battle, suspicion, confusion, wild riding, uneasy nights—and a certain trick with the sword. I offer that. Is it enough?"

Falcone smiled. "Well said!" he answered. "You have a great heart, my lord, and you know something of the matters that make the blood of a young man warmer. But—what is your answer, Tizzo?"

Tizzo, turning slowly from the Englishman to Falcone, looked him fairly in the eye.

He said: "Signore, I shall keep you in my heart as a father. But this man is my master, and I must follow him!"

CHAPTER

4

THEY had a day, said the baron, to get to a certain crossroads and they spent much of the next morning finding an excellent horse and some armor for Tizzo. Speed, said the baron, rather than hard fighting was apt to be the greatest requisite in the work that lay before them, therefore he had fitted Tizzo only with a good steel breastplate and a cap of the finest steel also which fitted on under the flow of his big hat. He carried, furthermore, a short, straight dagger which could be of value in hand to hand encounters and whose thin blade could be driven home through the bars of a visor or the eyeholes. He had taken, also, of his own choice, a short-handled woodsman's ax. This amazed the Englishman. He tried it himself, but the broad blade unbalanced his grasp.

"How can you handle a weight like that, Tizzo?" he asked. "You lack the shoulder and the hand to manage it."

Tizzo, with his careless laughter, loosened the ax from its place at his saddle bow and swung it about his head, cleaving this way and that. The thing became a feather. It whirled and danced. It swayed to this side and that as though parrying showers of blows—and all of this while in the grasp of a single hand.

"Practice will make even a bear dance!" said Tizzo. And then gripping the handle of the ax in both hands, he struck a thick branch from a tree under which the road passed at that moment.

The big bough fell with a rustling sound to the highway, and Tizzo rode on, still laughing; but the baron paused a moment to examine the depth and the cleanness of the wound and to try the hardness of the wood with his dagger point.

"God help the head that trusts its helmet against your ax, Tizzo," he said. "A battle ax is a thing I have used, but a woodsman's ax never."

"If a battle ax were swung for half a day to fell trees," said Tizzo, "the strongest knight would begin to curse it. But a woodsman will know the balance of his ax as you know the balance of your sword, and the hours he works teaches him to manage it like nothing. I've seen them fighting with axes too, and using them to ward as well as to strike. So I spent some time with them every day for years."

They came in sight now of a fork in the road, and as they drew closer a carriage drawn by four horses swung out of a small wood and waited for them.

"There are our friends," said the baron. "Inside that coach is the lad we're taking to a safer home than the one he's been in. His name is Tomaso, and that's enough for you to know about him. Except that to take him safely and deliver him will bring us a good, handsome sum of money for our purses."

"I shall ask no questions," agreed Tizzo, delighted by this touch of mystery.

About the coach, which was heavy enough to need the stronger of the four horses to pull it over the rutted, unsurfaced roads, there were grouped a number of armed men, two on the driver's seat and two as postillions, while another pair stood at the heads of their horses. And each one of the six, it seemed to Tizzo, looked a more complete villain than the other. They were half fine and half in tatters, with a good weight of armor and weapons on every man of the lot.

A slender lad in a very plain black doublet and hose with a red cap on his head was another matter.

"Tomaso, I've told you to keep inside the carriage," said the baron angrily, as he rode up.

"What does it matter where there's nothing but blue sky and winds to see me?" asked Tomaso, in a voice surprisingly light, so that Tizzo put down the age of the lad at two or three years younger than the sixteen or seventeen which had been his first guess.

"Whatever you may be in other places," said Melrose, sternly, "when you ride with me, I am the master. Get into the carriage!"

Tomaso, in spite of this sternness, moved in the most leisurely manner to re-enter the carriage, with a shrug of his shoulders and a glance of contempt from his brown eyes.

After he was out of sight, one of the guards refastened the curtains that shut Tomaso from view.

"Why," said Tizzo, "he's only a child."

The baron pointed a finger at him. "Let me tell you," he said, "that you're apt to find more danger in Tomaso than in any man you'll meet in the whole course of your life. To horse, my lads. I'm glad to see you all safely here; and I've been true to my promise and found a good man to add to our party. My friends, this is Tizzo. They call him Firebrand because his hair is red; but his nature is as quiet as that of a pet dog. Value him as I do—which is highly. He will help us to get to the end of our journey."

There were only a few muttered greetings. One fellow with a long face and a patch over one eye protested: "It's a bad business stirring up hornets and then waiting for them to sting; or making these long halts in the middle of enemy country. Already we've been noted."

"By whom, Enrico?" asked the baron. "Who would think of searching this place? And you covered the marks of the wheels when you drove the carriage into hiding?"

"I covered the marks well enough. But a dog uses its nose, not its eyes, and it was a dog that led the man into the wood."

"Did you catch the fellow?" asked the baron, anxiously.

"How could we? There was not a single horse saddled. He came on us suddenly, whirled about, and was off. I caught up a crossbow and tried for him but missed," answered Enrico. "He rode away between those hills, and ever since, I've been watching to see trouble come through the pass at us. I was never for making the halt."

"Tush," said Melrose. "Everything will be well. Did that stranger who spied on you—did he see Tomaso?"

[19]

"He did—clearly—and Tomaso shouted to him."

"By God, Enrico, do you mean that Tomaso recognized him?"

"I don't know. It seemed that way. Very likely, too, because a thousand men are hunting for—Tomaso."

The baron groaned and ordered an instant start. He left Enrico and Tizzo as a rear guard to follow at a little distance, out of the dust raised by the clumsy wheels of the carriage; for his own part, the baron of Melrose went forward to spy out the way.

As they started forward, their horses at a trot, Enrico turned his ugly face to Tizzo and said: "So my lord found his redhead, eh? You're the prize, are you?"

Tizzo had felt himself on the verge of a mystery. Now he was sure that he was involved in the mystery itself. For some definite and singular purpose, the baron certainly wanted him. It was above all strange that in Italy he should be looking for redheaded young men. Might it be that he intended to use Tizzo to impersonate another character? In any event, it was certain that the baron was not a man to bother over small scruples. And Tizzo determined to be more wakeful than a hungry cat. He had a liking for the baron; he respected his strength and his courage; he hoped that through him the golden door of adventure might be opened; but he half expected that the big man was using him as the slightest of pawns in some great game.

The carriage horses dragged their burden through the hills, where the road wound blazing white among the vineyards and the dusty gray of the olive trees, often silvered by a touch of wind. The day was hot, the work was hard, and presently the team had to be rested.

As they halted to take breath, the baron rode apart with Tizzo, and dismounting behind a tall stone wall, he pulled out his sword. "For the first lesson!" he said, and as Tizzo drew his own blade, Melrose showed him, with the slowest movement of the hand, the details of that maneuver which had opened the guard of Tizzo like a handstroke. For several minutes he studied and practiced that strange combination of ward and counterstroke. He had not mastered it with his hand but he understood it with his mind before they went back to the others.

[20]

Tizzo asked him, on the way, why he had not used the irresistible force of that ward and counter earlier during their encounter in the kitchen. At this the baron chuckled. "Because I'm a fool," he said. "I was enjoying the sight of your good swordsmanship too much to want the thing to end."

"Yes," agreed Tizzo, smiling. "And besides, you were wearing a lucky buckle."

"Luck is the best friend that any soldier ever had," answered the baron. "When you learn to trust it, you have learned how to be happy. But, Tizzo, trust me, also!"

He said this with a certain gravity that impressed his companion. But when the journey through the late afternoon commenced again, there was still a pregnant doubt in the mind of Tizzo. That matter of the search for the redheaded young man—that unknown role for which he had been selected weighed much on his mind.

He kept his concerns to himself, however, as they drew on into the cooler evening. A wind had begun in the upper sky, whirling the clouds into thin, twisted streamers, but it had not yet reached the surface of the ground.

The carriage was being dragged up a fairly easy slope when the baron halted it by raising his hand. He reined his horse back at the same time, calling: "Enrico, do you see anything in those trees?"

Enrico, staring fixedly at the small grove of willows—thick, pollarded stumps, exclaimed: "I can't see into the trees, but I can see a dust over them that the wind never put there."

Now that it was pointed out, Tizzo could see the same thing—a few drifting wisps of dust high above the tops of the trees. If the baron paid heed to such small tokens as these, it proved the intensity of his care.

"If we go on, the road takes us straight past that place," he said, "Cesare, ride into those trees and see what sort of birds you can stir up."

But before Cesare could stir to execute the order, something whirred in a streak through the air and Tizzo received a heavy blow against his breastplate. A broken quarrel dropped to the ground, the steel point of it fixed deeply in the armor; and Tizzo heard at the same time the humming clang of the crossbow string, which sounded from the edge of the wood. As though this were the signal, a shout burst out from many throats and the brush at the edge of the willows appeared alive with men.

CHAPTER

5

The baron shouted to get the horses turned. The team was swinging around when a full volley of half a dozen of crossbow bolts darted from the brush and stopped the maneuver. One of the team dropped dead. Two others, badly wounded, began to squeal and plunge, dragging the carriage to the side of the road and smashing a wheel against a rock.

"Charge before they reload!" shouted the baron. "Tizzo! Enrico! With me, friends!"

He set the example, yelling over his shoulder: "Andrea, hold Tomaso; the rest, follow me!"

The other fellows of the baron's troop left the carriage and ran on foot to help their master, four of them sword in hand. But Tizzo rushed at the side of Enrico toward the brush. Crossbowmen, usually lightly armored, would make easy game; but there were enemies of a different quality to deal with in the woods. For out of them rode no fewer than five men-at-arms in complete armor, lances at rest. Those on either side were equipped in the most complete fashion, but he in the center wore flowing plumes from his helmet and the evening light brightened on the rich inlay of his armor.

With closed visors, like five death's-heads, the horsemen charged, shouting: "Marozzo! Marozzo!"

It was a name that Tizzo knew very well. No man in Perugia, not even among the family of the high and mighty Baglioni, was richer than gallant young Mateo Marozzo, the last heir of his family name.

Anxiously, Tizzo glanced toward the baron, because it seemed a madness to engage, half armed as they were, with five fully equipped riders like these. Their long spears threatened quick death and an ending to the fight before sword or ax or dagger ever could come into play.

But Baron Melrose did not slacken his pace for all the odds against him. As the men-at-arms appeared, he merely stood up in his stirrups and shouted in a thundering voice: "Ah, ha! Melrose! Melrose! Strike in! Strike in!" And with this battle cry he rushed first of the three against his enemy, swinging his sword for a stroke. Enrico did not hang back; and Tizzo was last of the trio to come to action.

The spears were not so dangerous as they looked. Tizzo could see that at once. On smooth ground that charge of the five ponderous warriors would have overwhelmed the baron's men at once; but the brush, the uneven ground staggered the galloping horses and made the lances waver from a true aim. Tizzo, hurling himself toward that brilliant plumed figure in the center, grasped his woodsman's ax, rode seated high in his saddle, and at the last moment dipped low. The lance of his enemy drove over his shoulder; the backstroke of the ax, in passing, glanced off the polished shoulder armor, and descending on the mailed arm of the rider, knocked the spear from his grasp.

As he turned his horse, Tizzo could see the crossbowmen in the shrubbery struggling energetically to reload their weapons, but they were armed with those powerful arbalests whose cords were pulled back by the use of a complicated tackle of pulleys and rope. The fastest of them still did not have a second quarrel in place as Tizzo reined in his horse and flung himself again at the knight.

He saw, as he swerved, that Enrico's horse was falling; injured by a misdirected thrust of a spear; and big Baron Melrose had engaged with his sword two of the men-at-arms. As for the three fellows on foot, they had paused. They saw their master overmatched, one of his best fighters already dismounted, and the battle definitely lost, it seemed.

Those two glances were enough to discourage Tizzo. But, if he were to die, he was determined to die fighting. The plumed knight, wheeling toward him, had unsheathed a long sword and now drove in his horse at a trot, wielding the sword with both hands.

"Marozzo!" he was shouting. "Marozzo! Marozzo!"

And Tizzo answered with a yell of: "Melrose! Long live Melrose!"

Then he swung up the axhead to meet the terrible downward sway of the sword. A sure eye and a swift hand made that parry true. The sword blade shattered with a tinkling sound, splintering and breaking at the point of impact.

But Marozzo—if this were in fact he—was still full of fight. He could see his fourth companion whirling and running his horse at a gallop to come to the rescue, so the knight of the plumed helmet snatched a mace from his saddlebow and drove at Tizzo.

The first ax-stroke had glanced. The second would not, Tizzo swore—not if he had truly learned from the woodsmen how to strike to a line. He aimed at the central one of the three plumes and then struck like a whirling flash of light.

The blow was true and deep and good. As the blade bit in, a savage hope came up in Tizzo that he had cloven the skull of the leader of the ambuscade. But it was only the crest that he shore away, while from the heavier, conical steel of the helmet itself the ax glanced a second time.

The weight of that blow made the helmet ring like a bell; and Marozzo fell helplessly forward on the pommel of his saddle and the neck of his horse.

The course of the battle was instantly changed.

The trotting horse of Marozzo moved him from the next stroke of that flashing ax, which certainly would have been a death

[24]

blow. And as Tizzo swung his own horse about, with his cry of "Melrose! Melrose!" the four men-at-arms left off their individual battles and rushed to the rescue of their leader, who was sliding helplessly out of the saddle, stunned.

"Away!" shouted one of the ambushers. "Rescue the signore! Away, away! If he's dead, our necks will be stretched for it! Crossbowmen, cover us! The signore is hurt!"

In a moment the men-at-arms were withdrawing, one of them supporting their hurt master and the other three reining back their horses in the rear to keep a steady front against a new attack. The crossbowmen—there were eight of them in all—issued from the woods and fell in behind the riders, keeping their quarrels ready for discharge but making no offer to loose them at the baron's men. Quickly the entire troop was lost among the trees.

From the melee, two horses were left dead and one dying, but, what seemed a miracle, not a single man had received so much as a scratch. Luck had been with the baron and the plate armor of the men-at-arms had saved them. Only the leader had been injured to an unknown degree.

It was dusk before the dying horse was put out of pain; the carriage was abandoned; and with Tomaso mounted behind Melrose the party started on through the hills. The twilight gradually grew more and more dim and yet there had been light enough for Tomaso to look long and fixedly at Tizzo with a curious expression of admiration and hate in his brown eyes.

Baron Henry of Melrose was in high spirits in spite of the loss of the carriage. He said to Enrico: "You see what a redheaded man is worth, Enrico? And that was the famous knight Mateo Marozzo, you understand? Tell me, Tomaso! Was it not young Mateo? You ought to know his voice and he was shouting loudly enough until Tizzo tapped on his headpiece."

"I don't know," answered Tomaso.

He kept his one hand on the shoulder of the baron and the other gripped the high back of the saddle while Tomaso looked dreamily off across the hills.

"Answer me, Tomaso!" commanded the baron.

"My lord," said Tomaso, in his musical and quiet voice, "you

[25]

could not get an answer from me with whips. Let me be quiet with my thoughts."

This calm insolence seemed very strange to Tizzo; it was still stranger that the rough baron made no retort; but perhaps that was because the spirits of Melrose were naturally very high since their lucky escape.

Luck was the theme of his talk—luck and the swift hand and the courage of Tizzo—until the falling of night left them all in silence except for the steady creaking of the saddle leather. Finally Tomaso began to sing in a pleasant but oddly small voice, to which Tizzo listened with such a singular pleasure that he paid no attention to the words; the voice and the music fed in him a hunger which he had never felt before.

Presently on a hilltop vague towers loomed against the sky and toward these they made their way, entering the streets of a ruined village such as one could find frequently throughout Italy. Fire had ravished the place and all of the smaller houses were tumbled this way and that while grass had begun to grow in the streets. The castle which topped the height was only partially destroyed during the sacking of the place ten years before, and it was here that the baron intended to spend the night. In the courtyard they built a fire and roasted meat on small spits, like soldiers. Some skins of wine, warm and muddy from the jostling of the day's riding, were opened. And while they ate, Tizzo kept looking from the pale, handsome face of the silent Tomaso to the upper casements of the castle which stared down at the firelight with dark and empty eyes.

Melrose said briefly: "One more good night of watching, my friends, and we shall be far away from the grip of the Baglioni with our treasure. This night—and afterwards we shall be at ease. Keep a good ward. Tizzo will be here in the court until midnight, and Enrico at the door of Tomaso's room. At midnight I'll take the watch here. Tizzo, be wary and alive. If you hear so much as a nightingale's song, call me. Up, Tomaso, and follow me. You sleep in one of the rooms above."

"Why not here in the open, where it's cool?" demanded Tomaso.

"Because the night air might steal you, my lad," said the baron. And he led Tomaso from the court and through the narrow

[26]

black mouth of a postern door. Tizzo listened until the footfalls and the muffled chiming of steel had ceased.

But in his heart he had companionship enough. He had memories of this day which seemed to outweigh all the rest of his life. Two things stood out above the rest—the sword of the Englishman arrested in midthrust at his throat and that instant of incredible delight when the plumes had floated away from the crest of Marozzo and the steel helmet had rung with the stroke.

It must have been close to midnight when, as he turned the corner of the wall of the keep, he saw a slender shadow that trailed like a snake from an upper casement. He looked again, startled, and made sure that it was a rope of some sort which had just been lowered from the room of Tomaso!

CHAPTER

6

HE FOUND what the rope was by a touch—blankets cut into strips and twisted. And this fragile, uneven rope-end began to twitch and jerk suddenly. When he looked up, he saw a form sliding down the rope from the casement above.

Tizzo pulled the dagger from his belt and waited. He had that insane desire to laugh but he repressed it by grinding his teeth. Overhead, he heard a voice call out, dimly: "Tomaso! Hello—Tomaso!"

That call would not be answered, he knew, for poor Tomaso

was sliding, as he thought, toward a new chance for liberty. There was courage, after all, in the pale, brown-eyed boy. There was an unexpected force in the creature in spite of the undue softness of voice, whether in speaking or singing.

He kept his teeth gripped and grasped the dagger a little more firmly, also. He would not use the point; a tap on the head with the hilt of the dagger would be enough to settle this case.

Above him, the calling became that not of Enrico but of the baron himself, who shouted: "Tomaso! Where are you?"

Then Baron Melrose was bawling out the window above: "Ha! He is there! He is almost to the ground. Enrico, waken every one! Down to the court or the prize will be gone. Run! Run! Our bird is on the wing!"

The descending form, casting itself loose from the rope as it heard this cry, dropped the short distance to the ground that remained—and the arm of Tizzo was instantly pinioning the figure.

Tomaso, with the silence of despair, writhed fiercely and vainly; the head went back and the wild eyes stared up into the face of Tizzo.

And suddenly Tizzo breathed out: "Lord!" and recoiled a step as though he had been stabbed. Tomaso for an instant leaned a hand against the wall—the other was pressed to his breast. That hand against the wall carried a glimmer of light in the form of a little needle-pointed poniard.

"Listen, Tizzo!" stammered the voice of Tomaso. "You're only with them by chance. You're not one of them. Save me—and my people will make you rich! Rich!"

"Damn the wealth!" groaned Tizzo. "Madam—how could I keep from guessing what you are?—madam, I am your servant—trust me—and run in the name of God!"

Overhead, there were rapid feet rushing on the stairs; and "Tomaso" ran like a deer beside Tizzo around the corner of the keep and toward the horses, which had been left in a corner of the yard to graze on the long grass which grew through the interstices of the pavement. Some of them were lying down, others still tore at the grass.

"Can you ride—without a saddle?" gasped Tizzo.

"Yes—yes!" cried the girl.

He was hardly before her at the horses. Two bridles he found, tossed one to her, and jerked the other over the head of the best of the animals, a good gray horse which the baron himself had ridden that day. When that was on, with the throatlatch unsecured, he saw the girl struggling to get the bit of the second bridle through the teeth of another horse. He took that work from her hands, finished it with a gesture, and then helped that lithe body to leap onto the back of the gray.

Voices had burst out into the court, that of Enrico first of all. And he saw the forms running, shadowy in the starlight.

"Ride!" he called to the girl. "Ride! Ride!"

And as the gray horse began to gallop, Tizzo was on the back of the second bridled charger. The moment his knees pressed the rounded sides, he recognized one of the wheelhorses, the slowest of them all; and he groaned.

"What's there?" big Enrico was calling. "Who's there?"

"I!" he cried in answer. "Tizzo—and fighting for the lady."

It was too late for him to drive the horse through the gateway of the ruined courtyard; they were already on him, Enrico running first.

"The redheaded brat—cut him to pieces!" yelled Enrico. "The horses—get to horse and after her!"

And he aimed a long stroke at Tizzo, who caught it on his naked blade and returned a thrust that ran through the shoulder of the man. Enrico fell back, with a yell and a curse. Two more were coming; but in spite of its clumsy feet and bulky size, Tizzo had his horse in motion, now. He could hear the loud voice of the baron shouting orders as the heavy brute cantered through the gateway and then slithered and slid down the steep way outside, theatening to fall with a crash at every instant.

The girl was there—she was waiting just beyond the threshold of the first danger, crying out: "Are you hurt, Tizzo?"

She had heard the clashing of the swords, no doubt.

"Not touched!" he answered.

And they swept down the dangerous, bending way together. The huddled ruins of the town poured past them, like crouching figures ready to spring. They issued into the open country; and already the roar of pursuing hoofs sounded through the street of the village behind them.

Tizzo began to laugh. He sheathed his sword and waved his arm above his head. "We have won!" he shouted.

It seemed to him in the wildness of his happiness that he could pluck the brightness of the stars from the sky. But under him he felt the gallop of the carriage-horse already growing heavy. It would not endure. The poor brute was as sluggish as though running in mud fetlock-deep.

The girl had to rein in her light-footed gray to keep level with Tizzo.

"Go on!" he called to her. "This brute is as slow as an ox and they'll overtake it. But you're free. You've won. Ride for safety— go on!"

"If they find you, they'll kill you," cried the girl. "I won't leave you. If they catch you, Tizzo, I'll let them catch me, also!"

"They'd never spare me for your sake!" he shouted in answer. "Ride on!"

"I shall not!" came that clear voice in reply.

He drew the blundering horse closer to hers and leaned above her.

"I have started the work. Let me hope that it will be finished!" he exclaimed. "For God's sake and for mine, save yourself!"

As though to reinforce his words, the uproar of hoofs left the dull, echoing street of the village and poured more loudly across the open country.

"If they find you—" she protested.

But he laughed in that wild and happy voice. "They'll never find me. I have a lucky star—do you see there?—the golden one— it is favoring me now. Farewell! Tell me where to find you— and ride on!"

"Perugia!" she cried in answer. "You shall find me in Perugia. My name is—"

But here their horses thundered over the hollow of a bridge and the name was quite lost to him.

As they reached the roadway beyond, with loosed rein she was already flying before him, farther and farther in the lead; every stride that the fine gray gave carried her distinctly away from him. At the next bend of the road she was gone; and the flying hoofs from the village poured closer and closer behind Tizzo.

There was no use continuing on the back of that sluggard. He drew rein enough to make it safe to leap to the ground and then let the heavy blunderer canter on, diminishing speed at every jump, while the liquid jounced and squeaked audibly in its belly. Tizzo jumped behind a broken stone wall and lay still.

When the flight had passed him, he ran up to the top of the nearest hill, but the light was too dim for him to see anything. Only the noise of the galloping poured up to him from the darkness of the hollow, rang more loudly off the face of the opposite hill, and then dipped away and disappeared beyond.

Tizzo folded his arms and shook his head.

Ah, what a fool he had been not to see the truth before! Of course all of the others had known what she was. That was why their eyes had dwelt upon her in a certain way, following her hungrily. But he, Tizzo, had not known. And yet no matter what a fool he had been there remained in him an abiding resentment against the baron.

Neither was it all resentment, either. The heart of Tizzo poured out in admiration of that rash and valiant man who had set his single hand against such powers as those of the house of Marozzo. For with the name of Marozzo went that of Baglioni; the whole of Perugia was dominated by that noble family.

From Falcone, from Melrose, he had cut himself off. And if he went to Perugia—well, was it not likely that he would encounter the eyes of any one of the dozen men who had seen him with unvisored face in the battle of that day?

That did not matter. He knew that it was folly, but he also knew that nothing under a thunderstroke could keep him possibly from the town of Perugia.

She had made a handsome boy; she would be a gloriously beautiful woman. It seemed to Tizzo that there was nothing in the world he wanted so much as to hear, once more, her singing of that song which he had heard in the evening.

He walked down the hill, took the first road, and stepped along it at a brave pace toward distant Perugia.

[31]

———————————

It was a day of heat and of showers; and the old beggar at last drew in under a projecting cornice which kept him dry. His withered face was full of both malice and patience, and his throat was sore from the whining pitch at which he had been singing out his appeals for mercy since that morning. He had in his purse enough to buy him a good cloak, and wine and meat and bread for half a month, but he was disappointed because he had not picked up enough for an entire month. Old Ugo, secure under the cornice, leaning on his staff, was about to step out into the street again in spite of a slight continuing of the rain, but here a sprightly young man with a sword at his side and his hat cocked jauntily at an angle paused suddenly beside him and said: "Father, have you lived a long time in Perugia?"

"I have existed here for a little course of years, some fifty or sixty," said Ugo.

"If I describe a lady to you, shall you be able to tell me her name?"

"Try me," said Ugo. "But first why not advertise your name?"

"Because she has never heard it."

"She has not heard your name—but she will be glad to see you?"

"I hope so—I pray so—I earnestly believe so," sighed the young Tizzo.

"Well," said the beggar, "this is like something out of an old story. Perhaps love at first sight, love in passing, a look between you—and now you are hunting for her around the world. Describe her to me."

"I describe to you," said Tizzo, "a girl of about nineteen or twenty. She has eyes that are brown and big—gold in the brown like sunlight through forest shadows—and a sweet, pretty, perfect, delightful face—about so wide across the brow and with a smile that dimples, do you hear—"

"I hear," said Ugo, smiling steeply down at the ground.

"A smile that dimples in the left cheek only. The left cheek, you understand?"

"Perfectly, signore."

"Are you laughing at me?"

"I? By no means, signore. I was simply remembering certain things. Old men cannot help remembering, you know. Tell me more about her."

"The top of her head comes to the bridge of my nose. Her nose, by the way, is not exactly a straight, ruled, stupid line. It is altered from that just a trifle. It is tipped up a shade at the end. Just at that slight angle which makes smiling most charming. Do you understand me?"

"Perfectly, signore."

"Her complexion," said Tizzo, frowning as he searched for the proper words, "is neither too pale nor too dark. A trifle pale now, because of a little trouble, but with radiance shining through. She is slightly made. Not thin, do you hear; slenderly made but rounded. In her step there is the lightness of a cat, the pride of a deer, the grace of a dancer."

"Ah?" said the beggar.

"Do you recognize her?" asked Tizzo.

"Almost!" said the beggar. "Tell me a little more."

And he kept on smiling down at the ground.

"Her voice," said Tizzo, "is singular. Of a million ladies, or of a million angels, there is not one who can speak like her. And when she sings, the heart of a man grows big with joy and floats like a bubble. Do you hear? Like a golden bubble!"

"I hear you," said the beggar.

"Her hands," said Tizzo, "are small but not weak. They are hands which could rein a horse as well as use a needle."

"Ah?" said the beggar.

"And—I forgot—on her face, below the right eye, there is a little mark—not a blemish, you see—but a small spot of black; as though God would not give to the world absolute perfection or, rather, as though He would place a signature upon her; or as though through one fault he would make the rest of her beauty to shine more brightly. Am I clear?"

Ugo, the beggar, looked suddenly into the distance, squinting his eyes.

"Ah ha! You know her!" said Tizzo.

"I am trying to think. I shall go to see, signore. I shall go to a certain house and make sure. And then where shall I find you?"

"At that inn down the street. The one which carries the sign of the stag. I shall be there."

"Within a little while, I shall be with you, signore, and tell you yes or no."

"What is your name?"

"I am called Ugo, signore."

"Look, Ugo. You see this emerald which is set into the hilt of my dagger?"

"I see it very clearly. It is a beautiful stone."

"I swear to God that if you bring me to the lady, you shall have this stone for your own."

A faint groan of hungry desire burst from the lips of Ugo. In fact, he seemed about to speak more words but controlled himself with an effort.

"At the Sign of the Golden Stag—within an hour, I hope, signore."

And Ugo turned and strode up the street like a young man, because it seemed to him that, when he saw the emerald, he had looked into a green deeper than the blue peace of Heaven.

He continued on his way until he came to a great house where many horses were tethered and where there was a huge bustling from the court. Into this he made his way and said to the tall porter at the door: "My friend, carry word that Ugo, the beggar, has important word for Messer Astorre. It is a thing that I dare

[34]

not speak in the streets or to any ear except to that of Messer Astorre himself."

Then he added, "Or to my lord, Giovanpaolo."

At this second name the porter stopped his smiling.

"Messer Astorre," he said, "is engaged in talk with an important man. If I break in upon him, I must give some excuse."

"It shall be this," said Ugo. "Tell him that there is a beggar who is not a fool or crazy, but who dares to demand immediately to speak to him."

The porter hesitated, but the eye of the old man was burning with such a light that after a moment he was told to wait at the door while the porter went to announce him.

This was the way in which Ugo, after a time, passed through a door of inlaid wood and came into a room lighted by two deep windows, in one of which sat the famous warrior whose name at that time was celebrated throughout Italy—the great Astorre Baglioni. First the beggar glanced hesitantly and covetously all about him at the rich hangings which covered the walls of the room and then toward a pair of magnificent paintings done in the gay Venetian style. Afterwards he approached the noble Astorre, bowing profoundly and repeatedly.

"Your name is Ugo," said Messer Astorre, "and you have something to say to me?"

The second man in the room, a tall, darkly handsome fellow who had been striding around in an excited manner, shrugged his shoulders and looked out the window as though he could hardly endure the interruption.

"What I have to say is for the ear of my lord alone," said Ugo.

"Whatever is fit for me is proper for my friend, Mateo Marozzo, to hear," said the warrior.

"Messer Astorre," said Ugo, "it is a thing that concerns your sister, the Lady Beatrice, I believe."

Mateo Marozzo whirled about suddenly, with an exclamation and Ugo shrank a little.

"Be quiet, Mateo," said Astorre. "Don't frighten the man."

"The word was," said Ugo, "that the noble lady your sister was gone from the town, stolen away from it by thieves hired by some of the cursed house of the Oddi. But this very day a young man spoke to me in the street, described her, and offered me a jewel if I could find her for him."

"So?" said Astorre, smiling. Then he added: "My sister has been returned safely to the town. Who is this man who asked for her?"

"I do not know his name, my lord. He is a young man with red hair and eyes of a blue that shines like the blade of a fine sword, or like the blue underpart of a flame."

"Astorre!" Mateo called. "It is the man! It is the man! Give him to me!"

"Well, no doubt you shall have him if you want," said Astorre. "But who is he?"

"He is called Tizzo. I heard his name called out in the fight. He is the Firebrand. And it was he who knocked the wits out of my head with a lucky stroke of his battle-ax."

"Ah?" exclaimed Astorre. "Have the Oddi become so bold as this? Are they sending their agents like this into the middle of Perugia? Are they searching for Beatrice to steal her from us again? By God, Mateo, if we can catch this fellow, you *shall* have him. And if you don't tear out of him some information about the Oddi plans, call me a fool and a liar! My friend, where is this fellow?"

"At the Sign of the Golden Stag," said Ugo, beginning to tremble in body and voice as he realized that he had struck upon great news indeed.

"He is yours," said Astorre to Marozzo. "Go take him and do what you will with him."

CHAPTER

8

AT THE Sign of the Golden Stag a man whose face was roughed over with beard to the eyes was talking loudly in the big taproom. He had on a long yellow coat and pointed shoes of red; and he walked back and forth a little through the room, while all eyes followed him. The afternoon had grown so dark with rain that lamps had been lighted in the room and these cast an uncertain and wavering light. Tizzo followed the movements of the tall stranger with interest because he found the voice vaguely familiar, but not the face. He was wondering where he could have seen before that shaggy front; and in the meantime he sipped some of the cool white wine of Orvieto and listened to the stranger's talk. The beggar, Ugo, surely would soon return.

The man of the yellow coat was a doctor, it appeared, and he was peddling in the taproom some of his cures; for instance—"A powder made of the wing cases of the golden rose chafer, an excellent thing for cases of rheumatism. Let the sick man put four large pinches of this powder into a glass of wine and swallow off the draught when he goes to bed at night. The taste will not be good but what is bad for the belly is good for the bones." Or again the doctor was saying: "When old men find themselves feeble, their eyes watering, their joints creaking, their breathing short, their sleep long, I have here an excellent remedy. In this packet there is a brown powder and it is no less than the dried gall of an Indian elephant, which carried six generations of the family of a Maharajah on its back for two hundred years. And then it died not of old age but fighting bravely in battle. Now the merit, relish, and the source of an elephant's long life lies in its gall; and in this powder there is strength to make the old young again, and to make the middle-aged laugh, and to make the young dance on the tips of their toes."

Continuing his walk and his narration of wonders, the doctor happened to drop one of his many little packages on the floor beside the chair where Tizzo was sitting. And as he leaned to pick up the fallen thing he muttered words which reached Tizzo's ears only.

"Up, you madman! Away with me. Your face is known in Perugia and every moment you remain here is at the peril of your life."

The doctor, saying this, straightened again and allowed Tizzo to have a glimpse of flame-blue eyes which he remembered even better than he had remembered the voice.

It was the baron of Melrose who had come into the city of his enemies in this effective disguise. Was he risking his life only for the sake of plucking Tizzo out of the danger? The heart of Tizzo leaped with surprise and a strange pleasure. A moment later he stepped into a small adjoining room which had not yet been lighted. He had been there hardly a moment before the doctor entered behind him. He gripped Tizzo by the arm, exclaiming in a quick, muffled voice: "Go before me through the court and down the street toward the northern gate of the town. There I shall join you."

"I cannot go, my lord," said Tizzo. "I must wait here to learn—"

"You must do as I command you," exclaimed Melrose. "You have given me the pledge of your honor to serve me; we have made a compact and have shaken hands on it."

"I shall serve out the terms of the contract," said Tizzo. "I swear that I shall hunt you out tomorrow, but today I have to find the lady."

"What lady?" asked Melrose.

"That same 'Tomaso.'"

"You betrayed me, Tizzo," said the baron, angrily.

"It is true," answered Tizzo, "and I shall betray you again if

[38]

you give me the work of harrying poor girls across the country, robbing them from their homes, leaving their people—"

"Hush!" said Melrose. "Tell me—when did you know that Tomaso was a woman?"

"When I grappled with her at the moment she dropped to the ground."

"Not until then?"

"No."

"I understand," said the baron, "and any lad of a good, high spirit might have done exactly as you did. Tomaso turned into a lady in distress and the gallant Tizzo sprang to her rescue—but if I had overtaken you that night—well, let it go. She told you her name?"

"No," said Tizzo.

"But you came here into Perugia because she herself invited you!"

"I was to find her in Perugia, but I could not hear the name she called to me. The horses drowned it, thundering over a bridge."

"You came into this big city to hunt for her face? Are you mad, Tizzo?"

"I think I am about to see her," answered Tizzo. "I was able to describe her—"

"My lad," said Melrose, "if you try to reach her, you'll be caught and thrown to wild beasts. She is the Lady—"

But here a voice called from the lighted taproom, loudly: "He was in here. He was seen to enter in here. A young man with blue eyes and red hair. A treacherous murderer; a hired sword of the Oddi. Find him living or find him dead, I have gold in my purse for the lucky man who will oblige me!"

Tizzo, springing to the door, glanced out into the taproom and saw a tall, dark, handsome young man in complete body armor with a steel hat on his head and a sword naked in his hand. Behind him moved a troop of a full dozen armed men. They came clanking through the taproom, looking into every face.

"That's Mateo Marozzo," said Melrose, "the same fellow you bumped on the head yesterday. Run for your life, Tizzo. Try from that window which opens on the street; I'll make an outcry

[39]

to pretend that you've escaped into the court on the other side."

"My lord," said Tizzo, "for risking your life to search for me—"

"Be still—away! At the northern gate as fast as you can get there—hurry, Tizzo!"

Tizzo jumped into the casement of the window at the right and looked down into the rainy dimness of the street. One or two people were in sight; and the drop to the ground was a good fifteen feet. He slipped out, and he was hanging by his hands when he heard the loud voice of Melrose shouting inside the room: "This way! A thief! A redheaded thief! He has jumped down into the court—"

There came a trampling rush of armed heels, a muttering of eager voices. And Tizzo loosed his hold and fell. He landed lightly on his feet, pitched forward upon his hands, and then sprang up, unhurt. But from the entrance gate that led into the court of the tavern he heard a voice bawl: "There! That is he Messer Mateo wants. Quick! Quick! There is a golden price on his head!"

It was the old beggar, Ugo, who fairly danced with excited eagerness as he pointed out Tizzo to a number of loiterers about the gate.

The whole process of betrayal was evident now. One glance Tizzo cast up toward the high towers of Perugia, now melting into the blowing, rainy sky, and in his heart he cursed the pride of the town. But they were coming at him from the direction of the gate; and other yelling voices of the hunt issued from the tavern into the open of its court. They would be on the trail in another moment. He turned and ran with all his might, blindly.

It was clumsy work. He had to hold up the scabbard and sword in his left hand to keep it from tripping him; the steel breastplate which he wore under his doublet was a weight to impede him; but he held fairly even with the foremost of the pursuit until he heard the clangor of hoofs on the pavement, and he looked back to see mounted men behind, and one of them in the lead with three flowing plumes in his hat.

That would be Mateo Marozzo, of course!

He could not outrun horses, but he might dodge them for a moment, so he turned sharply to the left down a dark and narrow lane.

It was a winding way, as empty of people as it was of light, and when he turned the first corner he saw that he was trapped, for the foot of the lane was blocked straight across by a great building.

All other doors were blocked except to the right, where two figures in black hoods stood as if on guard, one of them constantly ringing a little bell. They made an ominous picture, and inside the open door of the house there was a yawning, a cavernous darkness. But Tizzo sprang straight toward this added moment of safety. In front of him, he saw the dark forms lift and stretch out their arms.

"Halt!" cried one deep voice. "Better to die in the open under a clean sky; death itself is waiting inside this house."

But Tizzo already had brushed past the restraining hands. He entered the dimness of a long hall with the ringing hoofbeats coming to a pause in front of the entrance to the place. And he heard a long cry from the street that might be triumph, horror— he could not tell what.

A stairway climbed on the left. He went up it on the run toward the greater light that came through the upper casements of the house. And at the landings of the stairway he saw bronze figures covered with the dark green patina of great age. That was sure proof that he had entered a house of the greatest wealth; none other could afford sculpture of the Greeks or of the Romans.

He sprang into an upper hall hung from end to end with magnificent tapestries, but empty of all life. There seemed to be no servants in the great mansion; none except the two grim doorkeepers at the entrance. And as he ran past a long table in the hall, he saw that the surface of it was dim with dust.

Through the first door he turned into a chamber with brightly frescoed walls and a number of crystal goblets set out on the table. The glasses were stained but empty. A decanter lay broken on the floor.

He ran on into a bedroom with embroidered hangings over the walls, the windows, the doors. The bed itself was raised on a dais above a floor of wood mosaic; a heavily carved canopy rose above but from it some of the curtains had been torn away. These and the covers of the bed streamed out on the floor as though some-

[41]

one, desperately struggling, had fallen from the bed not long before.

But the dust was deep, everywhere.

A strange, oppressive odor made the air thick to breathe. And a chill of dread passed suddenly through the body of Tizzo, and through his spirit.

He no longer ran, but crossed that room slowly. The doorway on the far side, yawning like a dangerous mouth upon the unknown that lay beyond, made him draw his sword before he would cross the threshold.

He listened for the sound of pursuit, but there was no beating of footfalls on the stairs. He heard no more than a dim whisper through the room, and this came, he saw, from the wind which he had brought with him as he entered and which still made the rich hangings of the apartment sway slightly.

When he had passed the door into the next room he found himself stepping on the skins of leopards. A service of massive silver, now dim under tarnish and dust, stood on a sideboard; and on a central table a huge jewel box lay overturned. Red and green and crystal-bright, the jewels streamed across the table and lay scattered on the floor. Here in the palm of one hand there was wealth to make an entire family rich forever. But the beauty frightened Tizzo more than it excited him.

He remembered what the man had called to him in the street —that within the house was death itself.

He saw a Madonna in a niche at the end of the room, a beautiful carved image, but there was no taper burning beneath it. And then, compelled by a sudden cold horror in his blood, he turned and thought that he was looking into the eyes of death itself.

CHAPTER

9

IT SEEMED to Tizzo an apparition which had not been in the chamber before; suddenly it appeared as a young man who sat in the depths of a chair near a casement. He was dressed very richly. About his neck shone a golden chain that supported a great jewel. But his hose lay wrinkled over his wasted legs; his neck was shrunk to hardly more than the bigness of a man's wrist; and his face was a death's-head in which the eyes were deep caverns of unlighted shadow. Like a death's-head he grinned, or seemed to grin, at Tizzo. And to crown the horror some great red patches appeared across his forehead and down one side of the face.

Then realization came over Tizzo, and blew through him like the empty howling of a winter wind.

"The plague!" he groaned.

He looked back.

He had crossed many thresholds since he turned in from the street and each one had, in fact, brought him farther into the maw of death.

Far better to have turned and faced the riders in the wet street, dying obscurely but with sweet air in his nostrils. Now he was confined where every breath might be planting the horrible infection deep in his lungs.

He gripped his head with both hands, and he set his teeth to keep back a yell of fear.

"Welcome," said a husky voice hardly louder than the stillness of thought. "The last of the Bardis of Perugia gives a kind welcome to the last of his guests!"

Such a sickness of spirit troubled Tizzo that he gripped the carved back of a chair and supported himself. He wanted to sink on his knees and implore Heaven for succor.

"I should rise to welcome you," said young Bardi, "but I lack the strength to do anything except crawl to the bed where my father and my grandfather have died before me. I should offer you wine, but it is consumed. I should offer you food, but there is nothing in the house—except the rats and even those must be a little thin, by this time. But if you can catch one of them, you are welcome."

Tizzo passed the tip of his tongue across his dry lips. He wanted to turn and flee but a powerful instinct made him walk straight up to the specter in the chair.

"If you come near my breathing, you are probably a dead man," said the young Bardi.

"If I am to die, I shall die," said Tizzo. "If I am to live, all the plagues in the world will not touch me."

"You talk like a brave man, but that is because you are cornered," declared Bardi. "But you will have this comfort: When I am dead you may throw me into the foulness of the cellars where the rest of the dead are lying; and then for a few days you will be the heir of the house and the master of it."

Tizzo, forcing himself to step still closer, peered at the red blotches on the forehead and face of the other.

"Those sores are dry," said Tizzo. "And that means you are recovering from the plague. It is starvation that kills you, my friend."

"It is as good a way to die as any other," said Bardi.

"You must have food," said Tizzo.

"I have prayed for it; there is no other way to come by it," said Bardi.

"If you are healed of the sores, all the world knows that you are a clean man again," said Tizzo, remembering the dreadful stories of the plague which he had heard.

"I shall be dead of the famine before the sores disappear from my face," said Bardi. "And you—whether you take the disease after the third day or not, you will starve here after me. And

[44]

another month will go by after your death before brave men will venture into this rotten hellhole. What is your name?"

"Tizzo."

"Tizzo, I have told you your future. Accept it."

"It is better to run out on the street and die fighting."

"So you think now; but every day a strange new hope will come up in you, and you will cling to your life for another twenty-four hours—until you are too weak to hold a sword."

"We could steal out through some secret passage underground."

"There is such a passage; and it has been blocked to close up the rattrap. My kind uncle, who wants this house and everything in it when the plague has finished its work, saw to it that the secret passage was stopped."

"We might be able to slip away in the dark of a rainy night like this."

"My good uncle and the city of Perugia keep guards at every door, day and night."

"Yet I was allowed to enter?"

"It would never occur to them to try to stop a man from entering; their care is to keep anyone from getting out."

Tizzo nodded. He attacked the last possibility.

"We may be able to get to a neighboring roof."

"From the eaves of this house to the nearest, there is a span of thirty feet. I have thought of all of these things. There is no hope. I sat at that table with my own father trying to plan. There was no hope—"

His voice, which had raised to a great outcry, suddenly stilled and the Bardi fell sidewise across the arm of his chair.

Was he dying? Was he suddenly and mercifully dead?

It seemed to Tizzo that he could not force himself to touch that body, still no doubt reeking with the mortal presence of the plague; but he could not stand by and leave the helpless man in that position.

Besides, since Tizzo was in the house, since there was hardly a chance in a hundred that he could pass the crucial three days without becoming infected with the sickness, he felt that he might as well open his arms to the horrible danger. He deliberately picked up the wasted, skeleton body of Bardi and carried it back to the bedroom which he had noticed before. There he stretched the senseless man on the bed where his father had died before him. He arranged the clothes, opened the window to allow more air to enter, and listened for a moment to the breathing of the sick man.

He was alive. He was barely alive.

Water would help. Presently Tizzo found the door which opened on the wellshaft and he wound up the long, long rope that carried the bucket up from the depths below.

It was good, clean, bright water. Tizzo took a swallow of it himself and then carried the bucket in to poor Bardi. A few drops on that bruised, tormented face roused Bardi.

"Ah!" he said, looking at Tizzo. "You are going to be fortunate. I dreamed that I was in heaven and saw you there."

It was a dream of a sort that Tizzo did not exactly appreciate. However, he talked with Bardi for a moment, bade him try to sleep, and then went back to the well. The length of the rope had given him thought. He unwound the long rope and put his weight against it; it held him easily.

So he stumbled and fumbled his way to the top of the house and there reached the roof.

It was not quite full darkness. The night, like an ugly smoke, steamed upward, as it seemed, to Tizzo. When he stood on the roof, he could see dim lights far down in the streets; voices rose to him very faintly.

CHAPTER

10

Tizzo looked upon himself as already dead; therefore life was a casual thing to be risked as he chose. Otherwise perhaps he would never have dared to attempt what he now tried.

There were watchers on the ground, an ample posting of guards, of course, as young Bardi had said. But were there watchers from the nearer houses? No, all of the windows had been closely shuttered as though to keep off the terrible breath of the infection from that pesthouse. So he measured the distance to the nearest roof and guessed it, with a fair accuracy, to be the full ten paces which Bardi had mentioned. Well, it was not an insuperable distance, after all.

He made a loop in the end of the wellrope and tried to cast it over the nearest chimney on the adjoining roof. But his stand was precarious on the slant of the tiled roof. The rope was heavy of its own weight and the damp it had absorbed; the frayed strands of it caught the wind and always it fell short or far away. He worked until his arm was weary before he surrendered that project.

There was some mystery behind the coming of Melrose. And Tizzo would be dead, of course, before ever he pierced the strangeness and found the answer.

He determined on another way of reaching the house adjoining. He went down the roof of the Bardi home until he was at the rear edge of it. It was perhaps ten feet higher than the roof of the adjoining house, at this point. Tizzo fastened his wellrope over the nearest of the chimneys and allowed some forty feet of its length to fall dangling over the edge. Down this length he lowered himself until he reached the big knot which he had tied in the end. Afterwards, like a boy in a swing, he began to sway his body back and forth until the rope commenced a pendulous motion that swept Tizzo farther and farther; in a greater and a greater arc across the rear face of the Bardi house.

Above him, he could hear the rope grating against the cornices, he could feel the shudder as the strands of rope began to fray out with this continual, heavy rubbing. At any moment the rope might part, he knew. But, since death was almost certain anyway, it was well enough for him to come to the end of life by the merciful swiftness of a fall to the hard pavement.

Higher he swayed. The rope flexed and bucked at the end of each rise. He could look up the slope of the adjoining roof, now. Then he could touch it with his feet if he cast them up.

Now, dimly, he could make out the hollow of the stone gutter that circled the edge of the roof.

A greater effort—and as the arc of the swing lengthened, he gripped a hand and arm inside the edge of the gutter. The strain was tremendous for an instant only; then he was up on the roof, holding an end of the rope in one hand. If it were impossible for him to find a way down into the house from the roof, the rope must serve as a bridge by which he could return to the house of Bardi. It was barely long enough to enable him to tie it around a chimney pot. It slanted up at a rather steep angle toward the Bardi roof above, but for one of his great activity of body and strength of hand, it could easily be traveled.

He began the search of the new roof at once. It was very wet, and where lichens had grown on the tiles, they were as slippery as though they had been oiled.

He had to watch himself carefully, for the pitch of the roof was, in addition, quite sharp. But he found on the other side of the crest of the roof what he had hoped for—a trap door which opened to the first pull.

He passed down a ladder into darkness thick as that of a wall. He found himself in a room cluttered with odds and ends, with a smell of moldy old cloth. Perhaps battered furniture was stored here. After he got to the wall he had to fumble carefully along it until he reached a door. It was not locked. He pushed it open and found himself in an upper hall, very narrow, long, bare. Down this he went to a stair which communicated with a far more spacious hall beneath, and here the odor of cookery greeted him. It was, of course, far past the time for the dinner of Italians; but the first door he passed was a big upstairs kitchen such as the clever Italians continually built in their larger houses so that the servants need not climb the great distance from the cellar kitchens to serve meals.

There was no one in this part of the house. Voices and laughter sounded farther down in the building, but Tizzo paused an instant at the kitchen, his teeth set.

He needed no food for himself; but he could not help remembering the gaunt body and the skeleton face of Bardi, in the pesthouse. To return to that place, now, seemed worse than giving up life itself. What man would be generous enough to dare such a thing? How could it be expected of anything in nature?

So Tizzo argued with himself, briefly—and then he remembered how the Englishman had adventured into Perugia—truly as dangerous as any plague spot for him!

He took a quick breath and made up his mind though his hair prickled in his scalp at the thought.

There was a slowly steaming bowl of soup near the embers of the fire, but of course such a weight as soup would be a waste of effort. Instead, he found a great ham such as might have come as the prize from a boar hunt. He cut a heavy quantity of this meat from the bone. There was good whole wheat flour. He took a bag of that, also, and even placed a flask of wine in his pocket.

He had some thirty pounds of provisions on his person, and if he could haul himself up the rope with that freight, it would keep the life of poor Bardi in his body for a fortnight, at the least.

He returned to the roof by the way he had come, found the rope, and began to climb, his body hanging under while with hands and pinching knees and a leg twisting into the slack of the rope he struggled up to the Bardi roof.

Down from the roof through the upper passages and into the dark of the bedchamber he went. But he had marked a lamp, before leaving, and this he now lighted. Young Bardi gave proof of life, groaning as he heard the clicking of the flint against the steel.

But not until the fragrance of the ham was in his nostrils and the savor of it was on his lips did he completely rouse.

He looked, then, from the food on the table to the red wine in the flask, and thence to the flame-blue eyes and the red hair of Tizzo.

"God of miracles!" said Bardi, and crossed himself. "Tizzo, have you worn wings?"

"I used the wellrope," said Tizzo, smiling. "It made a bridge for me to the next house."

"But after you reached it—after you were free to go—do you mean that you came back to me, voluntarily?"

He sat up; he stood up; and he supported his unsteadiness by grasping both the hands of the redheaded man.

"There's enough food here," said Tizzo, "to keep you alive until your kind uncle is certain that you are dead. And when he opens the house at the end of the appointed time—when he comes with his heart hungry for treasure—and finds you alive, well, with the scars of the plague disappearing from your face—that is a moment I should like to see."

"Tizzo," said Bardi, "you are going back to liberty. Why? Stay here with me. We'll divide the food. There will be enough for both of us until the time my uncle lets the house be opened. God will not permit you to catch the plague—"

He stopped himself as he uttered the absurdity.

"Whatever happens," said Bardi, "to the end of my life half of whatever belongs to me is yours. All, if you need it!"

He made a gesture toward the door.

"There are the jewels yonder," he said. "Even kings have heard of the Bardi jewels. Tizzo, pour them into your pockets. They are yours!"

And when Tizzo thought of those sparkling beauties, a sort of fire shot up from his heart across his brain. He actually turned toward the door; but then something stopped him.

"This is not for profit," he said. "This is an offering, Signor Bardi, and a little touch of charity—"

[50]

He paused and added, with a certain touch of astonishment: "Only the second kindness that I have done in all my life! May it be recorded! And God take care of us both!"

He slipped away from the gratitude of Bardi quickly. There was still trouble in his mind. And it was true, he could see, that all during his years he had taken, taken, taken, and never given. He had taken from the very beggars in the streets, when he was a child; he had taken from the long-continued charity of Falcone afterwards; and never until he ventured himself for the sake of "Tomaso" had he returned to the world its kindness.

When he got to the roof again, he looked up at the raining sky and breathed deeply. He had a sudden confidence. Fear left him. He could swear that not a shadow of the plague would adhere to him, and that he would make his way again safely down through the house of the neighbor to the street and to the new chance for life which he would find in it. He could not tell why this certainty was in him; but it was an odd feeling that, having paid, he had a right to expect from fate some kind return.

CHAPTER

11

He got down through the house without the slightest difficulty, through dim halls, past some brightly lighted doorways, until he came to the ground floor. There remained only the porter at the entrance to be passed, but this might prove difficult since the heavy door was locked. However, he had his sword to cut a way through difficulties and he was about to lay hand on it as he stalked the drowsy figure of the porter, when a door opened at his right and a flood of men and women, richly dressed, came out of a chamber that flared with many lights.

The surprise was so stunning that for half an instant Tizzo hesitated whether to run forward or back; and in that instant a man cried out in a ringing voice of horror: "The redheaded man of the Oddi; the man from the plague-house! We are all contaminated—we are dead!"

The women began a frightful screaming, but as Tizzo turned to flee, half a dozen resolute men sprang out, sword in hand, to pursue him.

He leaped to the nearest door, wrenched at the knob of it, and found it closed. He had barely time to whirl about on guard, with a sense that steel was already entering his body, and catch several swords with a sweeping parry.

His dagger in one hand, his sword busy in the other, he saw that he could not hope to win without a miracle. For the men of Perugia were all soldiers who had followed the banners of the Baglioni all up and down the length of Italy. These were swordsmen; and in the cramped space of the semicircle that fenced him in, Tizzo could not use that flashing, catlike footwork which was the chiefest grace of his fencing.

More men were coming. The big porter strode with a partisan in his hand, balancing the long-handled ax in a powerful pair of hands. In the meantime, feeling that the end had come, Tizzo threw back his head and laughed as he battled. For a frenzy was in him and the joy of the fight shut out past and future. He was to die, but he would do some execution even against all of those swords, before he fell. His body twisted from side to side; twice a lunging sword blade drove past him and shattered its point against the stone wall at his back. The dance of his wild sword parried many a downright cleaving stroke aimed at his head and flicked out a snake-tongue of danger that touched the others one by one. Here a fellow drew back with a slashed forearm; another was gashed across the forehead; a third was stung in the thigh by a lightning thrust.

This incredible resistance brought a great shouting. More men came flocking, and up the great stairway at the end of the hall he could see the ladies, bright as a garden of flowers, standing to watch the fight. Yet, for all their numbers, they drew back from his deadly work a little. Someone shouted to bring a crossbow and nail the redhead to the wall; but here the porter, stepping into the throng, brought down his partisan with a monstrous sweep.

Tizzo warded the stroke skillfully with his sword, but the blade broke at the hilt and the head of the long ax, turning, descended flat upon his skull. A red sheet of flame leaped across his brain; darkness swallowed him.

When he wakened, he rolled his eyes vainly to find light. All was thick blackness; water dripped, somewhere; and he was lying on a pavement greasy with slime.

He stood up, in spite of his spinning brain, and found that he could touch both walls of his chamber with his outstretched hands.

They had him cooped in one of the dungeon cells, far underground. They might leave him there to die, never opening the cell for a year for fear of the plague; or else they might take him to the torture chamber.

Tizzo sat down, cross-legged, and resigned himself to his fate. The sharpest, the most sudden regret that came to him was that he had not killed at least one man in the battle of his capture.

Afterwards, he began to think of "Tomaso."

He was very cold, very hungry, when a port in his door was opened, and a ray of light shone in at him. By that light, a loaf of bread and a pitcher of water were placed upon the floor.

"Where am I, friend?" asked Tizzo.

"Ay, you were out of your wits and talking dreams," chuckled the jailer, "when we put you down here. You are in the cellars of Messer Mateo Marozzo. We keep you here for three days to see whether or not the plague comes out on your face. If it comes, why, then we wall up this door and let you rest for a hundred years. If it does not come, you have the pleasure of meeting Messer Marozzo and the torture chamber."

It seemed to Tizzo that the part of good sense would be to end his misery by dashing out his brains against the stones; but he could not smash the bottle and spill the unique wine of life. Hope remained to him, foolish though it might be. And now and again, several times a day, he amused himself with a horrible interest by feeling the glands at the base of his throat. For these were the first to swell when the plague laid hold on a man.

Yet for a third time the shutter of the door opened, and the light struck on his face. Then said the voice of a man beside the jailer: "It is more than three days, and yet there is no sign of the plague in him. You may take him out at once. Let him be washed and have him dressed in clean clothes. He is to come before Messer Mateo!"

All of this was done quickly. Half a dozen armed men—a proof that the desperate courage of Tizzo was recognized—took him from his cell. Under their eyes and the points of their weapons, as it were, he was allowed to strip, bathe, and put on clean clothes. Then irons were fastened to his wrists and ankles with a chain that connected them passing through his belt; and in this fashion he was taken into the great hall of the Marozzo palace, and through this to a smaller room where a tall, very handsome, dark fellow walked up and down; several other men stood back, apparently attendants.

When Tizzo was brought in with clanking chains, the tall man stepped straight up to him; the guards on either side checked Tizzo by the arms.

"Do you know who I am?" he asked.

"You are Mateo Marozzo, I suppose," answered Tizzo.

"Have you ever seen me before?"

"With your visor down, Messer Mateo," said Tizzo.

"You know it was I that you faced that day?"

"Yes."

"Well," said Marozzo, stepping back with a smile of infinite satisfaction, "you are now in my hands."

"I am glad of it, Messer Mateo," said Tizzo.

"*Glad* of it, did you say?"

"I had rather be in your hands than in those of any other man in Perugia. You at least know that I fight as an honorable man."

[54]

"Ah, you've been reading stories about perfect knights. Is that it?" asked Marozzo. "Do you think that the spies and body-snatchers of the Oddi are entitled to be treated like men of honor?"

"I know nothing of the Oddi," said Tizzo.

"Am I to believe that?"

"I hope so," said Tizzo, frankly.

"On the contrary," said Marozzo, "I know that you are one of their men of greatest trust."

"I have never seen one of their faces," said Tizzo.

Marozzo laughed in his face in return. "Perhaps you never have seen the mad Englishman, Lord Melrose?" he asked.

"Yes. I know him. I am in his service."

"And he in that of the Oddi. In fact, my friend, I know that you are one of their most prized hirelings, in spite of your youth. Shall I give you the proof?"

"That you cannot do."

"Presently. When I have sent off to Astorre Baglioni himself a letter from Lord Melrose in which he offers anything for your release. Anything up to his own life!"

"His life?" exclaimed Tizzo, hoarsely.

"If that devil of a Melrose offers so much, you are worth a high price; you stand among the first of the servants of the Oddi. Admit that, my friend, and talk to me freely concerning whatever you know of the Oddi now—their location, their position, their plans—talk openly, and it may be that I shall be able to give you what I have a right to take—your life!"

His glance went hungrily over Tizzo as he spoke. It was plain that he hardly wished to surrender personal revenge to statecraft, no matter how he might be advanced in the eyes of the all-powerful Baglioni.

"Messer Mateo," said Tizzo, "I only repeat what I have said to you before; I know nothing about the Oddi."

"Well," said Marozzo, "then I shall have to see if I can persuade you to talk."

Tizzo knew what that meant. Torture would be used now, in order to force him to confess things of which he knew nothing. A fine sweat covered his body, gleamed on his face; and his eye looked inward on his soul, wondering how long he would be able

[55]

to endure the agony without screeching out shamefully. For wild savages would never be able to reproduce the exquisite master-pieces of pain of which the people of Italy were capable.

But before another move was made, a servant came in haste, carrying a letter on a tray.

"A message from Signor Bardi!"

C H A P T E R

12

THE VERY name of Bardi filled Tizzo with a sudden hope, but Marozzo cried out in horror to throw the letter into fire without touching it. The plague might be carried even in the ink with which it was written.

"Antonio Bardi," said the servant, "is pronounced by the doctors free and clean of the plague. This morning the house of the Bardi was broken open. It was thought that everyone must be dead of disease or of the plague, but by a miracle, Messer Antonio has lived and fresh food was found beside him. The terrible house is now being cleansed with wine and vinegar; and the first care of Messer Antonio was to send this letter to you."

"Read it to me," said Marozzo, his glance impatiently seeking his prisoner again, as though he was in haste to start a congenial work.

The seal of the letter was broken, and the secretary read:

MATEO, MY DEAR FRIEND:

By the grace of God and the charity of a stranger I have returned from the dead to the living. I was recovering from the disease by dying slowly of the famine when Tizzo, the Firebrand, brought to me food; my house is now open and life begins again. I hear that Tizzo is now in your hands. I know you will use him kindly for my sake until I am strong enough to come to you and tell you with my own mouth how great he is of heart.

(Signed in haste),
ANTONIO BARDI

Young Marozzo hesitated only a moment. His malignancy was too much roused to permit him to give up his cruel plan. He said: "Send word to Antonio Bardi that you found me engaged and that at my first leisure I shall read his letter; in the meantime I send him congratulations on his wonderful escape. And now we shall test the greatness of the heart of this Tizzo. Is that rare swordsman of mine prepared with armor in the court? Is he ready to put the question to this man?"

The answer was that Guido, the swordsman, was waiting; so the entire assembly adjourned at once to the courtyard of the palace. Here the superior servants of the household were ranged around the open colonnade; the female servants leaned from the upper windows of the house; and there were at hand half a dozen crossbowmen with quarrels ready on the string. In addition, Tizzo saw a tall man armed in complete steel from head to foot, the visor raised to show a lean face except for the bulge of the wide jaws.

"Where is that woodsman's ax?" demanded Marozzo. It was brought at once. "Set the prisoner free. And now, Tizzo, I have seen your tricks with an ax; I have felt one of them. You shall show them to me once more. Perhaps I shall learn from you something that will be worth knowing. Guido, there, will test your skill. And if his sword begins to enter you, remember that you have only to confess what you know of the Oddi in order to escape from more punishment. If you try to escape, the arbalests will send their bolts through you."

Tizzo, feet and hands free, grasped the ax and saw that in fact it was such a weapon as he had learned to use. And he answered:

[57]

"Messer Mateo, the ax is for striking blows, and the sword is both a weapon and a shield. I have no armor, but even without it, if you put a sword in my hand, I'll try my fortune against your champion."

"Do you begin to whine, you redheaded dog?" burst out Marozzo. "I should have you in the torture room, pulled by ropes and broken on the rack. Instead, I give you a chance to fight like a man. If you beat Guido fairly, you are a free man!"

Tizzo, running his eyes over the bright steel armor of Guido— whose visor was now closed and whose sword was drawn, with a dagger in the left hand—felt that his chance was smaller than that of a naked child against a mounted knight. But yet this was a far better way to die than to lie stretched in the torture chamber. And there was that ghost of a chance that he might escape, after all, to the promised freedom.

He flexed his knees, stretched his muscles as carefully and elaborately as a cat, and then said: "Guido, you have the advantage of weapons and armor; you would not be chosen for this part if you were not a good fighter; but God and luck fight on the side of the underdog. If you're ready, come on!"

Guido made no speech at all. He merely laughed through the holes of his visor, which was long and pointed like the muzzle of a dog. Then he strode forward with his sword prepared. Tizzo, instead of retreating, moved in a circle, carrying the weight of the ax in both hands.

"Action! Action!" called out Marozzo.

Guido, obediently, tried to close, feinting at the head with a thrust and then swinging his sword in a long sweep aimed at the legs. Tizzo, letting that blow go past him, withdrawing so that the keen edge missed his flesh by the least part of an inch, sprang in and struck.

The dimness of the prison was still in his eyes; and he felt the weakness of his diet for the past three days; otherwise that blow would have alighted exactly on the top of the helmet of Guido and finished the battle at the first stroke.

As it was, the stroke glanced from the head, slipped off the shoulder armor, and almost wasted. Even so, the brain of Guido had received a shock that set him reeling. The people who

[58]

watched began to shout; and a shrill, tingling cry went up from the women at the upper casements.

Marozzo yelled: "Guido, if you let yourself be beaten, whether you live or not I'll send you back to Assisi to let them hang you for your murders!"

Tizzo had followed the staggering Guido closely, ready to strike a finishing blow, when his foot skidded on a rolling pebble and he half fell to his knees.

Guido was by no means too far gone to throw away this opening. He struck a mighty blow. Tizzo half turned it with the up-flung head of his ax, but the sharp blade gashed the side of his head.

When he regained his feet and leaped back, blood was streaming down one side of his face and Marozzo began to laugh with joy.

"Now will you talk, red dog?" he called.

And he added: "Well done, Guido!" All the others who looked on were uttering harsh cries of satisfaction like so many savages. And Tizzo felt like a baited bull.

He began to circle Guido again until the man-at-arms, tired of the delay, pressed close in, showering blows. Half of them Tizzo dodged; the rest he put away with the incredibly swift movements of his ax. He seemed to be dancing in the midst of a fire, the sword of Guido flickered so rapidly. And when it was seen that Tizzo actually had escaped harm, a yell of astonishment went up from every beholder, Marozzo himself crying out: "Witchcraft! His life is charmed!"

But the red flow down the side of Tizzo's head was a sufficient answer to that accusation. He had been badly hurt; but with set teeth he tried a second chance. It was at the very moment when Guido abated his attack for a moment and lowered his sword a little. That instant Tizzo used to make one of his startling leaps forward. The ax flashed in an arc of fire but Guido, recovering himself with wonderful speed, threw up the ward of his dagger and armored left arm to prevent the blow while the sword flashed out in a long thrust. The blow of the ax snapped the blade of the dagger and then was wasted; but the sword of Guido slithered

[59]

across the ribs of Tizzo, biting into bone and flesh. One inch inside of his mark, and he would have riven the body of Tizzo straight through the heart.

As it was, it seemed to Tizzo that a great claw had ripped him. His body was poisoned with pain, and the blood gushed from this second wound.

Marozzo began to shout with pleasure: "Well done, Guido! Well done, my friend! You have caught the will-o'-the-wisp! You have notched the wild fire. Tizzo, has the time come when you will talk?"

Tizzo, drawing back a little, closely followed, answered: "The ax talks for me better than my tongue!"

And once more he had to fight desperately, leaping here and there among the thronging strokes and thrusts of Guido. The man was a master of his weapon, and his armor was so perfectly fitted that it did not greatly hamper the speed of his motions, yet the swerving body of Tizzo made a hard target to reach, and the magic dance of his feet carried him in and out from the verge of death as with his ax he strove to get close enough to strike a vital blow.

He retreated, limping, and the spectators suddenly ceased their yelling. The length to which that unequal combat had been drawn out, and the savage courage of Tizzo, together with his skill, had made all men sympathize with his battle. Only Marozzo in a frenzy of delight was shouting: "You have him now, Guido! He cannot keep on dancing with one leg gone. Kill!"

The bright helmet of Guido nodded in agreement, but even so he came in with caution, for his head must still have been ringing from the effects of the first blow of the battle.

Tizzo, favoring his wounded leg, stumbled as he retreated and sank upon one knee. He could have leaped up, though with difficulty. But instead, he raised the ax above his head as though he were incapable of keeping his feet and so waited for the final stroke.

A great call for quarter went up, now, from the onlookers, but Marozzo shouted: "Now, Guido! The dog is down. Kill! Kill!"

Guido took two quick steps forward and struck with all his might straight at the head of Tizzo.

He was so confident that his victim could not move that Guido launched his full force in that stroke; he was unprepared for the sudden spring that carried Tizzo to his feet, swerving barely aside from the blow.

Guido, grunting with fear, tried to recover and put himself on guard, but for the tenth part of a second his head was unwarded. And in that interval, as an arrow through a slot, Tizzo struck desperately with both hands.

The helmet was not his target, now, but a narrow crevice where the gorget plates fitted to the helm with rivets. If ever he had struck accurately to a marked line when he amused himself among the woodsmen of Falcone, so now he aimed his stroke with exquisite surety. Well and true the edge of the ax descended. The rivets snapped. The heavy blade of the ax shore almost through the neck of Guido so that his armored head dropped over on the opposite shoulder and a great gush of blood sprang up into the sunlight. Guido fell crashing on the paving, and lay still.

Marozzo himself, stunned with astonishment, found no utterance for a moment. He then yelled: "Drag Guido away. Federigo, arm yourself and take the sword. Witchcraft! Black witchcraft if ever I saw it!"

He was still shouting this speech as a crowd of people poured into the gate of the court, the porters instantly giving way before them.

Tizzo, looking up with dulled eyes, saw two men on horseback and a lady all in green, riding between them, with a plumed green hat on her head as though she were ready for hunting or hawking.

One of her two mounted companions, thrusting his horse suddenly forward, exclaimed: "What's this, Mateo? We need men in our army. Do you have them killed here for your sport?"

Tizzo looked up into the noble face of a man whose eye glanced and whose head moved as though he were born to authority. Marozzo grew humble before him at once.

"This little sport of mine, Messer Giovanpaolo," he said, "is something that should please you. Instead of using the torture chamber, to extract secrets from your enemies, the Oddi, I am letting my men use the sword—"

The name rushed strongly on the brain of Tizzo. For who had not heard, throughout all Italy, of Giovanpaolo Baglioni? With his brother, Astorre, he was a famous leader in war and in the councils of the city of Perugia.

Even now the fame of Giovanpaolo, and even the half-familiar beauty of the lady in green, was obscured for Tizzo by the sight of none other than Lord Melrose himself, who rode between two knights like a prisoner, the bridle of his horse made fast to those of the adjoining pair of riders.

The Englishman, like a madman, had come once by stealth to rescue Tizzo; and now he had come openly and put himself in the hands of deadly enemies!

He heard the lady cry out, and her voice staggered him with wonder: "Astorre! Giovanpaolo! It is he, and they have killed him! It is Tizzo—it is that man I have told you about—and you have let them murder him!"

It was that same "Tomaso." Fine clothes might alter her appearance, but her voice could not be changed even when she was calling out so familiarly by name upon the lords of Perugia. She slipped from her horse and came running, with her hands held out. One of those hands she laid in the blood that streamed slowly down Tizzo's side.

"Tizzo, they have murdered you! They have murdered you!"

But still there was life in Tizzo that made him break out in laughter.

"If I were dying, I would drink life again from your eyes, my lady!" he cried to her.

"Help him!" cried the girl. "Giovanpaolo! Astorre! If he dies I shall go mad! It was he who saved me! Do you understand? Astorre, if you are a brother of mine, let him be carried to a good leech. Tizzo, lean on me!"

There in the court, beneath the arcade of columns, they forced Tizzo to lie on blankets which were thrown down hastily, while a doctor came in haste. Baron Henry of Melrose crouched on one side of him and examined the wounds with a stern face and with cruel hands until he learned the truth and heaved a great breath.

"Why, Tizzo," he said, "you are going to be as gay as a lark inside of a fortnight. These are scratches that only make a bloody show."

And the lady, hearing this, cried out happily.

"Is it true?" asked Tizzo, looking up into the brown of her eyes. "Is it true that you are the sister of my lords, Astorre and Giovanpaolo? Are you the Lady Beatrice?"

She nodded, but added: "I am also your poor friend, Tomaso!"

"If you are the Lady Beatrice," said Tizzo, "in the name of God let no harm come to my friend who has given himself up for my sake!"

She lifted her head and looked a little coldly on the Englishman.

"I would rather be damned than be pitied," said the baron. "And I'm too old to catch the eye of a lady, Tizzo. Messer Giovanpaolo, you will be as good as your word and make him a free man?"

Giovanpaolo was frowning in deepest thought.

"I may even make a bargain with the pair of you," he said. "You, my lord, are serving the Oddi. But these are days of many changes. Why should you not enter my services?"

To this the Englishman replied: "If I had known you first, Messer Giovanpaolo, I would be with you. But I have given my word and my hand to the Oddi; and in England a man's hand is more than a written oath. I must serve the Oddi until they prosper or until I am dead."

"And this young man," said Giovanpaolo, "is he sworn to you in the same manner?"

"If it will help his fortune, I would release him from his oath," said the baron.

"Tizzo," said Giovanpaolo, "I have heard tales of you from my sister. I have heard other things, not an hour ago, from my dear friend, Antonio Bardi. I have many good men about me, but what one of them, himself a fugitive in a city of enemies, would have imperiled his life by returning to a plague-house carrying food to a dying enemy? You are a man of war; wars are the fortune of Perugia. I offer you a choice and a bargain also. You have heard Lord Melrose release you from your engagement to

[63]

him. Now give me your hand as you gave it to him and I shall on the one hand set Melrose free to go where he pleases, even into the camp of my enemies. On the other hand, you shall be my man and of your future I shall take good care. You already have a friend in my house." And he smiled at the girl as he spoke.

But Tizzo looked from her and from handsome Giovanpaolo to the grim face and the flame-blue eyes of the Englishman.

"My lord," he said, "you are my master. Tell me what I must do."

"Why, Tizzo," said the baron, "are you as blind as an owl? One of these days we shall meet again; but here is your fortune waiting for you. Take it, in God's name. We shall not forget one another. Remember the secret stroke; it is my legacy to you. But turn your face to the fortune that smiles on you!"

The loss of blood had made Tizzo weak and dimmed his eyes a little but the smile of the girl was so bright that it lighted up his soul. In her it seemed to him that he could see his future, his fortune, his happiness. He gripped the hand of Melrose with one of his, but the other, slowly, he raised to the waiting grasp of Giovanpaolo.

CHAPTER

13

SEVERAL evenings later, Tizzo was dressing with care, helped busily by Elia Bigi, a one-eyed cutthroat, now become his devoted servant. He had drawn on long purple hose, a green doublet heavily embroidered with crimson, green shoes of soft leather that came halfway up the calf of his leg; he had belted on his sword which was balanced at the right hip by a dagger. Scabbard of both sword and dagger were enhanced by rich golden chasings. Over his neck he hung a chain of massive gold, each link variously and curiously worked by a Florentine goldsmith, and supporting an intaglio which showed the noble profile of the famous Giovanpaolo, that Achilles of the condottieri of Italy. He was now swinging over his shoulders a black cloak which shone with an elaborate arabesqueing in silver when a messenger came to the door with a letter.

When Elia gave him the letter, he was about to throw it aside, but his eye saw the arms of the Bardi stamped into the seal and therefore he knew that it was a missive from his dearest friend in the entire city. So he opened the letter and read:

To my brother Tizzo, given in haste from my house; greetings, life, happiness, honor.

Tizzo, go not where you have willed to go on this night. Let your heart sleep. Do not follow it.

Ask me no more for my meaning or for the source of my information.

If I were free to come to you, I would be with you now and beg you on my bended knees to stay at home.

If ever you entered my house like a brave angel from heaven; if ever you saved me from a foul death beyond the holy hand of the church, alone, desperate, hateful to men; if ever I have sworn to you the eternal love of a brother for a brother, believe me now, ask me nothing, and lie quietly in your chamber tonight. It is your time of danger. If it passes, tomorrow will dawn brightly and the rest of your life may be spent in peace.

Farewell. My heart burns with anxiety. Be wise. Be prudent.

With all the blood of my body, thine,

ANTONIO

When Tizzo had finished the reading, he was so overwhelmed that he threw himself into a chair and bowed his head.

"He begs me as he loves me. . . . True, Antonio loves me. . . . 'Go not where you have willed to go on this night.' . . . How should he know where I am to go this night? Beatrice, my beautiful, noble, glorious, generous, brave, gracious, most perfect

[65]

Beatrice! . . . Let my heart sleep? How can I let it sleep when it strides like a lion through my body? . . . Ask not for his source of information, which means that he has it from a high and dangerous authority. . . . This is my time of danger? No, by God, it is my time of love! Elia!"

"Messer Tizzo?"

"I am called! And I must go. Is my horse ready?"

"It is, Messer Tizzo."

"Not the muleheaded bay for carrying an armored man, but the chestnut Barb that flies?"

"The Barb is saddled. The silver bridle is on him and the yellow housings with the bells."

"Bells?" said Tizzo. "Well, if they are waiting for me, let them hear me come! But give me that hat with the steel lining."

"And the breastplate of Spanish mail?" queried Elia.

"Yes. Let me have it. . . . No, I shall not take it. . . . What manner of man would I be, Elia, if I feared to die? Love of her is my armor. Arrows will turn from me tonight."

"I would put my money on a good crossbow bolt," said Elia, "or more still on a knife-thrust aimed at the back, or perhaps a little in a few dozen tiles, dropped from an overhanging roof."

Tizzo, staring for a moment at his servant, suddenly broke out of the room and ran hastily down the stairs. In the courtyard he found the slender chestnut Barb standing, a gift from the richest of all the Baglioni, that Grifone who was the most fortunate of men, married to the loveliest of ladies, with the whole world of happiness already in his hands, as it seemed. The occasion of the gift hung now beside the saddle in a case of embossed leather, a common woodsman's ax. The deceptively slender frame of Tizzo had seemed incapable of great efforts and yet with that ax he had cloven the massive jousting helmet, the finest product of the Milanese armorers. It had been put on a horse-post and he had split it from top to bottom with that deft, quick swing which he had learned from Falcone's foresters in his boyhood. The reward had been a loud exclamation that ran all the rounds of Perugia—and this beautiful Barb mare which now put out her lovely head and whinnied for her new master.

Once in the saddle, he flew the mare down the crooked, winding, paved streets of Perugia until the dark and massive arch of a city gate appeared before him.

"Open! Open!" he shouted, as he came up.

The captain of the gate stepped into his path, a tall man in complete armor except for the head, which was shaven close and gray with premature age.

"Are you drunk or a fool?" he asked bluntly, for the soldiers of the Baglioni were at ease in their manners to the townsfolk. "Is it my duty to open the gate to every young hothead who wishes to take the country air at night?"

"Does this help you, captain?" asked Tizzo, thrusting out a hand on which appeared a ring with a large incised emerald on it.

The captain saluted instantly. "Messer Tizzo!" he said. "The light is dim; I could not see your face; forgive me!"

He ordered the small portal to be unlocked and it was done at once.

"Give me fortune, my captain," said Tizzo.

The captain of the gate laughed. "If I don't give it to you, you'll take it anyway. I give you fortune, Messer Tizzo. May she be the daughter of the richest merchant in Perugia!"

The last exclamation came as Tizzo leaped the Barb through the barely opened portal and let the mare speed away down the slope. He crossed the hollow at the same wild gallop, but let the mare draw down to a trot as he climbed into the hills again. It was the face of Beatrice Baglioni that filled his mind, it was her remembered voice that silenced the hoofbeats of the mare as he drew near the high, dark shoulders of a great villa.

He did not go directly to the big house, but tethering the mare at a short distance from the corner of the stone wall, he climbed that wall like a cat, and dropped lightly down inside it.

Already he was well inside a realm of danger. It was true that he was a chosen friend and supporter of both Astorre and Giovanpaolo Baglioni, but the armed guards they maintained were apt to strike an intruder dead before they looked into his face or asked for his name. Besides, no matter how they valued him, they could not be expected to smile on a romance between him and their own sister, a lady rich enough and famous enough in

[67]

name and in beauty to marry a prince of a great estate. The Baglioni were, he knew, generous, brave and true to their friends; but they were also ruthless in matters of important policy.

The fragrances of the garden flowers came as intimately as voices to the heart of Tizzo.

There was almost infinite peril about him, but to him it was the spice in the wine, the savor in the breath of life. He would not have altered anything.

When he looked up, he took note of the position of the moon and saw that it still lacked perhaps half of an hour of the position in the sky on which he had agreed with Beatrice. But now she was filling her heart with expectancy in the great villa. That was her room, there at the upper corner of the building that one with the two lighted windows.

Yes, she was there, preparing to steal from the house.

And now she must be coming down the little winding steps which were cut into the wall. She would wear a dark cloak to hide her beauty and defy the moon. Slipping over the lawns like a shadow, she would enter the summerhouse and then he would see, from his place of covert at the hedge above, the signal which they had agreed upon: the triple passing of a light across the face of a window.

He had to sit down on the grass and bow his head in his hands and tell himself stories of his past to make the time pass. When he looked up, the moon was already at the proper place in the sky. The moment had come!

But no signal flashed for him! He waited with a sudden coldness of the heart.

Strange things are done by the great to the humble. What if she had been playing with him? What if she had named the hour for him and, afterwards, had told the story to her maids, laughing pleasantly, wondering how long in the chill of the night the poor redheaded fool would wait in vain?

The window of the summerhouse which faced him was, to be sure, unshuttered; but perhaps it was habitually left open to the cool of the night.

Impatience suddenly overwhelmed him, swept him away. He ran swiftly as the shadow of a stooping hawk across the lawn and peered in through the window. The moonlight made a slant path before him, and in the midst of it saw nothing except a chair which lay on its side.

He was through the window instantly.

The air within was warmer, softer, and a perfume breathed in it that sent an ecstasy through his brain, for it was that fragrance which his lady preferred, he knew. That one chair overturned— that sparkling eye—he leaned and picked from the floor a small ring set with diamonds and knew it for one of the jewels of the Lady Beatrice. At the same time shadows moved softly from the dark corners of the room; he saw them by instinct rather than with his eyes.

CHAPTER

14

As FULL awareness leaped into the mind of Tizzo, he heard a voice more hateful to his ears than any other in the world, the young Mateo Marozzo crying: "Now! Keep him from the window! Now! Now!"

And those shadows were lunging from the corners of the room with a sudden thundering of feet.

This was the danger of which Antonio Bardi had warned him, faithfully. He heard the peculiar grating, clanging noise of the steel plates of armor; he saw the sheen of naked weapons already sweeping past the open window behind him.

There was no refuge in that direction. And since he could

see no means of flight he followed the first impulse of a very brave man: with his sword swinging he leaped straight into the face of danger and charged the men immediately before him.

Their own numbers clogged their efforts. Two blades struck at him almost in the same instant. He caught one with the sword, one with the dagger, and burst straight through the fighting men. There was a door before him, barely ajar. Through it he leaped as a hand grappled his cloak and a sword smote the ledge of the doorway above his head. That assailant he heard crying out in the voice of Marozzo, once more.

He turned and struck the man to the floor with the pommel of his sword. Those others, recovering from their confusion, had turned to follow at his heels but he slammed the door and shot home the bolt. By the moonlight he saw a point of steel struck straight through the heavy wood and heard the impact of armored shoulders against the barrier.

It held firm and he turned to the senseless form on the floor. By the hair of the head he raised Marozzo and laid the back of the man's neck across his knee.

"Take the rear way; cut him off; a thousand florins for him!" he could hear voices shouting.

But with the point of his dagger, with cruel deliberation, he cut a cross in the forehead of Marozzo. The point of the keen weapon shuddered against the bone, so strong was the pressure. And the blood looked black as it flowed down the face of Marozzo.

He, wakening with a groan, heard the voice of Tizzo saying: "Where is the lady? Marozzo, here is your death waiting in my hand if you lie; but you live if you tell the truth."

"The convent of the Clares!" groaned Marozzo.

Tizzo flung the helpless body from him and sprang up. A fellow with an ax was smashing in the outer door to this room and there was a clamor of many voices near him. So Tizzo drew back again the bolt which he had just shot and leaped back into the first room.

Two soldiers were still in the place, but totally unprepared for this sally, and Tizzo leaped through the window and raced over the gentle slope of the lawn.

They were hopelessly lost behind him, in a moment, those

fellows in the anchoring weight of their armor. He leaped the first hedge, gained the wall, and was over it and in the saddle of the Barb, while the clamor still poured aimlessly toward him from the distance.

The swift mare carried him from all danger, now, like a leaf in a strong wind.

And still, as he looked up, he saw the same moon which had promised him happiness sliding over the wide arch of the night and tossing a meager drift of clouds into shining spray.

But in an hour the entire prospect of his life had changed. He had been the friend of the Baglioni; what was he to them now? The red hair which had been his passport through the city gate might be his death warrant now. And Lady Beatrice was closed inside the icy walls of a convent until it pleased her lordly brothers to set her free!

He could not cast forward to any conclusion; the speed of the mare had brought him back to the same gate of the city before anything was settled in his mind; he was knocking again at the portal with an instinctive hand, and he heard a voice calling through the shot-window: "Who is there?"

"I've come through this way once before, tonight," said Tizzo.

"Ah, it is he!" Tizzo heard a quieter voice mutter before the hole in the gate.

The middle door was opened at once, and he saw that same tall captain approaching, now with a naked sword in his hand and a helmet on his head.

"Messer Tizzo," said the captain, with a certain happy unction, "I arrest you in the name—"

"Of my foot!" cried Tizzo, and driving a spur into the side of the Barb, he made her bound like a deer while he drove the heel of his other foot straight into the face of the captain.

"Crossbows! Crossbows!" shouted the captain in a muffled voice as he staggered and fell.

The crossbows were quickly at the shoulder, but before a single quarrel could fly, the Barb had rounded the corner of the first building and was raising loud echoes down the narrows of the street.

So Tizzo came back into Perugia easily enough, but would he

[71]

find it such a simple matter to get out again? If he were wanted, he probably would be caught, because the Baglioni knew how to turn their city into a bird net which was capable of catching even the swiftest hawk in the highest sky.

But here he was riding on the street which contained the convent of the gentle order of the Clares, that sisterhood which followed the mind of St. Francis. But however good their lives and sweet their ways, the gray of their habits was not so gloomy as the bitterness in the mind of Tizzo. The gray gowns seemed to Tizzo to have claimed his lady, and she was shut away from him already as though by the veil of twenty years.

And now he sat the Barb under the lofty wall of the convent, staring hopelessly up at the barred casements. Somewhere inside the building a bell was striking, as though to hurry penitents to their prayers. The knees of Tizzo weakened, also. He would have been glad to throw himself down on the pavement of the street and to ask God for mercy in the midst of his wretchedness.

It was now that a figure detached itself from the arched shadows near the door of the building and came slowly across the street toward him, a ragged beggar, walking with a staff. When he came closer, he lifted his tattered hat.

"Messer Tizzo?" he asked, humbly.

"Well?" demanded Tizzo.

"This is for your hand, *signore*."

And he handed to Tizzo a letter from which there came the slightest scent of perfume, a fragrance more grateful to Tizzo than all the music of the spheres.

He ripped open the letter and read the writing by the dim moonlight.

Tizzo, we are betrayed. Astorre is wild with rage. Even Giovanpaolo has struck his hand on his sword and sworn an oath. A wretched woman of my own household has told everything. I shall spend my days kneeling, praying for your life. Fly, Tizzo, fly! My love follows you.

BEATRICE

[72]

CHAPTER

15

THE GIFT of a florin made the beggar begin to bless Tizzo and all his ancestors.

"I don't know their names," said Tizzo harshly, interrupting the long benediction, "so keep your prayers for your own spindle-shanks."

Out of the letter came two great facts: that his lady loved him, which lifted earth to heaven and spread blue fields of eternal happiness before him; and that Giovanpaolo had struck his sword hilt with rage—which swept all of this happiness out of existence again.

Tizzo sat his saddle musing through a long moment until he heard the clanking of armor down the street and saw the dim swinging light of a lantern approaching. Then he turned the head of the Barb mare and rode on the wildest errand he had ever attempted in all his wild life.

Danger came to him from the Baglioni. The innermost brain as well as the strongest striking hand of the Baglioni was Giovanpaolo. Therefore he intended to go straight to that man of many devices.

Giovanpaolo, he knew, was spending the night at the house of his cousin, Grifone, in order to discuss with him, late and early, the plans for the reception of Astorre's wife, who was to arrive the next day from Naples. The whole city was to be given over to a great fiesta in honor of the newly married pair and already the preparations were making the town hum day and night.

Toward the house of Grifone he went, therefore, and rode his horse slowly past the great façade. At all the corners of it were posted small groups of men-at-arms to keep watch, for the Baglioni were masters of the city, though Perugia was full of danger to them. The exiled house of the Oddi still retained a great number of adherents within the walls and these were likely to strike whenever the opportunity was good. What bait more tempting than to find within the walls of one house both the richest and the wisest of the Baglioni?

Since it was obvious that he would not be able to enter the house through one of the lower windows, he determined to take the place in the rear. So he went to the next lane, left the good mare tethered in it, and looked up the gloomy height of the side wall of that house which adjoined Grifone's.

He took off his hat to have the weight of the steel lining from his head. He put away the heavy cloak, also. In doublet, hose, and the soft green leather shoes he prepared to climb, but first he hung his sword by its shortened belt from around his neck. So lightened he went up the side of the house with ease. As a cat climbs, at home in the branches, swift-footed and confident, so he ran up the window bars which were like ladders, clawed his way over the great projecting ledges, and came at last to the high cornice, which thrust well out from the wall of the building. Balanced on a mere edging of stonework that girdled the house, he looked up to study this hazard, and made sure that he could hardly hope to surmount the barrier. Then he saw a projecting coping stone on which he might be able to fasten, but it was well beyond his reach.

He slipped off his sword and stretching out his arm, hooked the belt over the stone. As well as he was able, he tested the strength of this anchorage; he looked to the fastening which, except in time of action, held the sword blade to the sheath.

However, he was a fellow who usually found the first thought better than the second. In another moment, setting his teeth, he grasped the sword blade and allowed himself to swing out from the wall of the building. Above him, he felt the belt slide on the stone and made sure that he would drop the next instant into thin air.

That was why he looked down and saw in the street, made

narrow by the height at which he hung, two lanterns and a dozen men gathered about his mare.

Would they glance up and find that dim, small object dangling under the great eaves of the house?

The belt no longer slipped. It had stuck precariously, at the very end of the projecting stone, and Tizzo pulled himself up gingerly, hand over hand, until he could grasp the stone itself. Then, in a moment, he had swung himself onto the steep slant of the roof, gathering the sword up after him.

Lying flat, he peered down and made out the mare being led away, while one lantern went swaying down the street and another was hurried up its length. For all he knew, they might well have seen him above their heads and they were now going to spread the alarm. Nevertheless he went forward.

That moon which had appeared to him like a bright face of promise earlier in the night was now sloping into the west and the stars were wheeling slowly after it. He gave them one glance and then crossed the roof to its farther side. The roof of the great house of Grifone Baglioni began here, with hardly a ten foot gap between the two cornices.

He bounded across that chasm quickly and nimbly.

A flat roof-garden stood in the center of the space with a door leading downward. The door was locked, but the bolt was so flimsy that it gave at once to the pressure of his shoulder, and so he passed down into the house of Grifone. Past the upper corridor, he went down to the second hall and through this to the end because he knew perfectly where Giovanpaolo would be lodged. It was not the first time that Tizzo had been in this palace and he knew that the suite of honor adjoined a fine open loggia which overlooked the piazza. Here he expected to find Giovanpaolo.

He turned to the loggia. The door was not locked and he stepped into the open, peering down from between the columns into the width of the piazza.

No one stirred across that great pavement; he could hear the sound of the fountain waters in the middle of the place like the soft rushing of a wind.

From the loggia he turned through the next door and found

[75]

himself in a large anteroom lighted clearly enough by two lamps which no doubt had been supplied with oil to burn all the night through. There lay the hat of Giovanpaolo, shining with an incrustation of pearls all over the crown. On a chair were piled the cuirass, the leg armor of finest steel; a two-handed sword leaned in its sheath against the chair. On the table were a pair of golden spurs with immensely long rowels. And beside the spurs lay an open book, beautifully printed according to the new art which had been introduced through Italy from Germany, that distant nation of northern barbarians. It was strange, thought Tizzo, that any art could come from that misty, northern region!

Through a doorway adjoining he passed into a chamber far more dimly lighted by a single small lamp from whose wick a mere tremor of flame rose, so that the shadows washed up and down the walls ceaselessly and the entire apartment became a ghostly thing.

The paintings along the walls seemed more real than the figure of the man who lay on the great bed. It stood huge as a house at the side of the chamber.

The sleeper must have had restless dreams, for even now he was stirring uneasily, gripping a hand above his head, and muttering. Half of the covers had slipped from him and spilled toward the floor.

Tizzo leaned over him and recognized the strong, handsome face of Giovanpaolo.

He had come to the end of his short quest!

His sword was naked in his hand, now. He placed the point of it close to the throat of the sleeper and, leaning still closer, heard Giovanpaolo muttering: "Once more, men of Florence, brave fellows! If you are hungry, remember that there is bread and wine in their tents. The fat, red wine of Siena, comrades! Charge once more with me and we shall have it!"

The warrior was fighting again some battle in his sleep as Tizzo murmured: "Waken, my lord! There is a sword at your throat."

CHAPTER

16

THE ROUSING of such a warrior as Giovanpaolo was like the rousing of a lion, Tizzo knew, and he watched with apprehension and curiosity. Giovanpaolo, opening his eyes, looked without a start along the steady gleam of the sword and up into the eyes of the youth.

"So, Tizzo?" he said. "Murder?"

"If I'd wanted to murder you," said Tizzo, "as much as you've wanted to murder me, I could have drawn the edge of this sword across your throat or dipped the point of the dagger into your heart. I have come to talk to you."

"Let me reach the sword in that chair and I can answer all your questions," said Giovanpaolo.

He sat up in the bed, looking earnestly at Tizzo.

"Why have you wished to murder me?" asked Tizzo.

"I've had no such wish," said Giovanpaolo.

"You knew that armed men were posted at the summer house of Messer Astorre, waiting for me," said Tizzo.

"I knew that a trap was baited. I could not believe that such a clever cat as Tizzo would play the mouse and walk into the danger."

"But if I were fool enough to go—there was the end of me, so far as you are concerned?" asked Tizzo.

"My dear Tizzo," said the warrior, "what use have I for fools in my life? I knew you were a brave man and a good fighter, so I valued you; but if you were fool enough to throw your eyes on

Lady Beatrice with hope, you are no more to me than a dog that bays the moon."

Tizzo regarded the Baglioni with a curious eye. There was no fear in this man, and there was a ruthless frankness of truth in his remarks, as though the long, keen blade of the sword were no more than a pointing finger.

"Sir Giovanpaolo," said Tizzo, "if I have looked at the lady it is because I love her as other men love angels in heaven."

"My friend," answered the Baglioni, "every pretty girl is as bright as a star—while she is at a distance. I want to keep you from Lady Beatrice."

"Who means to you," agreed Tizzo, gloomily, "a strong marriage with some powerful house."

"She means that to us," answered Giovanpaolo. "Men who rule cities, Tizzo, cannot be governed by ordinary motives. Beatrice is a pretty thing, and moreover she is a Baglioni, therefore she has to be of use to the house. And what are you? A fellow with a fine flame on his head and a fine spark in his eye—but no more."

"My lord," said Tizzo, straightening, "the reason I came to you was to ask for an explanation."

"I have given you one," said Giovanpaolo, looking both at the sword and the man without fear.

"I was sworn to your service," said Tizzo, "and yet you were willing to throw me to the dogs of Marozzo."

"It was he who had the forethought and the information," answered the other, shrugging his shoulders.

"The Lady Beatrice was to be the bait, and I was to be the rat for the trap!"

"If you play the rat's part, you must die the rat's death."

"And you, my patron, for whom I have fought with my sword— you let me go to my death?"

"No. I gave you a fighting chance but a good one. To a man who loves you like a brother, to that same Bardi who owes his life to you, I let a hint be given that you should keep at home tonight."

Tizzo started. "And if I had done as he advised me to do?"

"Then, when Marozzo's trap had closed on nothing, I should have seized his house and his possessions, given a moiety of them to you, and had him beaten from Perugia with whips; as a man who dared to conspire against and falsely accuse my nearest followers."

Tizzo was staring, now. There was a queer, crooked, cruel morality in this attitude of mind that he could not fathom. He could see the fact, but he could not feel any understanding of it.

"Instead," he said, bitterly, "the lady is closed inside a convent until you choose to bring her out for a political wedding, and I am an enemy of your house forever."

"Not unless you wish to be one," said Giovanpaolo. "All the qualities that I saw in you before are in you still. I have removed the temptation of Lady Beatrice from your way and I have flashed a sword in your eyes. There is no reason why we should not carry on as we have done before."

"There *is* a reason," said Tizzo, his heart beating high.

"Name it to me, then," answered Giovanpaolo.

"You have set a trap for me and therefore you are a traitor to me, my lord. What keeps me from driving this sword through your heart, then?"

"A certain foolish set of scruples prevents you," said Giovanpaolo. "And the light in your eyes, Tizzo, is the love of battle, not of murder. You cannot strike an unarmed man."

"It is true," said Tizzo. "But there is plenty of light in the next room. You have a sword there and another on this chair. These apartments are set off from the rest of the house so that the clashing of swords will bring no interruption to us. Your highness, we will fight hand to hand and wash our stained honors clean with our blood."

"That," said Giovanpaolo, "is as childish and mad an idea as I have ever heard, but I like it."

He rose from the bed and picked up from the chair beside it a sheathed sword. The scabbard fell away with a hissing sound and left in the hand of the Baglioni a blade as like that of Tizzo's as a twin brother. Giovanpaolo led the way straight into the next room and from the scattered clothes selected hose, doublet, and slippers. Now that he was dressed, he took his position and weighted the balance of his weapon. His sleeve, thrust back to the elbow, showed a forearm alive with snaky muscles. The wrist

[79]

was perfectly rounded by the distention of the big tendons. Stories of the terrible cunning and strength of this man rushed back upon the brain of Tizzo; for in Giovanpaolo there was the brain to plan great battles and then the courage of a hero to lead his soldiers through the fight.

"Now, Tizzo," said Giovanpaolo, "I'm to thank you for this pretty little occasion. How often do we have a chance to fence with honest, edged weapons? How often does blood follow the touch?"

He began to advance, slowly.

"I shall have to let the world know that you burst in on me like an assassin," he said, "but I shall have you honorably buried. Tizzo, I salute your courage, I smile at your folly. Defend yourself!"

On the heel of these words, he rushed suddenly to the attack. Tizzo, having marked everything in the big room, gave back before the assault, and at the first ringing touch of steel against steel, he knew that he had met a great master.

The lightning feet of Tizzo were his defense and his attack. The sleights of a magician's hands were no more subtle than the flying of his feet, the intricate dancing measures through which they passed.

Twice, in as many minutes, Giovanpaolo cornered his man and set his teeth with a grim, furious purpose to drive the sword through the body of the enemy; and twice, with hardly a parry, Tizzo swayed from the darting point and was away.

Giovanpaolo began to sweat. He drew back to take breath, measuring his man and the work before him.

"By God, Tizzo," he said, "you are such an exquisite master that my heart bleeds to think that I must lose you through my own handiwork. Defend yourself!"

He leaped again to the attack. The man was as cunning as a fox, leaving apparently wide openings to invite the point of Tizzo's blade and flashing a murderous counterattack the moment Tizzo lunged at the opening. But Tizzo, holding back, with a carelessly hanging guard, met the assaults, moving his sword arm little, his feet much. There seemed to be an intricate pattern on the floor, in every one of whose divisions he had to step. Death darted past his face, his throat, his body, but it always missed him by a hair's breadth.

And then Tizzo began to attack in earnest. He had fathomed the consummate science of his man, by this time. Now he pressed steadily in, until Giovanpaolo began to groan faintly in his breathing. His face turned pale; it was polished with sweat.

Here a heavy beating came against the door.

"Who is there?" called Giovanpaolo.

"In the name of God, your highness, we have heard swords clashing in your rooms!"

Giovanpaolo looked at Tizzo for an instant. A faint, cruel smile dawned on his face.

But he answered: "I am fencing with a friend. Be gone and leave us in peace."

"There is one other thing, your highness. The noble Mateo Marozzo is now in your house, his face horribly wounded. Tizzo, men say, has escaped from a dozen men, branded the face of Mateo Marozzo forever, and escaped. But he is still in Perugia. Shall all the gates be guarded for him?"

"No!" called Giovanpaolo. "He is already gone! Let me be in peace!"

Footfalls obediently withdrew.

Tizzo said: "Your highness, I have always known that you must be such a man as this. You could have let your servants in to kill me like a blind puppy. I thank you. Your highness is troubled; your breath is short and your arm is tired. Shall we end this fighting?"

"End it?" exclaimed Giovanpaolo. "Do you think that I shall ever give over a battle I have entered upon?"

He came in with a desperate, last strength. Twice the leap of his sword blinded the very eyes of Tizzo. And he, half down upon one knee, used suddenly the secret stroke which the baron of Melrose had given to him as a treasure.

The sword of Giovanpaolo, knocked from his hand, wheeled brightly in the air and then descending, thrust straight through the cushioned bottom of a chair.

Giovanpaolo himself, unabashed, hurled himself straightfor-

[81]

ward at Tizzo, in spite of the level gleam of the weapon that pointed at his breast.

And Tizzo could not strike the final blow! His arm turned weak and senseless to make the stroke. Giovanpaolo, brushing past the bright point of danger, grasped the doublet of Tizzo at the neck and thrust him back against the wall. The other hand caught Tizzo's sword hand at the wrist.

So for a moment they stood, with the glare of savage beast in the eyes of Giovanpaolo.

But this fire died out. His hands left their holds. His head dropped forward wearily on his breast. He turned from Tizzo and, slipping into a chair, rested his forehead on the heels of his hands.

Tizzo sheathed his sword and felt gingerly the bruised muscles about his throat.

"To be beaten—and then spared—like a dog!" groaned Giovanpaolo.

Tizzo went to the loggia door and paused there.

"Your highness," he said, "I cannot fight under you any longer; and it is seen that God will not let me strike against you. Therefore I leave Perugia forever. Farewell. To the Lady Beatrice, say that I send my prayers—"

"Be silent!" commanded Giovanpaolo. "Pour wine for us at that table, and bring it at once."

CHAPTER

17

"Now, Tizzo," he said, "you have taken service under me before. In the meantime, you have dared to look past your height to the Lady Beatrice. In reward for that, I have allowed you to be trapped. You were a step from death in the summer house of Astorre tonight. I have been half an inch from death in this room. Tizzo, for the evil I have done you, forgive me."

"Forgive you?" said Tizzo, overcome by the humility of this fierce master of Perugia. "Highness, I have forgotten all offense!"

"You have beaten me," said Giovanpaolo. "It could be in my heart to hate you, Tizzo; it is also in my heart to love you. I cast the hate away"—here he spilled a little of the wine purposely on the floor—"and I take the love, instead. This cup, Tizzo, is filled with immortal friendship. Beware before you taste the wine. If it passes your lips it is as though you drank my blood. Do you hear me?"

"I hear you, highness," said Tizzo, beginning to tremble with a great emotion.

"Are you prepared to be with me two hands, two hearts, two souls of friendship?"

"I am!" said Tizzo.

"Then give me your hand!" said Giovanpaolo, grasping that of Tizzo at the same moment. "I drink to you, Tizzo, in token that so long as blood runs in my body, it is your blood and ready to flow for you."

They drank, and setting down the silver goblets stared at one another for a moment, as men who already saw a strange future stretching before them.

"Giovanpaolo," said Tizzo, "this is a beginning. Whether it be a dry death or a wet one, by steel, or fire, or bullets, or starvation, may we come to the same ending together."

Giovanpaolo, picking up from the table a heavy ring of gold, laid it on the floor and stamped on it. He lifted it, snapped it in two parts.

"Take this," he said to Tizzo. "Whatever message comes with it, night or day, if the half of the ring fits with my half, I shall go at once to answer you."

"If your portion comes to me in the same manner," answered Tizzo, "by the blood of God I shall come to you in spite of ten thousand."

"So, so!" said Giovanpaolo. "We have spoken in a very high strain for a few moments. Sit down, my friend. But—sacred heaven! When I think that a moment ago I stood with a naked breast in front of the point of your sword, I am still amazed. Where did you learn that last trick of the blade, Tizzo? Or did some devil of an enchanter teach you the thing? Will you teach it to me?"

"Whatever I know I shall teach you—and that same stroke as soon as I have the permission of the man who taught it to me."

"Who was that?"

"Henry, baron of Melrose."

"That wildheaded Englishman loves you, I know, Tizzo. He put his head in jeopardy to keep you from death when he rode into this city and gave himself into the hands of Astorre to have you set free. Do you give medicine to make them love you, Tizzo? What is Henry of Melrose to you—except that he is the chief leader of the forces of the Oddi and plots daily against the lives of the Baglioni?"

"He is," said Tizzo, "a friend of the Oddi, for what he chiefly serves is chance and the bright face of danger. To follow danger, he has left his country and ridden around the world. At last he came seeking for me; and for what mysterious reason I still cannot tell. He values me, I know, and again I cannot tell why. And that not in modesty, but because the strange love of this man amazes me! I only know that he came one day into my life, dashed me away from all the future I had come to accept, and swept me away at his side in the pursuit of adventure. There the Lady Beatrice crossed my way. You know how I set her free from the Oddi and followed her here. You know how that pursuit of her almost won me my death at the hands of Marozzo. And now it has led me to the rooms of your highness—and made us pledge our hands together."

"All spoken like a prophet," said Giovanpaolo. "It is true that you are a wildheaded lover of the Lady Beatrice. Now tell me what you would have me do? Marry you to her?"

"Five minutes ago," said Tizzo, "I would have stolen her with poison or swords. Now I would not lift a finger to come near her without your special permission."

"So?" said Giovanpaolo. "If men were like you, I should have to give up war and my old way of living; I should have to take to frankness, honesty, truth, and mercy. Let me tell you this— if the time comes when I can persuade old Messer Guido, the head of our house, you shall marry Beatrice on that day. And I'll carry you to see her this moment."

"You will?" exclaimed Tizzo.

"This moment," said Giovanpaolo, "she shall be set free from the house of the Clares and permitted to see you."

"Wait!" said Tizzo. "Before I take so much from you, tell me in what way I shall be able to serve you? Tell me, quickly, before my heart bursts, that service of which you are most in need."

"I should have to drop you like a plummet into the sea, deeply into the heart of a man who smiles in my face but who is, I fear, my greatest enemy," said the Baglioni.

"Let me go to him then," cried Tizzo, "and I shall read his mind and you shall know his present attitude."

"Tizzo, if you could do that, the weight of the world would be removed from me!"

"What is his name?"

"Jeronimo della Penna."

"But he is one of the chief friends of the Baglioni."

"So he seems," said Giovanpaolo, "but as a matter of fact he is known to have been kind to our enemies, of late."

"For all that is known to others," said Tizzo, "I have been pursued through the city by your riders—"

"There I was at fault," said Giovanpaolo.

"It is forgotten," answered Tizzo. "But suppose that tomorrow you put a price on my head and proclaim me an enemy? I return to the house of my foster father. There is an estate of this della Penna close by. If he truly hates you, and learns that I also am your enemy, will he not try at once to make me his friend?"

Giovanpaolo laughed, suddenly and loudly.

"Our friends are the eyes that look into the hearts of the world; the ears that listen to its mind. With two more like you, Tizzo, I should be able to conquer Italy in six months.—But wait—there is a frightful peril. You and I alone will know the truth. All of my family will hunt you down like a wild beast the moment I put the price on your head; and you know already that the Baglioni can be cruel enemies."

"You, and I, and the Lady Beatrice will know the truth," said Tizzo. "That is enough for me. Nothing is gained without danger. If della Penna is your enemy, within two days I shall know the degree of his hatred. You may depend on that."

"It is done!" said Giovanpaolo. "Here, cloak yourself with this and pull the hood down over your head. Already it is dawn. We shall go to Beatrice now!"

Wrapped in a length of blue velvet that muffled his body and his sword, with the hood pulled down over his face, Tizzo a moment later was passing down the halls, down the great stairs, through the tremor of life which the night lights revealed along the painted walls of the house of Grifone and so out onto the street, where he walked eastward with Giovanpaolo toward a great, golden Venus which blazed in the green forehead of the morning sky. But the lesser stars already were withdrawing to their distances like the lights of a retreating army.

So they came to the high, bald front of the convent of the Clares, where the porter saw the face of Giovanpaolo and bowed very lowly as though he would strike his forehead against the floor.

CHAPTER
18

TIZZO, striding anxiously up and down in the reception room, looked again and again toward the shimmering bars of iron which set off the room from the little cell in which the sisters of the order might appear to converse with their friends. He had waited, he was sure, for hours, before hinges moved with a dull, grating sound, and then a candle was carried into the cell by a veiled girl with a beautiful face.

Tizzo leaped to the bars and grasped them.

"Beatrice!" he said.

"Beatrice," said Giovanpaolo, "Tizzo is now my sworn brother. He has forgiven my sins; will you do the same?"

"How did you buy him, Giovanpaolo?" asked the girl.

"With my right hand," said Giovanpaolo.

"Has he given you his hand?" she asked suddenly of Tizzo.

"And I have given him mine," said Tizzo.

Her face softened suddenly.

"Did you hate me, Beatrice? I came to the place honestly, as I told you I would, and before the time. And there I was!"

"Do you know what I found there?" she asked.

"Marozzo?"

"Yes. My wretched maid had sold my secrets to him; and Giovanpaolo let him use what he had learned."

"I was to blame," said Giovanpaolo.

"Some day," she said fiercely, "I shall pay you home for that, my handsome brother!"

"Hush!" said Tizzo. "I have put my mark on Marozzo.

"With the point of my dagger I have drawn a cross on his forehead that will make him a crusader the rest of his life. No doctor will ever rub that mark away."

"Tizzo, I love you!" said the girl.

The mulberry, orange, and lemon trees flavored the airs that blew over the house of Luigi Falcone, and through the lawns of his garden great-headed plane trees gave shade and spear-headed cypresses marked the walks and circled the fountains. There was an artificial lake expensively produced by diverting the water from a creek among the hills and leading it here to fill an excavated hollow in the midst of the garden. A Venetian gondola with a gondolier waited there on the convenience of the master.

This fellow now started up, for his name was called.

"Olimpio! Fat-witted, lazy Olimpio!"

"Mother of heaven!" said Olimpio. "It is my master!"

And he leaped up to the deck and to the handle of his oar. As soon as he saw the flaming head of Tizzo under the shadows of the trees that crowned the bank, Olimpio began to lean his weight on the long oar and drive the little bark furiously forward.

"Wait here," said Tizzo to Elia Bigi. Before he left the town of Perugia he had said to the one-eyed servant: "Elia, I am about to leave Perugia as a proscribed man with a price on my head. You can sit here and keep my rooms, or you can ride with me and risk your neck." And the grotesque answered: "Well, if I stay here I shall lose my appetite and the only eye that's left to me will grow dull as an unused knife. But if I go with you, every day will have a salt and savor of its own." So he had ridden with Tizzo, each with a shirt of the finest Spanish mail, and a steel-lined bonnet, and the pair of them got hastily from the town.

The gondolier, bringing his boat swiftly and gracefully along the side of the little pier at the edge of the lake, held out both hands with a shout, but Tizzo leaped from the pier exactly into the center of the gondola.

"Tizzo!" cried Olimpio. "Ah, two-footed cat. You could drop from a treetop and never break the leaves that you landed on.

[88]

Welcome home! Welcome, welcome! You have been dancing with the devil in Perugia and still he has not turned your hair gray!"

Tizzo shook the greeting hands warmly and laughed: "The best day is the day of the returning. Is your master on the island?"

"He is there with a Greek manuscript," said Olimpio. "He will make it a fiesta when he knows you have come!"

From the columns of the temple, as the gondola touched the shore, there ran out a tall, bald-headed man who threw up his hands with a shout when he saw Tizzo.

For a moment it seemed to Tizzo that he was again the nameless waif of the village streets, standing agape as the "lord of the castle" went past him. And then, like the blurred flicker of many pictures, his memory touched the years when he had entered this house as the humblest of pages and grown at last to the position of foster son and heir.

Now he had fallen into the arms of Luigi Falcone. Now he was being swept into the little summer house where the harp stood aslant against a chair and, on a table, were scattered the yellow parchments of old manuscripts.

"What have you been doing with your Greek, Tizzo?" demanded Falcone.

"I've been using it to sharpen my sword," said Tizzo.

"I've heard that you and Giovanpaolo Baglioni are like two brothers together; and a man must have a sharp sword to be a brother to Giovanpaolo. But Perugia is a city of murder."

"I'm a proscribed man with a price on my head," said Tizzo. "Haven't you heard that?"

"Proscribed? By the Baglioni? Tizzo, what are you doing lingering here so close to Perugia? Wait! I'll call for horses! We'll send you as fast as hoofs can gallop—"

"I've fled all this distance from Perugia and I'm tired of flight," said Tizzo. "I'm going to stay here."

"They'll come in a drove and slaughter you, lad!"

"Perhaps they will. But the fact is that a man has to die some time, and it's better to be struck down from in front than stabbed in the back. I'll run no farther. It's as easy to die young as it is to die old."

"Of course it is," said Falcone. "But are you really resolved to run no more from the Baglioni?"

"Not another step—today," said Tizzo, and laughed.

Falcone laughed in turn. "The same blue devil is in your eyes and the same red devil is in your hair," he said with a smile.

"We'll go into the villa. I have some French wine for you. You shall tell me everything; and I'll give orders that every man on my place shall take weapons and be prepared to fight for you!"

"Not a stroke! Not a stroke!" said Tizzo. "I've made my own fortune and whatever is in the cup I'll be ready to drink it, alone."

They went back in the gondola, and as he left the boat Tizzo gave some golden florins to Olimpio. "Turn them into silver," he said, "and scatter them among all the servants. Tell them that the Baglioni want my life and that if it is known that I am here in the Villa Falcone, I'm not better than a dead man."

"Ah, *signore*," said Olimpio, his eyes still startled by the sight of the gold, "we all are ready to die for you; not a whisper will come from one of us."

But as they went on toward the large house, Falcone said: "Tizzo, that is the act of a child, really! You tell them that the Baglioni are hunting you, and you ask the servants to say not a word. But how can they cease from talking? They have heard no gossip like this for many years! You have come back from Perugia with the atmosphere of a hundred duels about you.

"So how can they keep from talking about you?"

"Let them talk, then," said Tizzo. "Even mute swans have to sing when they die. Let them talk."

"In fact," said Falcone, suddenly stopping, "it is a part of your plan to have them talk?"

"Perhaps it is," agreed Tizzo. "But don't ask me what the plan may be."

"I shall ask nothing," said Falcone. "Even when the wasps begin to hum, I'll try to brush them away and merely go on rejoicing myself in you, Tizzo. Tell me everything! What have you learned in new swordplay? Are you content in Perugia? Why don't you decide to travel across the world? There are great new things to see, in these days. But you hear everything in Perugia, because it is on a main road to Rome. Tell me all the news of the world, Tizzo! I hunger to learn it!"

They sat in an open loggia near the top of the large house, looking over the green rolling of the Umbrian hills; the sun-flare shimmered over all. They drank white wine of Bordeaux, cooled with packings of snow.

So they sat talking and laughing together while the day ran on toward the evening. The dusk was descending blue and soft after the hot summer day when a whistle sounded from the trees near the villa and Tizzo bounded to his feet.

"Is it danger? Wait for me, Tizzo!" exclaimed Falcone. "I catch up my sword and follow you instantly—"

But Tizzo was gone, flashing through the bright, painted rooms, leaping down the stairways and then out the door into the garden.

There he found a big, gray-headed man whose eyes shone even through the dimness of the twilight. He wore heavy riding boots; his doublet was wide open at the base of his great throat. A small round hat, plumed at one side, sat jauntily on his head, and at his side a heavy sword made a light shivering sound of steel against the scabbard as he moved to greet Tizzo. Even Luigi Falcone, even Giovanpaolo Baglioni were no greater in the eyes of Tizzo than this man who had made him the gift of one consummate trick of swordplay.

CHAPTER

19

THEY greeted each other as men who have owed their lives to one another. Then, as Baron Melrose pushed himself back to arm's length, he surveyed the younger man with care.

"You are no bigger in the bones than when I last saw you," he said. "But neither is the wasp as big as an eagle, and yet it can trouble a man more. Still, I could wish that there were twenty English pounds of extra beef on you. Then you could spend more muscle and less spirit in your wars."

"My lord," said Tizzo, "I am what I am—a starved thing compared with you, but ready to guard your back in any battle. Tell me, how do you dare to show yourself so near to Perugia? Are the Oddi rising to try to retake the town? How did you know so quickly that I was at the Villa Falcone? Where have you been since I last saw you?"

"If I had four tongues and four separate sets of brains, I would begin to answer all those questions at once," said the big Englishman, laughing. "But as the matter stands, I have to speak them one by one. As for the Oddi, their secrets are their own. I am no nearer Perugia than I have been for a month. And I knew you were here because a whisper ran through the hills and came to my ears. Now for one question in my turn: Have you broken with Giovanpaolo, Astorre, and all the Baglioni?"

"I've crossed swords with Giovanpaolo," said Tizzo. "I've had my life attempted in the garden of Messer Astorre. And a price has been put on my head."

"Have all of these things happened?" asked Henry of Melrose. "You can pick up trouble faster than a pigeon can pick up wheat. But if the Baglioni have closed one door in your face, another opens of its own weight behind you. Tizzo, Jeronimo della Penna wishes to speak to you."

"About what?"

"He will open the subject to you himself."

"Tizzo!" called the anxious voice of Falcone.

"Say farewell to Falcone," said Melrose, "and meet me again here. That is, if you wish to face della Penna tonight."

There was nothing that Tizzo wished to see less than the long, dark face of Jeronimo della Penna, but it was for the very purpose of sounding the depths and the intentions of this man that Giovanpaolo had schemed with him. Therefore: "I return in one moment!" said Tizzo, and hurried to meet Falcone.

"I'm called away," said Tizzo.

"Into what?" demanded Falcone. "Tizzo, you shall stay this night, at least, in my house."

"I have to go. I am compelled," said Tizzo. "As surely as a swallow ever followed summer, so I have to follow the whistle that sounded for me tonight."

"It's a thing that I don't like," said Falcone. "But the devil befriends young men. Good-by again. Wait—here is a purse you may need—no, take it. God bless you; come to me again when you can!"

And Tizzo was away again to the side of Melrose.

They walked on through the gardens until they heard the ringing strokes of an ax in a hollow, followed by the crashing of a great tree. The fall of the heavy trunk seemed to shake the ground under them.

"There are friends of mine, yonder, working by lanternlight," said Tizzo. "And I must speak a word with them. Wait here—or at least keep out of their sight."

Tizzo, hurrying on, came on three foresters who worked by a dim, shaking light which had been hung from the branch of a small sapling. Unshaven of face, ragged in their clothes, the three were preparing to attack another huge pine tree with axes.

[93]

"My friends!" called Tizzo, stepping into the faint circle of the light. "Taddeo—Riccardo—Adolfo—well met again!"

The three turned slowly toward him. Old Taddeo began to nod his bearded head.

"Here comes the Firebrand again. What forests have you been burning down, Tizzo? Is it true that the Baglioni are leaning their weight and ready to fall on your head?"

Tizzo grasped their hands. "I've had my hands filled with something besides axshafts," he admitted. "But I'm happy enough to see you all again."

"Your hand has turned soft," said Taddeo.

"It is harder than my head, however," laughed Tizzo. "Why are you working so late?"

"Because the overseer drives us like dogs."

"I'll speak to my father. You shall not be enslaved like this!"

"No man is a slave who has mastered an art," said Taddeo. He waved his great ax with one hand. "And we are masters of ours!" he added. "But have you touched the haft of an ax since we last saw you?"

"An ax has helped me more than a sword," said Tizzo. "Give me a mark and let me show you that my eye is still clear."

Old Taddeo struck the trunk of the tree a slashing blow and left a broad, white face, large as the disk of the moon and shining brightly.

"There is the target. Make a mark for him, my sons," said Taddeo.

Big Riccardo, chuckling half in malice, drew out a knife, picked up a straight stick to make a ruler, and calmly drew a five-pointed star with the sharp steel edge. Where the knife cut the white of the pine wood it left a thin, glistening streak, hardly perceptible except to a very fine eye.

Old Taddeo ran the tips of his hard fingers over the design and laughed loudly.

"Let me see it done, then!" he said. "It has never been managed before even by the oldest woodsman in the forest. Strike at that target freely, Tizzo. There are ten strokes to make and with the tenth the star should leap out from the tree. And then see that every one of your strokes has hit exactly the ruled line. Ten

[94]

strokes without a single failure—here is my own ax to use, and if you succeed—why, the ax is yours!"

Tizzo accepted the ax and looked down on it with attention. Of old, from his boyhood, he had heard about that ax, and he had seen it swung, more than once, in the hands of Taddeo. The steel had a curious look. It was blue, with a strangely intermingling pattern of lines of gray. And the story was that once a fine Damascus blade had been brought back from the Orient, and being broken it had been rewelded by the father of Taddeo, not into a new sword, but into an axhead. That matchless steel, supple as thought, hard as crystal, had been transformed into a common woodsman's ax. The blue shining of it seemed to be reflected, at that moment, in the flame-blue of the eyes of Tizzo as he swayed the cunningly poised weight of the ax.

For two lifetimes that ax had been in use, the handle altered, refined, reshaped, so as to give it a gently sweeping curve. The balance was perfect. It grew to the hand like an extension of the body.

Tizzo threw down on the ground the purse which he had just received from Falcone.

"I take the challenge, and if I fail, that purse is yours, my friends. Watch me now, Taddeo. Watch, Riccardo, Adolfo! There are ten enemies; if I miss one of them, the gold in that purse is your gold, and you will all be rich for ten years!"

So, measuring his distance, swinging the ax lightly once or twice to free his muscles, he suddenly attacked the dim target with no calm deliberation, but with a shower of strokes, as though he stood foot to foot with fighting antagonists. With each stroke the ax bit in deeply; and with the tenth a block of solid wood leaped out from the blazed surface of the tree and fell upon the ground—a perfect star with five points!

The three foresters raised a single deep-throated shout and actually fell on their knees to examine the work that had been done. But neither on the fallen star nor on the edges of the blazed surface appeared a single one of the lines which Riccardo had drawn with his knife. True to a hair's breadth, the ax had sunk into the wood.

[95]

Old Taddeo, standing up, pulled the cap from his head and scratched the scalp in meditation.

"Wise men should teach only the wise," he stated. "I have wasted my time teaching these two louts. But when I taught you the art of the ax, I taught two hands *and* a brain. Take my ax, Tizzo. Take my blue ax, and God give you grace with it. If it will not shear through the heaviest helmet as though it were leather and not hard armorer's steel, call me a fool and a liar! Keep the edge keen; let it bite; and the battle will always be yours."

Tizzo picked up the purse and tossed it to the old man.

"A gift is always better than a bargain," he said. "Turn this money into happiness, and remember Tizzo when you drink wine."

So he was gone, quickly, and found Henry of Melrose chuckling in the woods not far away.

"I followed closely enough to see what you did," said the Englishman. "You understand one of the great secrets; coin is made round so that it may keep rolling. And the best of buying is a giving away!"

CHAPTER

20

JERONIMO DELLA PENNA had a dark, yellow skin, and a mouth which the earnest gloom of his speculations pulled down at the corners. He had large properties, but he was both penurious and absent-minded. His hose was threadbare over the knees, on this evening, but his brocaded cloak was fit for a king.

He kept striding up and down, and when he greeted Tizzo it was with a stare that strove to penetrate to his soul.

"Do you vouch for this man, my lord of Melrose?" he asked.

"I vouch for nothing," said Melrose, "except for the state of my appetite and the cleanness of my sword. Here is the man I told you about. I found him willing to come. I know he has been driven out of Perugia. Perhaps that makes him fit for your purposes. For my part, I withdraw and leave you to find out about him as much as you please. Come to me later, Tizzo. I have a room in the south tower. We can have a glass of wine together, before you sleep."

He went away in this abrupt fashion, leaving della Penna still at a gaze.

He said: "My friend, it is said that there is a price on your head?"

"That is true," said Tizzo.

"It is said that you have been wronged by Giovanpaolo. But he has a way of winding himself into the hearts of men so that they serve him more for love than for money. If he has dropped you today, can he pick you up tomorrow?"

"Perhaps," said Tizzo.

Della Penna started. "Do you think that he *can* take you again when he chooses?"

"How can I tell?" asked Tizzo, calmly. "I am not a man who knows the mind he will have tomorrow. The days as they come one by one are hard enough for me to decipher. Every morning, I hope to find a pot of gold before night; and how can I tell what will be in the pot? The hate of Giovanpaolo, or his friendship? It is all one to me."

"And yet Melrose brought you to me!" pondered Jeronimo della Penna. "Tell me, Tizzo—because I have heard some rare tales of your courage and strength and wild heart—are you a man to pocket an insult?"

"I am not," said Tizzo.

"Are you a man to return wrong for wrong?"

"I am," said Tizzo.

[97]

"Are you a man I could trust?" pursued della Penna.

"I've never betrayed a friend," said Tizzo.

"Ah! You won't answer me outright?" exclaimed della Penna.

"*Signore,* you are a stranger to me," said Tizzo. "Why should I boast about my faith and truth? You must do as I do—take you as I find you. If you can use me for things I wish to do, I hope to shine with a very good opinion. If you try to ride me uphill against my wishes, you can be sure you'll be sooner weary of spurring than I of following the road."

Della Penna scowled.

"You are one of these fellows," he said, "who have been praised for speaking your mind right out, like an honest man."

"Sir," said Tizzo. "I think that only a fool trusts the man who is out of his sight."

"Do you know why I have sent for you?"

"I guess that you plan something against Giovanpaolo or some others of your own family who have the control of Perugia."

"If that were the case, what do I know of you?"

"Nothing except that you think I have a grievance against the same people. I make no promises; I ask none from you. If there is mischief abroad, perhaps each of us will make his own profit."

Della Penna smiled, faintly. He had found something in the last speech that appealed to him very much. Now he said: "There is one man in the world who can tell me the truth about you. But before he is through searching you, you may wish that you had let your soul be roasted on a spit in hell. Come with me, Mr. Honest Man."

They went down a corridor which communicated with winding stairs and came up these to an open tower from which Tizzo could look across the dark heads of the hills to a little group of lights which, he knew, shone from the village of Falcone. On this top story of the tower there was a fat old white-headed man with a red nose and a very cheerful smile, who greeted della Penna warmly, turning from an iron kettle in which he was stewing some sort of a brew over a little corner hearth.

"Messer Baldassare," said della Penna, "I have brought—"

"A good sharp blade that will be useful unless it cuts the hand which tries to use it."

Della Penna was so struck by the saying that he turned sharply about toward Tizzo, but Tizzo was too busy staring into the white circle to pay the least attention. It seemed to him that great white sign upon the floor was as dangerous as the entrance into hell itself. It was a pit of damnation on the verge of which he stood and, covertly, he crossed himself.

"How do you know," asked della Penna, "that I wish to use this man? You have cast no horoscope for him nor even consulted your herbs on his behalf or on mine. Explain what you mean?"

This sharply inquiring tone did not upset the magician in the least, and he turned his red, jovial smile on della Penna as he answered.

"I have served your father and you for so long that when great good or evil come toward you my invisible agents are apt to whisper something in the air, indistinct words. I was about to make those words become clearer. I was about to force the spirits to speak to me in real language. I had drawn the circle on the floor and heated the broth, as you can see for yourself, when you appeared with the very man about whom I heard the whisper."

"How do you know it is the very man?" asked della Penna.

"Look!" said the magician.

He extended his hand above the steaming pot. In an instant the steam had turned crimson, and the hand of Messer Baldassare was gilded red, also.

Tizzo uttered a faint, choked exclamation. His knees grew weak. He was terribly certain that now he was beholding the handiwork of the devil.

"When I saw the red light strike my hand," said the magician, "I knew that you were near—on the very stairs about to open my door. I had barely time to put my hat on my head before you came into the tower."

He was wearing a square, yellow, high hat with certain cabalistic signs worked in black upon it; Tizzo remembered the saying that it is not safe for common men to look upon an enchanter when he is serving the devil with his arts.

"Look into this man, Baldassare," said della Penna. "Shall I have good or evil fortune from him?"

"Better than for me to speak, I can force him to speak for himself and to utter the truth."

"Force him, Baldassare?" demanded the patron.

"Give me three drops of your blood, young man," said the enchanter. "Come, and let me put them into the pot. Come without fear. In the circle, there is no harm for you!"

But Tizzo nevertheless chose to edge cautiously around the circle and so come to the caldron.

"Give me your hand!" said Messer Baldassare in a sudden, loud, and terrible voice.

He caught the right hand of Tizzo and stared straight into his eyes. The very soul of Tizzo was shaken, but he looked back and thought that the face of the enchanter had turned into the face of a frowning lion. The eyes were sparks of fire.

"Now," said Baldassare. And drawing the hand of Tizzo until it extended over the pot, Baldassare plucked out a bodkin and pricked a finger until the blood ran. The running of the blood he watched carefully and suddenly threw the hand from him.

Then, stepping to the circle in haste, Baldassare drew certain signs with a rapid piece of chalk. Tizzo, frozen in his place with horror, felt the hair prickle and rise on his scalp.

Baldassare, dropping on one knee, held out both hands, palms down, close to the floor. It was the gesture, Tizzo knew, of one who prayed to the infernal powers.

What would be revealed, now? In what manner would the enchanter learn of the plot which Tizzo had made with Giovanpaolo to come at the truth of any machinations which this same scoundrelly della Penna was practicing against him?

It was time to prepare for an escape with foot and hand and sword; but Tizzo found that he could not move. The spell of the enchantment—was it already working upon him?

Then out of silence in which there was only the faint bubbling of the caldron, a voice issued, faint and far away, half stifled, but seeming to proceed from the steam of the pot itself. In obscure doggerel the voice said—and it was like the voice of Tizzo himself:

> I have found no greater lord
> Than the brightness of a sword;
> I have found no lady's grace
> Sweeter than high danger's face;
> I shall serve no higher power

Than the stealthy midnight hour;
Trust me in the hour of sorrow
But beware of me tomorrow . . .

Here the voice ended. The enchanter, faintly groaning, rose to his feet and then sank wearily into a chair where he remained with his head bowed, as though exhausted by the labor of his spirit.

"Trust you in the hour of sorrow? That is my answer!" said della Penna, triumphantly. "If I can trust you in the hour of sorrow, let the devil carry you off wherever he pleases on the adventure of tomorrow. Messer Baldassare, here is something for your hand. I am very well pleased with you and the spirit that sang from the steam. Come, Signor Tizzo; there is much that I must say to you!"

CHAPTER

21

Tizzo, his body and his face darkened by the almost indelible stain of walnut juice, a sleek, black wig on his head, and his face aged at least ten years by the introduction of certain dark shadows in the natural lines of his features, finished dressing, looked at himself in a mirror, and turned with a laugh to Henry of Melrose and della Penna.

"If I had a mother, she would never know me," he said. "If I had a father, he would deny me."

"No," said the baron. "He would see the same blue devil looking out of your eyes."

"It would take more than a father," said della Penna, critically, "to look into that face and see the blue of the eyes. He is safe, my lord. He can enter Perugia now, and walk straight through all the halls of the Baglioni, if he wishes, without drawing a second glance. This handiwork of Messer Baldassare, who is there that can see through it?"

They all agreed to this.

"There are horses ready," said della Penna. "Ride as fast as you can to the town of Camerino. Go to the lord of Camerino and show to him this signet ring of mine. He will know it well. Ask him this question: How many? And when you have heard his answer, return to the city of Perugia as fast as you may. Go to the tavern of the Sign of the Golden Stag. There, wait until you see in one of the public rooms a man with a red band drawn around his head. When you see him, go to him privately and say: 'Camerino.' That will be enough to win his ear and he will instantly ask what news you bring. Repeat to him then the number which the lord of Camerino has given to you. And leave him at once. When this has been done, remain at the Sign of the Golden Stag until you receive word from me, directly. As for your means of entering the town of Perugia, show at any gate the same signet ring which I have given to you, and you will be admitted without question. I am not without power in that city, and before long my power shall be greater. The time may come before many days when they will have a cause to think of me—the fat rats, the citizens of Perugia!"

Here the Englishman remarked: "I shall wait for you at the Sign of the Golden Stag, my young friend. Look for me there."

"No, Henry," protested della Penna. "You are too well known. You run too great a risk if you enter that town. They would rather see you dead than have all the Oddi stretched lifeless at their feet. For, without you, they know that the Oddi would be powerless."

"I have ways of going into the city and coming from it safely enough," said the Baron Melrose. "Remember, Tizzo. I shall see you at the inn."

"Now hurry," exclaimed della Penna. "Your servant is already waiting at the head of your horse. I have fetched him from the house of Falcone. Be swift, be faithful, and your fortune is made as well as your revenge."

That was how Tizzo found himself mounted and on the road in another minute.

The one-eyed warrior, thief, and servant, Elia Bigi, merely said to him: "What am I to know, master?"

"To know nothing is to be wiser than I am," said Tizzo, frankly.

They rode constantly through the night. And still there were relays of horses waiting for them at appointed places along the road, strong horses which beat the summer roads to dust as they galloped steadily on. It was a weary pair of riders who, at last, climbed into the mountain town of Camerino, dignified by the presence in it of the old university. And chance brought them straight on a procession of riders who had come back from hawking with some short-winged hawks on the wrist, and, above all, a beautiful pair of peregrine falcons.

One of these was on the wrist of a middle-aged man who rode with a downward smile of crafty thought on his fat face.

"That," whispered Elia Bigi, "is the lord of Camerino."

So Tizzo, hurrying his horse to meet the aristocrat, held out his hand in greeting, having turned the signet face of della Penna's ring around to the inside of his finger. He made sure that those crafty, downward eyes were fixed on the signet as he spoke.

Instantly the eyes of the lord of Camerino lifted to the face of Tizzo.

"What news of my friends?" he asked, quietly.

"How many?" questioned Tizzo, with a smile.

There was half a second of pause before the other answered: "Two hundred and fifty. If time is given."

And Tizzo fell back at once from the group of riders and let them go on with their tired, sweating horses.

Camerino was half a mile high in the mountains; Tizzo and Elia Bigi dropped by looping roads through the valleys and climbed again toward Perugia. It was night when they came before the dark height of the gate of Marzia. The lights of the guard showed vaguely, the three Etruscan busts above the gateway and the heads of the two proud horses which flanked the group. To the captain of the gate, Tizzo showed the signet ring. There was no asking of questions. The gate was opened to them at once, and they entered into that narrow, winding way, so capable of defense, so sure to check the onrush of attackers, and so advanced into the narrows of Baglioni Street.

It was well-named; because to either side the lofty tops of the palaces of the Baglioni lifted toward the stars, fencing a narrow, crooked way through heaven.

Elia Bigi said at the ear of his master: "Here are the seats of the mighty, and the mighty are asleep. They are so rich, these Baglioni, that poison is beside every bed; a knife is sharpened for every throat. And yet they can sleep."

"Not all of them," answered Tizzo.

For, as he spoke, a number of retainers bearing lights rounded a bend of the narrow street with several horsemen behind them. The fellows who were on foot in advance kept calling out: "Room for the noble Semonetto! Room for his highness!"

At these calls, the crowd in the street shrank back at once into entrances.

This Semonetto, as Tizzo knew, was of all the Baglioni the fiercest blade, the greatest warrior with the single exception of Giovanpaolo and, perhaps, the great Astorre, for whose wedding the city of Perugia was now in a tumult. He was still in the middle twenties and the expectation of the time was that he would go on to a greatness even surpassing that of the older members of the family, for already he showed the brain for war as well as the courage of a true lion.

He was now seen with two young companions on horseback behind the group of his forerunners, who kept the crowd back from his nobility. They were laughing with one another.

"Back!" said Elia Bigi, at the ear of his master. "Quickly, *signore*. This is the great young Semonetto himself, the wildest and strongest blade in Perugia, unless Giovanpaolo himself be counted. Give him free passage. His temper is fiercer than any fire!"

"It should have something to feed on, then," said Tizzo, laughing. "A fire that is starved of wood soon dies."

[104]

And he kept his horse fairly in the middle of the street.

The forerunners of the Baglioni were instantly about him. Two or three of them sang out for him to keep from the path; one man laid his hand on the bridle of Tizzo's tired horse.

"Keep your hand back, brother," said Tizzo. "Even if there is a helmet on your head, I have a hand heavy enough to knock a dent in it."

The man-at-arms, hearing this threat, instantly sprang into a posture of defense and snatched out his long and heavy sword.

"What's the matter there?" cried a loud voice. And young Semonetto rode up to the van on a great white horse. Of all the men Tizzo had seen, this was the most magnificent. Such shoulders, such a head and such a bearing were beyond comparison.

"Here is a fool of a stranger," said one of the servants, "who refuses to make way for your highness."

"What do you mean, fellow?" asked Semonetto. "I am Semonetto of the Baglioni. What will you have?"

"My share of the street, even if you were the lord of the sun and the moon," said Tizzo. And he looked fixedly at the other, as a hunting hound might have looked at the throat of a lion, wondering if just there a touch of the teeth might not give an ending to the battle.

"Are you drunk?" demanded Semonetto.

"Only with a little wine," said Tizzo. "But you are drunk with pride, Semonetto. You have too much blood in your body. You are swollen."

"Master, master!" groaned Elia Bigi, in terror.

"If I have too much blood, are you prepared to let some of it?" demanded Semonetto.

"My friend, I'll gladly be your doctor," said Tizzo, fingering the handle of old Taddeo's ax which hung beside his saddle.

"Have at you, then!" shouted Semonetto, in a sudden and uncontrollable rage, and he spurred his big white horse straight down the street toward Tizzo. A sword had come into Semonetto's hand as he spoke. His height, the bigness of his horse, the sharp down-slope of the street made him loom like a giant above Tizzo. And the long sword darted like a silver snake at Tizzo's breast.

Taddeo's ax was swiftly in the hand of Tizzo. It feathered as true and as light in his grasp as though it had been made of painted wood.

He had little time. In a flashing semicircle the head of the ax went up and met the deadly lunge which was aimed at his heart. As he parried, Tizzo laughed, and as he laughed the axhead struck the sword away. The violence of the parry knocked the long blade high up; and then Tizzo struck in turn, with one hand, a lightning fast circling of the ax.

Semonetto might well have been cloven to the chin by that blow, but his was the instinct of the true fencer, and he turned his sword into a parry to guard his head.

The descending weight of the ax met the long steel and snapped it. But the shock turned the blade of the ax so that it glanced flatling from the head of Semonetto. The shock hurled him prostrate across the bows of his saddle.

And at this, a wild yell of despair and rage and anguish came from all the followers and companions of the young noble. They drove in a flock, straight at Tizzo.

The ax, which was perfect for the dealing of a single stroke, was less valuable in such a melee as this. Tizzo, hooking the heavy weapon beside his saddle, instantly pulled out his sword, which was blade and shield at once in his perfect hand. And here Elia Bigi proved the goodness of his fighting heart by pressing in beside his master in this hopeless quarrel against overmastering numbers.

They put aside a dozen strokes. The clashing of steel began to resound through the street when the voice of Semonetto called out, loudly: "Swords up! Hold every hand."

His order was obeyed. And Semonetto, riding weaponless through the crowd of his friends, came up to Tizzo and held out his hand.

Semonetto was pale. A thin streak of blood coursed down one side of his face, but he was smiling as he said: "My lord of the moon and sun, that was a good, swift trick of the ax. And I see that you are the master of a sword, also. My friend, come to see me tomorrow. I yearn with all my heart to cross blades with you again. In any case, I wish to call you a friend, whether living or dead. You know my name. Find your way to my house and a wel-

[106]

come. Now, my friends," he added to those around him, "beware of lifting a hand against this dark-faced stranger. He is my companion from this moment. He is my confederate and friend."

He added, in a voice that was probably louder than he intended to make it: "Get me home, some of you. My head is broken, and I am half sick from that blow! Fool that I am to venture out with no steel to guard this thin pate of mine!"

CHAPTER

22

THE press was gone instantly from the street and Tizzo, riding on unhampered and unfollowed, at the side of Elia Bigi, said: "That was very well done, Elia. When the fellow with the halberd took that swing at my head I was sure that it was my last moment. I saw the flash of the steel from the corner of my eye, but never in time to make a parry. You were the hand that saved me then. I thank you from my heart."

"What am I to say, then," remarked Bigi, "about the man in the green and red hose who ran in with his target and sword and would have cut my throat if you had not knocked his blade aside from the true thrust which he was making with it?"

"Say nothing," said Tizzo, "except to thank God, with me, that we are both men, and true to one another."

"That's a very handsome thing to say," declared Elia, rubbing his big hands together and chuckling, "but your way of searching for trouble is something more than manly. It is more like an angel's; and an angel you are apt to become, one of these days, if you continue always as you have begun. If you keep on sowing the teeth of dragons every day of your life one of them will stick you in the heel and poison your life."

Tizzo laughed in turn. They had come now within the sight of the Sign of the Golden Stag, and now rode through the entrance into a courtyard which Tizzo could remember very well.

It seemed to Tizzo that the very man who showed him to a room looked closely and covertly at him. But, as Elia said afterwards this was a mere trick of his imagination.

"The hunted rabbit sees a wolf in every strange hare," said Elia. "Now we are as safe as any other man in Perugia to drink wine at our ease until the devil and your own weariness with life cause you to get us into more trouble."

"You shall have your wine," said Tizzo, "but now I give you the smallest part of an hour to go out and find exactly where the Lady Beatrice is now lodged. Go quickly, and return to me."

He went out while Tizzo looked about his room and examined the windows which opened on the one side upon the paved court and upon the other, just beneath the eaves, overlooked the outer street. There was no country in the world, at that time, which offered so many conveniences to travelers as the inns of Italy.

And Tizzo, after he had tried the softness of the bed with a backstroke of his ax, and tasted the pitcher of red Umbrian wine which was brought to him, decided that he would have a few hours of happiness, no matter what would follow.

It was at about this time that Elia Bigi re-entered the room.

"I've been stopped by a hard-faced captain of infantry," he said, "who remembers that I was once employed by a certain Tizzo, the Firebrand."

"What did you say to him? Tell me honestly," said Tizzo.

"I told him," said Elia Bigi, grinning sourly, "that although I was a male cat I had already spent eight of my lives and that I did not wish to pay down the ninth of them for the sake of a flame-headed, wild-brained fellow with an eye crazier than that of a warhorse. So I now had service with a quiet young man who did not fight with swords or axes above once a day, except on the Sabbath, when he might blood himself twice; and who never played at dice for more than five hours at a sitting, or drank more than two gallons of wine before rising from the table. The lieutenant said that I was wise to find such a quiet master and that he would pay his respects to you tomorrow.

"He asked me if I knew that there was a price of two thousand florins on the head of that same Tizzo. I swallowed twice before I was able to repeat the words after him."

Tizzo laughed. "But did you come back to me without news of the Lady Beatrice? However, of course you would not have word of her at a common tavern."

"Would I not?" asked the servant. "The poor people are always the ones to talk about kings and lords and ladies. The Lady Beatrice cannot so much as crook the little finger of her left hand without the report of it going the rounds of Perugia. There is a certain French lord who swears that if he could have enjoyed the privilege of killing you he might have taken your place in her favor."

"Enough of that," said Tizzo. "But tell me the name of the frog-eater, the forked carrot, the damned *parlez-vous* who dared to handle my name and that of the lovely lady in the same breath?"

"If I told you that you would have him dead and yourself hanged before morning," said Elia. "However, it is true that the Lady Beatrice now sleeps in the house of her cousin, the rich Grifone. Her room, since she left the convent and you left Perugia, is the third room on the south side—the room with the three little columns of white marble, banded with blue, in front of each window."

Instantly Tizzo was drinking wine with his left hand and scribbling with his right:

Adored and most beautiful, queen of the world and of Tizzo, spitfire and nightingale, flirt and angel, most exquisite Beatrice of whom waking I dream, and for whom sleeping I wake, hear me and forgive me:

I am at the Sign of the Golden Stag, come to see the wedding of my lord Astorre, and would to God that it were yours and mine.

I love you past thought. I shall see you before I leave Perugia or die attempting it.

[109]

Farewell for a moment, which to me is an age, loveliest, maddest, sweetest of women.

Thy servant that will one day be thy master by the help of God, two spurs, and a good right arm.

TIZZO

This letter he sealed, kissed, and presented to Elia.

"Tie a pebble to it and throw it in at one of those same columned windows of which you spoke," said Tizzo. "Remember that if you are seen making the throw, your throat will be cut. If the letter falls into any hands but hers, *my* throat will be cut."

At this, Elia was gone quickly from the room and left his master walking up and down in an agony of impatience.

It was still the greater part of an hour before Elia returned and gave his master a letter from which a light and delicate fragrance came to the enchanted senses of Tizzo, but when he opened the letter he found written, merely:

I had forgotten that you were living; your letter reminds me that you will soon be dead if you linger in Perugia.
Farewell.

There was no signature. Over the brutal words Tizzo pored for a long time but could not extract from them any semblance of a tender meaning.

CHAPTER

23

THE sleep that tumbled at last over the excited brain of Tizzo was a storm of nightmares. When he wakened, it was with sun in the window, a fanfare of trumpets ringing through the street outside, and a joyous voice of citizens crying through the air.

And far and near through the city there were high sounds of music.

"Hai, Elia!" cried Tizzo. "Is it the end of the world and are we all going to heaven?"

And running to the window he looked out on the most splendid sight that had ever graced his eyes, for directly beneath him he saw twenty knights riding up the street in gilded armor that shone like fire, while trumpeters paced before them, blowing their blasts in great, strident harmonies. And after the knights walked girls each as gay as a wind of spring that dances at once all the wild flowers in the field, so bright were their costumes. In between the out-roaring of the trumpets, the girls were dancing, and from their filled aprons scattering roses, roses, nothing but roses white and yellow and crimson on the pavement. Behind them, in turn, came eight horses as white as snow, each led not by a mere page or groom, but by a man of noble birth.

The eight horses drew a great carriage canopied loftily with flowing velvets fringed with gold and silver, and under that canopy sat Messer Astorre Baglioni and his bride.

It seemed to Tizzo, at that moment, that Astorre Baglioni was the most glorious man he had ever seen or dreamed of, because he was dressed from head to foot in blazing gold, and with a great golden collar oversprinkled with jewels, the gift of My Lords of Venice, whom the famous warrior had served in their time of need.

In fact, the eyes of the world were fixed, for this day, upon Perugia and on this almost royal wedding.

As for the bride, Tizzo could hardly tell whether she was beautiful or no. At least she bore the great name of the Orsini, dazzling to the mind that knew its famous history, and the pearls that covered her sleeves and her hair dazzled the eye of Tizzo.

Behind that chariot of fame rode, in advance of all the rear escort, a single figure on a great black horse, armed in chased steel completely except for the stern young head. That was Semonetto. As he went by, there was almost as great an outcry in his honor as in that of the bridegroom and the bride. For all of Perugia had been beautified by the great undertakings of this youth in honor of the marriage.

As young Semonetto rode by, the voice of Tizzo was among the most shrill as he leaned from his window, so Semonetto looked up. Instantly he shouted a greeting, waving his arm, and still was waving it to Tizzo as the black charger carried him from view around the next bend of the street.

Tizzo was out in the throng at once, with gaunt Elia Bigi striding behind him. The weight of Beatrice's letter was heavy on the heart of Tizzo, but in this time of public rejoicing, he could not help but rejoice, also.

They were coming into the yard of the Golden Stag when Tizzo saw, suddenly, a tall man about whose head was tied a scarf of crimson silk with fringed tassels falling down behind his neck. In the wild riot of that day such a Turkish bit of decoration passed for nothing, but Tizzo remembered the instructions of della Penna.

He passed close to the tall fellow and, as he did so, he was startled to see the disfigured face of the most poisonous of his enemies: Marozzo.

A dagger stroke would have been a proper greeting for the scoundrel, but instead, Tizzo walked slowly past, fingering his cap so that the great signet ring of della Penna showed clearly on his hand. Marozzo could not miss it.

[112]

Instantly he was touched on his shoulder.

"How many?" demanded the voice of Marozzo, huskily.

"Two hundred and fifty," said Tizzo.

"Ha!" exclaimed Marozzo, and Tizzo turned around to find his eyes blazing.

"They have drawn you in, Master Tizzo, have they?" sneered Marozzo. "A fine bargain they have made, when nameless dogs are to hunt at the sides of gentlemen!"

"Mateo," said Tizzo, calmly, "the next mark I put on you will not be a thing which a rag can cover. Go carry the news to your masters and stop snapping at my heels. There will be a time for our own private brawling, but this is not the day."

He walked on into the tavern and went singing up the stairs, with Bigi behind him, but when he threw open the door of his room he was amazed to see a jaunty youth in a green doublet and parti-colored hose, half red and half yellow, lolling in a chair near the window and sipping wine.

"You take your ease, my friend," said Tizzo, "but you take it in the wrong room."

"A fig for you and your rooms," said a rather husky, boyish voice, that sounded on a familiar chord in the memory of Tizzo. Anger brought the old flame-blue into the eyes of Tizzo as he answered: "A fig for me and my rooms? Young lad, I give you while I count three to get from that chair through the door. . . . Elia, where is your whip!"

"Whip?" said the figure that still lolled in the chair. "Whip—to me?"

And a slender poniard, a mere gleam of light, came into the hand of the stranger.

The sight brought the sword of Tizzo whistling from the scabbard.

"You have a sword as well as a knife. Draw it and we'll have a little game together!" he challenged.

"Have at you!" cried the stranger, and was instantly up, and sword in hand. But at this moment the sunlight fell on the face which had been darkly shadowed and Tizzo sprang back with a cry.

"Out of the room, Elia!" he said.

"What is it? A saint or a bit of the true Cross?" asked Elia, and strode grumbling from the room, slamming the door heavily behind him.

Tizzo, throwing his sword onto the bed, ran forward with his hands stretched out: "Beatrice!" he said. "Mother of heaven, you have not come here? Beatrice, if a whisper comes to the ears of Perugia your reputation is ruined, blackened forever; so quickly —go—"

She dropped her sword back into its sheath, the poniard clanked home in the scabbard.

"Tizzo," she said, "my reputation will still be good with you, and what do I care about the rest of the world?"

"And what did you care for me," he asked, "when you wrote to me last night?"

"That was last night," she answered, "and this is a new day."

He took her in his arms.

"Don't kiss me, Tizzo," she said, her brown eyes looking straight into his.

He released her with a great effort.

"I do as you will," said he.

"So much as a touch," she told him, "and I leave my home forever, and follow you through the world. Oh, in the name of my good father, why are there not other men like you? Not in looks, Tizzo, because I loathe red hair. Not in fortune, because I hate poverty. Not in dimensions, because you are half a head shorter than the hero I would like to have. But why are not other men, like you, compounded of equal parts of madness, laughter, extravagance, and swordplay? If I could find one, I would never look at you again, never think of you, never dream of you, but until I can find another, I have to love Tizzo until my heart aches and my head spins."

24

HE WAS like a man who sees a jewel but dares not touch it. He could not move without stretching his hands toward her. He could not speak without a rush of emotion that threatened to destroy his words.

"Whatever you think of me, tell me what you have done this afternoon," he insisted.

"Put on boy's clothes and left the house of Grifone."

"You have been living there?"

"Yes, I've been living there."

"How could you leave unnoticed?"

"By a rope. I slid out of a back window."

"And left the rope hanging?"

"No, it was a double length, so when I got down, I pulled it all after me."

"How long before you'll be missed?"

"They won't miss me before dark."

"Beatrice, I love you to a madness."

"You were mad before, or you would never have loved me."

"What are we to do?"

"Giovanpaolo loves you, and with his love you can do anything. He swears that you are one of the immortals."

"Will he let me marry you, Beatrice?"

"He says it would be poor policy, but he will never oppose it too much if he can make the rest of the family agree. I've told him that if I cannot have you, I will have nothing. They have showed me a beautiful French duke with more estates than there are between Perugia and Rome, a face like a statue, and a brain like a statue's, also. They want me to choose him. But I tell them that if I marry such an ass we'll have mules for children."

"Beatrice, stop talking a moment and let me look at you."

She put back her head and assumed a proud attitude, but in a moment she was smiling at him.

"You had to keep yourself in exercise by fighting the proudest, highest, harshest, sternest, wildest of the Baglioni—my cousin Semonetto. I heard that you cracked his head for him."

"How did you know that it was I?"

"Who else would dare such a thing? Who else could do it, with an ax like a woodchopper working on a tree? Besides, I talked to Semonetto, and he told me about it; when he saw that a blue lightning came in your eyes as you fought, when he told me that you fought laughing, I knew that it was my Tizzo, the happy madman. Tizzo, when *we* marry we shall not have mules for children—they will all be born with a cap and bells."

"My God, my God, how happy I am! How I love you, Beatrice! I could forswear wine, or anything, for your sake. But listen to me. I have news for Giovanpaolo."

"I know that. That is what has waked me at night in a cold sweat."

"Tell him that I saw della Penna."

"The long-faced, sour, discontented grumbler!"

"He is more than a grumbler. He is a traitor. Besides, he works with a wizard!"

"Do you believe in such stuff?" asked the girl, her proud lip curling a little.

"I tell you, Beatrice, that in della Penna's house I heard things and I saw things beyond credence."

"Every man is sure to see as much as his superstition enables him to believe. Tizzo, don't tell me that you are taken in by the childish tricks of juggling magicians."

"I heard my own voice speak out of the rising steam of a magic caldron!"

"Magic fiddlesticks."

"I tell you, I heard it. And afterward, della Penna gave part of his trust to me. He sent me to the lord of Camerino to ask him one question: How many? I went there and asked, and the lord of Camerino told me: Two hundred and fifty."

"Did Camerino speak of two hundred and fifty armed men?"

"He named the number; he did not speak of the men."

"This is horribly serious, Tizzo."

"Murder, murder, or I miss my guess. That news from Camerino I repeated today to a designated man in the court of this tavern, a man with a red scarf around his head—and that was Mateo Marozzo."

"He was never known for any good."

"I have sworn to have the killing of him—but this leads on. I shall see more of them, I'm sure. Before long, having done one mission, I shall be employed on another. When and where they mean to strike we still do not know. There must be other heads of the plot than della Penna. Tell Giovanpaolo that before long I hope to have seen the bare faces of the plotters; and then I shall be able to send him word."

"In the meantime, you go in a double danger, Tizzo. A price has been put on your head by my family; and also if the traitors of della Penna's company suspect you, you will die like a dog."

"Danger is the air I was born to breathe. Beatrice, go back with the news I give you."

"I cannot leave you, Tizzo. See—I try to walk to the door but my feet will not carry me there."

"How can even God have fashioned a thing so beautiful, a mind so noble, a spirit so high? I shall spend my life worshipping you."

"We shall spend our lives having tiffs and quarrels, I'm sure. But we love each other, and that's worth a barrel of French dukes."

Here there was a soft, quietly murmuring sound from the corridor, a thin humming noise which Tizzo, his head suddenly high in the air, seemed to recognize as the stir of swords in scabbards. The girl, too, suddenly thrust the bolt home in the lock and whirled about.

[117]

"There are armed men in the hallway, Tizzo!" she whispered, turning white.

And at that moment the bolt of the door clanked a little; after that followed a quiet, discreet knocking. Tizzo moved slowly to make his answer, when the inner door of the chamber was thrust suddenly open and Elia Bigi appeared looking like a hungry wolf. His one eye was shrunk by fear.

"There are a hundred men come to find you!" he muttered. "Come with me quickly. There is still time to escape. The traitor Marozzo is among them to point you out. Quickly, my master. There is still time to pass through this door and down the winding stairs."

"Take the lad—the girl—and carry her along with you."

"Lad? Girl? You shall come with me!" snarled Bigi, and laid a hand on her arm.

"Do you know what you do, you fool?" she asked savagely. Then she added in a whispering passion: "I shall not leave you, Tizzo! I know you mean to protect my good name or my life, or both. But I shall not leave you! I shall not leave you here to be a rearguard—and to die—"

Her voice broke, while Elia Bigi stared gloomily down at her and bit his lip.

Tizzo did not argue. He merely said: "Elia, it is the Lady Beatrice Baglioni. Take her; save her; and quickly."

"Hai!" muttered Elia Bigi, and instantly he had grasped her with both hands. "Come with me, my lady! There is no use in argument. You come while I have the strength to take you. You are too fine a hawk to be found in this nest. A Baglioni in a common tavern! Aha! You will struggle? This ends all struggling! Away! Away!"

Here he literally caught her up in both arms and bore her out of the room.

The door swung softly shut behind him, and now a heavier hand beat on the door. Tizzo called out: "What's there?"

"A friend to see you, *signore*."

"What friend?"

"A messenger from Antonio Bardi."

"How many are with you?"

[118]

"I am alone, *signore*."

"You are alone in your lie, only," said Tizzo. "The hall is filled with the murmur of armed men."

A distinct though faint voice now said out of the distance: "Guard the lower hallway and the winding stairs. He may try to break out through that way."

Then a louder voice exclaimed: "Open the door, traitor and dog! It is I! It is Marozzo!"

The moment he spoke, there was a distinct clinking of steel as the many men who had stolen into the hall with him gave up all pretense at secrecy.

And a moment later an ax was struck into the door with such force that the edge of it gleamed on the inner surface of the wood!

CHAPTER

25

Tizzo looked swiftly around him, then sprang for the inner door of the room. He had waited long enough, now, to assure the retreat of the girl and Bigi in safety. But when he snatched the second door open, he heard, distinctly, the clanking of steel on stone as many armed feet ascended the winding stairs beyond.

He swung that door shut and thrust home the bolt. There remained the window, which offered to him the blue sky of twilight as a promise of peace. He leaped to the window and looked out, but he saw what he had known he would see—the eaves projecting too far for him to reach them, and under him the sheer, flat surface of a wall of cemented masonry. Not even a cat could have climbed to safety in this direction.

He turned again, to face the darkening room and the certainty of death. And then the rising night wind blew through the window upon him and gave to him a new inspiration.

He had noticed, glimmering around the room, a number of large oil-fed lamps. The olive oil in the big bowls must be measured in many a liter. He seized those lamps now and emptied them one after another on the clothing of the bed until the mass of cloth was soaked.

In the meantime, the wood was being hewn away in chunks. And the voice of Marozzo at the door was calling out: "Busily, axes! One moment and we bear down the door with our shoulders and get at the rat. Remember that he has teeth! Beware of him. Use the point before the edge! Remember, there is a reward of two thousand florins and that's enough to keep you all drunk for six months. I give you my half share in the reward. I put it all into your hands! Cheerily now, axes!"

Tizzo swept the bedding onto the floor of flags and with the flint and steel beside the fireplace, struck a shower of sparks onto the oil-drenched material.

The flames caught, ran lazily, cast upward a thick smudge of black smoke that rapidly began to cloud the room.

"Tizzo!" shouted Marozzo, as a hail of blows fell upon the door thickly. "Do you hear? It is I! It is Mateo Marozzo! I have come to see you at your finish, Tizzo! Do you hear me laugh?"

In fact, the loud, long laughter of Marozzo rang mocking above the tumult.

Tizzo, the woodsman's ax in his hand, pulled the flaming mass of the bedding closer to the door. Then, with his left hand, he thrust back the bolt, hurled the door open. He saw before him a closely packed mass of steel-armored men-at-arms. On this occasion, Mateo Marozzo was taking no chances, but having cornered his quarry he was making sure that he had enough trained soldiers beside him to finish his game.

Into the faces of these men, with the hooked blade of the ax, Tizzo flung the flaming mass of the bedclothes.

Before the fire, the dense, thick, oily smoke was blown by the draft into the faces of the men-at-arms. And now the flames themselves followed. Even drawn visors were no sure protection against the spattering drops of flying, flaming oil which searched every crevice of all the armor instantly. The surcoats were flaring fires at once. And the gust from the window, pouring through the door, fanned the fire and drove all the smoke in a headlong cloud.

Through that whirling, dense mist Tizzo leaped with his ax. He dealt blows right and left and the shock of the impacts on the heavy steel helmets dropped a man before him at every blow.

But it was not from his fighting that they turned. It was the sudden appearance of a flaring hell-mouth at the door of a common tavern room that made the men-at-arms bolt.

"Magic! Black magic!" one of them yelled.

That shout was taken up by all the rest. It was an ample excuse for flight, and the whole mass of men poured down the hall.

Tizzo, by dint of his ax-work, was ahead of the rest. He was down the stairs like a leaping wildcat. He was in the courtyard where stupid-faced grooms held the bridles of horses and stared up in wonder at the black smoke pouring through the windows of the corridor above them.

Not the blow of the ax but the merely swinging flash of it was enough to give Tizzo a horse. He raced the animal through the gaping gate of the courtyard and out onto the street. And behind him he heard the wild cry begin to go up: "Treason! Treason! Treason to the Baglioni! Follow, in the name of God and two thousand florins!"

Down half a dozen of the swift-sloping streets of Perugia which turn and angle dizzily, like the courses of mountain torrents, he twisted and turned his way until the noise of the pursuit was dimmer behind him. Then he leaped to the ground and let the horse gallop furiously down a slope, sliding and twisting and slipping over the smoothness of the pavement.

But Tizzo had gone on straight to the house of the rich della Penna.

Compared with the country villa of the same family, this house was small. But it offered him the one point of safety he knew about, unless he chose to make his way a greater distance to the residence of his dear friend, Antonio Bardi. But to go to Bardi's place was to involve Antonio in the same difficulties which faced him, and this he preferred not to do.

To the two armed porters who kept the main door of the house, he merely flashed the face of the signet ring of their master and they let him pass through at once. One of them conducted him to a hall on the second floor above the street; and then went to fetch della Penna himself who, he said, had just returned from the country that day.

He heard a swift stride, presently, and into the hall came the tall frame of della Penna.

He was one of those men who like to stand close to any conversational partner, as though to awe the other by the keenness of his eye and the dignity of his presence. He might as well have stared into the eyes of a hawk as into the eyes of Tizzo, where the faint blue flame of battle was still dancing.

"Did I tell you to make my house your resort?" demanded della Penna.

"I was chased from the Sign of the Golden Stag," said Tizzo, "and I came here to report the thing to you."

"As for your tavern brawls," said della Penna, "they do not enter into my accounting."

"Does the honesty of your brother traitor, Marozzo—does that enter into your accounting?" demanded Tizzo.

The whole phrasing of the sentence was such an affront that della Penna fell back a stride, as though from a blow.

"Marozzo?" he said. "What has filled your mouth with language like this? In what way do you dare—"

"Listen to me, my friend," said Tizzo. "That you are older than I, I admit; that you are wiser, I am ready to grant; but if you try to beat me with your tongue first, you will have to beat me with your sword in real earnest afterward. I've come to bring you news. If you want to hear it, well; if not, may you and your entire faction be damned. I leave you at once."

"Wait—wait!" panted della Penna, yellow with rage and yet hard bound with curiosity, also. "You forget that men who are deep in dangerous affairs—"

"Have dangerous tongues? Well, I'm willing to forget the first

[122]

manners so long as the second ones are better. Do you wish to hear me?"

"If you please," said della Penna, still breathing hard.

"I tell you that I gave your message from Camerino to Marozzo—"

"What was it?"

"Two hundred and fifty."

"Good! Ah, that is news which men who are now in the house will be glad to hear. Two hundred and fifty?"

"That is what he said."

"You gave that to Marozzo? Why did not the madman carry me the word at once?"

"Because he recognized my voice, if not my face in spite of walnut stain and black hair. Hatred washes the eyes very clear, Signor della Penna. And a little later he was back at the tavern, outside my room, with twenty armed men."

"Twenty? How in the name of God did you escape? Through a window?"

"I'm not a bird," answered Tizzo. "I managed to throw some fire in their faces, and then I came away. It does not particularly matter how. The important thing is that you now know what the lord of Camerino will do for you."

"Two hundred and fifty!" muttered della Penna. "Then the thing is as good as done—ah, Astorre Baglioni! May I see your face before you have ended dying!"

As he spoke, forgetting himself in a transport, he shook his clenched fist above his head. Then he took Tizzo hastily by the arm.

"You have done enough," he said. "You have done quite enough. You shall come in among the others with me and tell your news. If Camerino is with us, we shall surely win!"

Tizzo followed, his mind whirling. Whatever he had guessed before, the naked truth, as the first glimpse was revealed to him, dazzled his eyes with horror. For it was plain that an attack on Perugia was planned and that Astorre was to be murdered in the midst of his wedding festivities.

But now he was taken through a doorway into a large room,

well lighted. The first face he saw was that of Henry, baron of Melrose.

With the sight of the second face his brain reeled and refused all thought. For the host in whose house Astorre, Beatrice, Giovanpaolo, Messer Guido, and more than half the great names of the Baglioni were gathered as guests for this night, himself the richest of all the name, young, famous, beautiful Grifone Baglioni stood there among the plotters against his own blood!

CHAPTER

26

AFTERWARDS, slowly, by glimpses, other faces were identified by the stunned eyes of Tizzo. Grifone was not the only traitor to the name of Baglioni. There was Carlo Barciglia, poorest and proudest and most spendthrift of the Baglioni, but a famous fighter. There was Filippo de Braccio, descended from the high and mighty family by the left hand. There was that other Jeronimo, della Staffa, young, foolish, but a devil in daring, and Berardo da Corgnie and his brothers, Pietro Giacomo and Ottaviano hardly past twenty years of age. Others among the noblest in the city were in that hall, and hardly a one of them but had been supported and favored by the great leaders, Giovanpaolo and the great Astorre. But the face to which the eyes of Tizzo repeatedly turned was that of handsome Grifone, who still was housing in his own great palace the heads of his family.

Henry of Melrose, whose very life was lived for the sake of

danger, plot and counterplot, came striding to Tizzo and grasped his hand.

"Well met in the hornets' nest, my fine bird," he said.

"My friends," said della Penna, "there is handsome news for you. It is brought to us by a confessed enemy of the Baglioni, by a man with a great price of two thousand florins on his head. Tizzo has ridden to the lord of Camerino. He will tell you himself how many men-at-arms Camerino will send to our help."

Tizzo, so appealed to, said in a clear voice: "Two hundred and fifty is the number that he named, without fail."

There was a faint shout—it sounded rather like the growling of a great beast with a single throat. On all sides the number was repeated. "Two hundred and fifty!"

Not that the number was large, but for the execution of a secret plot, in the narrow streets of such a city as Perugia, a well-armed band of two or three hundred could do almost more than a large army. Besides, they would come in a unit, under a strong command. They could be even more trusted than the nearest members and originators of the plot.

Another man stepped up to Tizzo from the shadows in the corner of the room. It was young Antonio Bardi who clasped his hand in turn. The fine, intellectual face of Bardi was flushed with emotion and happiness.

"Tizzo," he said, "my hands have never felt quite clean in this enterprise before tonight. But now that I see you, I am sure that the cause is just!"

"Still I am amazed, Antonio," said Tizzo. "Because I thought that you and your family have been for generations great friends of the Baglioni."

"So the world has thought; and so I thought until my father opened his heart to me when he died. He told me of many slights and brutalities to which the Bardi had had to submit. He made me swear to use the first opportunity of striking for the lost honor of my house. But more than all else, if I had known that you were joined to this plan, I should have been happy to come into it. In fact, my dear Tizzo, when I heard you had been driven from the city with a price upon your head, at that moment I determined to join myself with della Penna and the rest."

Tizzo, hearing this speech, groaned inwardly.

But here there came an interruption that made a great stir, for the door of the big chamber opened, and Mateo Marozzo entered with a plume burned from his helmet, his cloak scorched, and half his mustache singed from his face. Soot of the oil smoke was still streaked over him.

"Seize that man!" called out Grifone Baglioni.

Baron Henry of Melrose went up to Marozzo with his hand on his dagger.

"You are my prisoner, Marozzo," he said.

"Am I?" said Marozzo, and laughed cheerfully.

"I'll change that laughter; I'll widen the stretch of your mouth for you," said Melrose, in one of his quick tempers.

Jeronimo della Penna strode to Marozzo and lowered upon him.

"Mateo," he said, "you received great news for us this long time ago. Why have we not heard from you about it? What does it mean that you gratify a private spite by attacking one of the best men in our enterprise?"

"Best?" said Marozzo, still laughing scornfully. "You call him best? This fellow—this man without a name—this Firebrand, this Tizzo! Bah! He is a spy in the midst of you!"

The blood congealed in the body of Tizzo and the nerves ran tingling shocks through his brain.

The Englishman, Melrose, with a sudden shout of rage raised his hand to strike Marozzo, but della Penna intervened just in time.

"Mateo has something to say. I, also, remember a voice that was not of any fleshly throat, saying ambiguous words—to trust Tizzo today but not tomorrow! Mateo, what is it you know?"

"What is it you guess, rather—you singed cat!" said Melrose, in such a passion that Tizzo, even with all the fear in his heart, was struck with wonder.

"I tell you," said Marozzo, "that this fine Tizzo, this stray dog in Perugia, this red head and blue eye that never came from honest Italian blood—this same Tizzo is hand in glove with the men who still own the city."

"Talk! Talk! Empty talk!" exclaimed Melrose. "We want proof, not words."

[126]

"Shall I give them to you?" asked Marozzo.

"Or die for the lack of them!" cried Tizzo, warming himself into a pretended anger.

"I shall not die for the lack of them," said Marozzo calmly. "But first I ask you—what sort of proof will do? How much proof do you need, my friends, to show you that you are on the brink of a precipice and about to fall? How much proof do you need? What should its nature be?"

"Any proof," said Grifone, "that Tizzo is playing false with us."

"Look first at the cunning of the trick!" said Marozzo. "A pretended quarrel between Giovanpaolo and this Tizzo sends Tizzo out of the town as a fugitive. Where does he fly? To Jeronimo della Penna. Naturally, you will say, because the world knows that della Penna for a long time has been no friend of Giovanpaolo, who thinks himself the master of the world!"

"He did not come directly to me. I sent for him," said della Penna.

"You found him conveniently in a neighbor's house. He showed himself to you as a man who hated Giovanpaolo in the hope that then you might invite him into any scheme that might be on foot."

"Do you think that Giovanpaolo dreams of our plans?" demanded della Penna. "No, we should long ago have been minus our heads if he had had the least suspicion."

"There has been talk for a long time, and even whispers come finally to the ears of the rulers of the city," answered Marozzo. "But it was not a certain knowledge. That is, it was not certain before tonight. Now, however, it is sure in the mind of Giovanpaolo; or almost sure."

"We have had Tizzo watched. He has not been near Giovanpaolo since he came into the city," said della Penna.

"Are you sure that Giovanpaolo has not been near him, however?" asked Marozzo.

"How can Giovanpaolo move, in these days, without having a crowd around him?" asked Grifone Baglioni.

"Not he himself, but his own flesh and blood!" exclaimed Marozzo. "What do you say when I tell you that the Lady

Beatrice herself went to the tavern to speak with Tizzo this night."

"Liar! Liar and dog!" shouted Tizzo, and drew his sword.

But della Penna held him back from running at Marozzo. The last words of that man had made a great stir through the hall. He continued now, forcefully: "She was there. She was seen to leave the Golden Stag after spending a long time in the room of Tizzo."

"I give you the lie!" panted Tizzo. "She is a lady pure as snow and higher than heaven is above your head!"

"You hear him?" said Marozzo. "This is the language he uses about a woman whose brothers we intend to put to death, and he assisting. Come, come! The thing is patent, and the man is a spy."

Della Penna exclaimed: "I begin to smell a rat, it is true. But how could the great beauty, the famous Lady Beatrice enter a tavern and visit the room of an unknown man? It is not possible, Mateo!"

"Not for her in the dress of a woman; but in the dress of a boy —what do you say to that? I tell you, the poniard she had worn was found in the room where Tizzo had stayed. It was her own weapon. An emerald which Giovanpaolo had given to her was set in its hilt.

"Not a thing from which she would be parted lightly. A delicate little dagger such as most of these ladies of Perugia have about them. And—here it is!"

He held it out suddenly in his hand. And in the silence that followed Tizzo felt his heart thundering. It was a damning proof.

"How are we to know," said Henry of Melrose, "that this Marozzo, who has been shamed by Tizzo and hates him, as all men know, has not stolen the poniard on purpose?"

"Who was the pretty boy who went to the room of Tizzo in the tavern, then?" demanded Marozzo. "Who was the boy so important to him that he sent his own servant to carry the lad away to safety while he, like a brave fool, remained behind to cover the retreat? Yes, remained there until he would surely have fallen into our hands except that a touch of the devil and black magic got him away in the midst of flames?"

"It is true!" exclaimed della Penna. "The scoundrel has betrayed us—the hand of Giovanpaolo is about to close over our throats!"

He added, with a shout: "Seize him!"

"Kill! Kill!" cried Marozzo.

The baron of Melrose was suddenly in front of Tizzo, sword in hand.

"Justice, here, and a little common sense," he roared.

The Italians in a semicircle that glittered with naked steel faced the baron; and then Antonio Bardi, throwing away his scabbard, took his place at the side of the Englishman, calling out: "I shall lose my faith in God sooner than in this man!"

These three with resolved faces confronted a score of fighters, as Melrose said: "My wild-headed friends, are you turning a boy's love affair into treason? This same Lady Beatrice—when I was serving the Oddi and taking her stealthily away through the hills—did he not steal her from me and give her liberty? Is it a wonder, then, that the silly wild hawk of a girl should come running to his arms when he shows himself in Perugia? Bah! Young blood is hot and it will have its way. But the lad has served us all, and he will serve us again. Della Penna, you are not a child. Be reasonable."

"You take a strong position with a drawn sword, Melrose," said della Penna. "But the fact is that I'm not altogether convinced that Tizzo is a traitor."

"He is, by heaven!" insisted Marozzo.

"Be quiet, young man," answered della Penna.

Melrose broke in: "There has been time. If Giovanpaolo had news of this gathering, do you not think that his men-at-arms would have surrounded the house long before this? We would all be dead men, and the house would be running blood."

This was a remark so convincing that Grifone Baglioni cried out: "That is true. Up swords and have an end of this argument.

"We need all our weapons tonight for the work before us."

"God above us!" cried Marozzo. "Are we to turn the villain loose? Are you all mad?"

"No," said della Penna. "Let him remain here with Marozzo to guard him while we do our night's work."

"Agreed," said Grifone Baglioni. "So it must be."

ANTONIO BARDI, after this scene, remained standing at the side of Tizzo, who had been tied firmly with silken cord and then bound into a chair to keep him from moving too freely. And Bardi, resting a hand on the shoulder of his friend, said over and over: "I am your surety that you shall come to no harm. Trust in that, Tizzo."

And now one explanation began to form, suddenly, in the mind of Tizzo, taking his breath; but before the idea could grow clear, the words that were being spoken in this room drove from his mind all else. For he was hearing the details of the plot by which the Baglioni were to meet their death on this night.

Each was assigned his part.

Henry of Melrose, saying simply: "This damned business smells more of murder than of fighting!" promptly refused to undertake any of the midnight work, and therefore to him was assigned the guarding of the gate of San Ercolano, through which the men of Camerino were to be admitted.

Balks of wood heavy enough to dash in the doors of the bedchambers were prepared and in readiness. To each of the leaders was assigned fifteen men and a definite mission. Grifone would give the signal for the united attack by dropping a huge stone from his balcony into the street.

So Tizzo listened, his eyes on the floor for fear lest he might lift them and the horror be seen that worked in his mind.

Jeronimo della Penna made the last speech. He said: "My

friends, we hope to give to ourselves power and wealth, to Perugia a new rule. Let us be true to one another. And remember that if either Astorre or Giovanpaolo escape, we have not killed the snake—we have only scotched it. Midnight is the hour. Be prepared. All must go well!"

So they went out from the room. Henry of Melrose, before he left, dropped a hand on the shoulder of Marozzo and said, sternly: "If harm comes to Tizzo while you are his guardian, I shall call you to an accounting afterwards, Marozzo!"

Then he strode from the room and left Tizzo alone with his enemy.

The latter sat down in a tall chair upholstered in red velvet and stared for a long time at his captive. Then he began to smile.

"What is the taste in your throat, Tizzo?" he asked at last.

"It is a little cold, Mateo," answered Tizzo. "Why do you ask?"

"Because I wish to know how death seems in its coming, what weight is on the heart, and what taste in the throat."

"It is a taste you'll enjoy in the morning," said Tizzo, "when Baron Melrose finds that you have murdered me."

"I? Murdered you?" laughed Marozzo. "Ah, Tizzo, what a simple fellow you must think I am! No, the truth is that you yourself tonight showed me exactly how the thing should be done. With fire, Tizzo. Here, do you see, I place a small table with a lamp on it. It seems that I have left the room. When I return, I find Tizzo has overturned his chair in a vain effort to escape—traitor that he is!—and not only is the chair overturned but the small table beside it has fallen. Besides, with the fall of the lamp, the flaming oil has spilled over the clothes of Tizzo, and he is burned horribly—too horribly! Death is a mercy to him. My wild cries have brought the servants, and they carry the dead body away. They fight to put out the fire, which luckily is quite harmless on this tiled floor."

"What is the hour?" said Tizzo.

"It lacks a few minutes of midnight."

"Let me die as you please, Mateo," said Tizzo. "But the truth is that there is still time for you to do one great and noble thing. Burn me, stab me—that does not matter. But when you have done that, run to the house of the traitor Grifone. Fly to the room

[131]

of Giovanpaolo. Rouse him. Tell him his life is in danger. Believe me, he will reward you more for the saving of his life than all the scoundrels of tonight will ever reward you for the taking of it. Think, Marozzo! Jeronimo della Penna will have all the power in Perugia in his own hands after the Great Betrayal has taken place. And you will again be one of the lesser citizens, undistinguished, as weak as ever you were. But go to the Baglioni now and you will become a giant in Perugia!"

Marozzo, who had started to sneer, finished by scowling in a serious fashion out the window toward the night.

"True," he muttered, "true—" And then he groaned: "But it is too late. If I try to give the warning, the trap which is about to close over Giovanpaolo will close over me, also. It is too late to repent. Much too late! And besides—I'd rather have these five minutes alone with my dear friend Tizzo, than to possess all the wealth in the world and be king of France besides!"

"Aye," said Tizzo, looking curiously at him. "You hate me as much as one man may hate another, I believe."

"From the moment I looked into the blue of your eyes, like the blue tremor of flame before the yellow of it begins—from that moment I have hated you, Tizzo. But today came the crown of thorns for me. Not that you escaped from me. No, that was bitter poison to swallow, but that you should have been visited in your room by my Lady Beatrice!"

He groaned aloud.

Then, without a word, he picked up a small table and stood it close to the chair of Tizzo. On the table he set a lamp and stood for an instant enjoying the sight of Tizzo's face with almost affectionate eyes.

"What shall I do in this world when I no longer have you to hate in it, Tizzo?" he murmured.

Then he added: "But first I shall have to seal your mouth, my friend, for otherwise the screaming might make too much noise in the house and call too many servants here. They would be surprised if they saw a squealing pig being roasted alive, eh?"

He stepped to the window and began to tug at one of the long, silken cords.

[132]

And Tizzo held his bound wrists over the flame of the lamp on the table beside him.

The instant agony knocked his chin against his breast. He remembered that old tale of the Roman hero who had allowed his right hand to consume in the fire in order to prove his love of his country. But he, when his skin was barely hissing with the heat, could hardly endure the torment.

But in a moment, the pressure of his wrist caused the cord to snap. He tossed it into the fireplace and, in another instant, he would have managed to untie the other cords which fastened him into the chair. But it was too late for that. Marozzo, turning from the window, came jauntily across the room to his prisoner.

"A ha!" said Marozzo. "What's been burning? There's a stench in the air."

Tizzo kept his scorched wrists close together in his lap, in just that position in which the cords had held them.

"You smell your own idea," said Tizzo.

Marozzo paused, close to the chair.

"By heavens," he said, "there's a cloud of smoke in the air across the ceiling! What does it mean?"

He was about to draw back to pursue his inquiry when Tizzo, leaning as far forward as he could, reached out with both hands. One of them quite missed a hold; but with the left he caught the cloak of Marozzo close to the throat.

The latter, wildly starting back, pulled Tizzo after him, chair and all. The hand of Marozzo was very swift. Still striving to free himself from Tizzo, he snatched out his dagger to strike, but here the plunging forward weight of the chair drove Tizzo toward the floor. He flung his arms around Marozzo's knees and brought him crashing down at full length.

Then, reaching upward, he caught frantically at the dagger hand of the murderer.

But the hand was relaxed; the dagger hilt fell from inert fingers. Marozzo lay stunned from the blow which the back of his head had struck against the tiles.

CHAPTER

28

A few slashes with the sharp edge of the dagger and Tizzo was free.

He caught Marozzo by the hair of the head, jerked up the loose weight of the body, and bent the neck back over his knee. There, with the knife poised, twice he tried to stab and twice his will failed him. If so much as a glimmer of open eyes had showed, the blade would have been instantly in the heart of Marozzo, but it was a limp, lifeless form that lay there, and Tizzo sprang again to his feet.

There was a flight of time like arrows past his ears. With each second of his delay, death was drawing closer in the house of Grifone Baglioni.

There in the corner stood his ax. The sword had been left belted about his hips when he was tied into the chair. He reached the ax with a bound, dashed open the doors, and fled down the stairs and was instantly out in the street.

He knew the way well. And, ah, for a horse to shorten the distance!

But there were only his straining legs to carry him up the steep way, through the dipping, staggered course of an alley, and so into the wider street and the piazza where the great house of Grifone stood.

He had almost reached it when a thin shadow streaked down the face of the palace. A stone crashed on the pavement below with such force that it split into a hundred pieces, recoiling and then lying scattered.

It was the appointed signal of Grifone, and in this instant the heavy balks of wood would begin to dash against the bedroom doors. Those poor sleepers, startled by the sound of the falling stone, would perhaps rouse for a single instant with wonder in their minds. And then death would burst in upon them.

Through the open doorway of the house he leaped and heard, with one terrible, resounding crash, the sudden thundering of the battering rams against a dozen doors.

The great lower hall stretched before him, dim with the flicker of a few lights. And at the foot of the main stairway a full dozen of men-at-arms, in complete armor, barred the way.

"Halt!" called a voice that broke out above the frightful turmoil of the house. And a pair of swords crossed in the path of Tizzo.

The agony in his heart needed some outlet. With all the might of his body and the strength of his charge he swung the woodman's ax. The exquisite Damascus steel alighted full on the ridge of a heavy helmet, and the steel split like wood—steel and skull beneath it.

That tall, knightly body, falling, cleared a small gap in the crowd, and through that gap Tizzo sprang. The force of his leap wrenched the lodged blade of the ax out of the wound it had dealt; Tizzo was up the steps far before the soldiers, weighted with their armor, had moved a stride in pursuit. And, in fact, they did not rush after him; they remained at the post which had been assigned to them, merely thrusting the body of the dead man out of the way. On a night like this, with so much murder in the air, one more death here or there made very little difference. And what could a single man perform against the hands of the scores who swarmed through the upper part of the house?

Tizzo, as he reached the hall above, saw a confusion of tossing lights and men and heard the crashing of the heavy beams of wood against the doors of various rooms. For more than he could see, he could hear, and from the left the wild screams of a woman plunged like a burning dagger again and again into his brain.

Giovanpaolo, sworn blood brother, was his objective; but he

could not resist that frantic screeching of terror and sprang through the open doorway.

What he saw was a female servant groveling on the floor and trying to fight off the burly man-at-arms who was tearing the jewels from her hands and neck. It was she who screamed so terribly, but at the farther end of the room stood the slender figure of the Lady Beatrice who, with a delicate French sword in her hand, fought as valiantly as a man and with some sense of fencing against another big invader, who laughed at her efforts and made half playful gestures with his sword.

The cry of Tizzo rescued her from danger before he reached the spot. As for the brute who was plundering the serving maid, he received one of those stunning hammerstrokes with the back of the ax, and was spilled like a heap of old iron junk upon the floor.

The man-at-arms in front of the girl, whirling as he heard that cry, swung his sword with a fine strength and made a downright stroke at Tizzo. He might as well have struck at a dead leaf which is thrust aside by the mere wind of a blow. His sword actually descended with such violence that the point of it lodged in the floor; and the circling ax of Tizzo once more cleft steel as though it had been wood. The man-at-arms, struck through the brain pan, fell forward, crashing, and the voice of Beatrice was ringing at the ears of Tizzo: "Run, Tizzo! For your life! You are unarmed, madman, among all the swords. It is murder—Tizzo—this way—through the window—"

"Save yourself if you know a way!" he panted. "Giovanpaolo—"

He had that one glimpse of her as she stood beside the table on which the scroll of an unfinished letter lay. She could not have spent the evening in that male costume. How did she happen to have it on now? He had only the millionth part of a second to give to that thought and to the picture of her beauty as she stood by the flame of the lamp. Then he wheeled from her and rushed again into the hall.

He could hear a great voice shouting: "To me, friends! Hail Semonetto! Semonetto! Hail Baglioni! Down, traitors! A hail!"

And through the hall rolled a tangle of men whose swords flashed and fell, aimed at a tall, white figure.

It was the young Semonetto himself, of whom men said that among all the Baglioni there was not a better blade, hardly in Giovanpaolo himself. Now, clad only in his shirt, he struck such giant blows that the armored fighters broke back from him then rushed forward to cut him down. Still with a warding buckler and with a living sword of light, he struggled against them.

"Semonetto! Semonetto!" shouted Tizzo, and hurled himself into that fray.

The unexpected attack from the rear, the great, ringing, hammerstrokes of the ax which stunned brains or smashed shoulders, split the crowd in two and let Semonetto leap through the gap.

Never would Tizzo forget that figure. For Semonetto had been wounded in the head so that one side of his face ran crimson; and from a rent in his shirt high on the breast another torrent of blood was flowing.

"Brother!" he gasped to Tizzo.

"Flee!" shouted Tizzo, and from the lightning circles of his ax the murderers shrank for an instant.

Semonetto, with one wild glance about him, sprang down the great staircase with Tizzo yelling: "No, no! That way is blocked! Semonetto!"

But Semonetto, crazed with his wounds or deafened by the uproar which rang through the house as through a brazen cave, fled on down the stairs, and Tizzo turned to run upward. He found, as he returned, that Lady Beatrice was beside him with that delicate splinter, that long dagger of a French sword in her hand.

"Beatrice, save yourself!" he groaned to her. But she was already fleeing before him to show him the way through a narrow little door which was set flush against the wall, and so to the windings of a secret stairway. As Tizzo slammed that door behind him, he heard steel clash and break against it.

He thrust the bolt home and fled upward, pursuing the girl.

"Do you hear me? Beatrice!" he panted.

She waited for him at an upper landing, where a little narrow arched window opened over a roof.

"Here is escape, Tizzo," she cried, "and yonder, in that hell— yonder is Giovanpaolo! Will you save yourself?"

Beyond the roof, beyond the rough tiling, he saw the moon hanging like a red flag of murder in the west, above the city of Perugia.

There was the road to safety, and the girl pointing the way to it. He could save her and himself, perhaps, but in the meantime the man to whom he was sworn must be fighting for his life. He turned his back on the window with a shout.

"Giovanpaolo!" he cried, and raced down the hall.

CHAPTER

29

WHEN the assault began, Messer Astorre was roused, and called out to know what had happened. There was the vast crashing and shouting all through the house, as though the place were seized upon by thunder, but at the door of Astorre himself, and his wife, there was no disturbance. Only the voice of Filippo, the traitor, called out to him from the hall: "My lord! Your highness! It is your friend, Filippo! Open in the name of God! There is murder loosed through the house."

At that, Astorre took a sword in his hand and turned the key, with his own hand opening the door on his destruction. As the door yawned, Ottaviano da Corgnie struck savagely through the opening and made a great wound in the head of Astorre, striking him to his knees. While he was still down, Filippo, who had called to him like a friend, plunged a sword into the body of Astorre.

[138]

That hero, though he was dying, was not yet dead. He managed to gain his feet and struck some great stroke with his own sword, so that for a moment the press of men failed to get through the door. He might even have succeeded in driving the scoundrels out of the room, except that his poor wife, in a frenzy of screaming terror, came like the wind and threw her arms around him to save him from further blows.

Then Filippo—it was he himself—with his sword ran the poor woman through the shoulder and with the same stroke drove the blade of his weapon right through the body of the Baglioni. Then Astorre felt that he had his death. He put his bloody arms around his wife and kissed her.

He fell, and as he fell his wife was dragged down with him because she was still pinned to his body by the sword of the traitor.

They seemed to feel that his glory must be as strong as armor about his naked body and that they would have to hew at him as at a man clad in steel plate. Over fifty wounds were received by his senseless body, so that he was hewed almost to pieces, but as though by a miracle—it was in fact the work of a kind saint, said some men—the face of Astorre was not touched, so that when he lay in death with his body covered he looked like a glorious Greek hero, asleep.

When his highness, the young Semonetto, had escaped in the upper hall by means of the battle ax of Tizzo and his own strong sword, he fled down the staircase, dripping blood as he ran, and so came to the men-at-arms at the bottom of the stairs.

They tried to stop his flight, but he struck down two of them, killing one, and the force of his attack carried him straight through the armored crowd.

They followed and clung to him, however. His sword struck showers of sparks from their armor, as he raged among them, and for a moment they fell back, in awe of this man.

In that moment, he leaped into the street and, perhaps, might have escaped. But here he saw a poor serving lad, a mere page of twelve or thirteen years, who was driven by the swords above to leap from a window, and this poor boy was crushed to death on the stones of the street in front of Semonetto. He only lived long enough to gasp out: "Semonetto—my lord—avenge me!" Then he died.

They say that Semonetto, when he saw this death and heard those dying words, turned straight around, forgot all care for his own safety, and rushed back against the men-at-arms from whom he had just escaped.

Before he fell, he laid on the ground five armored men, and his sword was broken in two before they managed to push in close and overwhelm him with blows.

It was a second miracle that he, like Astorre, was never wounded in the face, during all this terrible medley of blows.

Men said that if this Semonetto had lived, not even Nicolo Piccininni would have accomplished such feats, because in all things, even in his cruelty, he was above other men. After his death, his absence was felt like a curse, and like a blessing, in Perugia.

Berardino of Antignolle had already burst into the room of the old man, Guido Baglioni, the father of so much strength and valor and himself, men said, among the wisest of the men of his time.

When the door was burst in, the murderers found that the old man had risen from his bed and that he had taken up a sword in a corner of the room. So many blades came at him, that he had to use both his blade and his left arm to ward off the strokes. And then a soldier leaned and stabbed the old man in the breast.

The chief object of all that midnight attack was the person of Giovanpaolo, the most famous of all the house. Astorre was perhaps as widely known for his commanding of mercenary armies in the service of various cities through Italy, but it was known by all that Giovanpaolo was the great brain of the house of the Baglioni.

For his destruction his treacherous host and cousin, Grifone, had taken special order.

Also Carlo Barciglia and some of the house of da Corgnie went hurrying from their other special tasks of murder to assist in the killing of that famous man, because, as Jeronimo della Penna had said, if that one brain escaped with life, all the business of the slaughter was disappointed and undone. Here are some of the chief heads of the enterprise gathered before the door of Giovanpaolo, and it was said that just as Filippo, the traitor, called out to Astorre, so Carlo Barciglia called to Giovanpaolo and wakened him.

He begged to be let into the room, because there was destruction in the house, but the wise Giovanpaolo said: "Traitor, if there is destruction in the house, you are a part of it!"

In fact, there were great suspicions in the breast of Giovanpaolo because, on the night before, his sister, Lady Beatrice, had brought him assured word from Tizzo that in the hands of della Penna there was some murderous scheme for which the lord of Camerino was sending two hundred and fifty men-at-arms.

Just after Giovanpaolo had cried out in this manner, the traitors in the hall outside his room saw that there was no way except to beat in the door of his room. As they gathered and lifted the heavy beam, they heard him cry out, inside the room: "Tizzo! I have been like a blind fool for failing to heed your warning! I have allowed murder to come into my family!"

With the heavy balk of wood, the assassins dashed against the door. At the first stroke they smashed it down. They dropped the beam of wood which they had used to crush the barrier and they were about to pour into the room to finish their black business when they were amazed by a voice crying out loudly, behind them: "Giovanpaolo! Giovanpaolo! I come!"

At this Giovanpaolo raised a great shout of joy.

At the same time a slender man with a still slighter youth beside him, the first armed with a terrible ax and the second with a light sword, sharper than a needle, rushed through the group and threw them all into a slight confusion. Here a young man of the house of da Corgnie, trying to close with the newcomer, received from the ax a tremendous stroke which glanced from his helmet, clove through his shoulder armor, and almost severed the arm from his body.

But Tizzo and Lady Beatrice were now in the room of Giovanpaolo, who had taken time to draw on a few clothes between the first alarm and the beating down of his door.

When he saw Tizzo, he cried out: "Brother, you should have lived to revenge me; now we must die together!"

To Lady Beatrice, he merely said: "And it was I who tried to keep two sparks from flying in the same wind!"

For there was a certain touch of laughter in Giovanpaolo, even on a battlefield. But he with his lunging sword and Tizzo with the terrible, beating ax, kept the doorway clear for a moment.

CHAPTER

30

LADY BEATRICE exclaimed: "The way is still open to the loggia." In a pause in the fighting, Giovanpaolo said: "There is no use in that unless we all had wings!—Ha, Grifone, do I see your face, traitor and dog? Have you joined yourself with villains?"

Then he saw Carlo and shouted: "Carlo Barciglia, come closer. If we cannot touch hands, at least let us touch swords!"

"Pay no heed to him, Grifone," said Carlo Barciglia. "He has the tongue that will persuade honest men that red is white! Death to him!"

The whole body was about to rush again at the doorway when Tizzo said at the ear of his friend: "Giovanpaolo, I know a way from the loggia which even men can take. Follow me!" He added: "Beatrice, go first and open the doors from here to the loggia. If you see a strong cord or a rope, snatch it up. If not, take the long red cloth that lies across the table in the second room."

She obeyed those orders at once.

And Giovanpaolo and Tizzo met the second rush against the doorway. Again the sword flamed in the hands of Giovanpaolo, the ax circled in the grasp of Tizzo, and those blows, together with the narrowness of the doorway, held back the attackers for a moment.

Grifone called out that crossbows were coming, and that they should hold their hands.

But as the assailants fell back, the two inside the room fled suddenly across it and, passing through the door to the outer room, they locked and bolted it behind them, throwing some furniture against it to delay further the murderers.

In the same way they passed out onto the loggia and closed and locked that strong outer door behind them.

They could now look down through the last of the moonlight upon the piazza beneath, where loud shouts were ringing, and the hoofs of horses struck sparks out of the pavement, galloping back and forth. The continual cry was "Camerino! Camerino!" as though the men of that town had actually taken Perugia by assault.

There was neither cord nor rope, but the girl had brought the red cloth from the table of the second room. And Tizzo, grasping this, threw it like a long scarf over his shoulder.

Then he made Giovanpaolo hold him up on the low wall at the edge of the loggia in such a fashion that with his hands he could swing out and grasp the edge of the roof just above.

With a mighty effort, he tried to pull himself up, but one hand failed to hold and left him dangling by a precarious grasp. Lady Beatrice, trying to reach out to save him, herself almost fell head-long into the street below, but her brother caught and held her.

Behind them, they heard the conspirators smashing down the door to the outer room, the furniture which had been piled against it, yielding with a groaning sound as it was pushed across the floor.

Tizzo, listening to that uproar which shook the house, made a new, great effort and swung himself up onto the edge of the roof. There he lay precariously on the steeply slanting surface, looking down into the piazza as into a deep well.

Above him, the roof of the loggia rose to the higher wall of the house with a window in the midst of it. He reached that window, presently, smashed it open, and peered into an obscurity of

[143]

shadow in which he could see nothing. He had no time to make sure of what was about him. Beneath him events were flowing like a wild river, and he was close to ruin with Lady Beatrice and Giovanpaolo. He merely tied the belt of his sword about a chair that could not slip through the window, and then fastened the safety catch which held sheath and blade firmly together. He had been able to trust his life once before to the strength of that catch. He would have to trust three lives to it, now.

Sliding down to the end of the scabbard, on which he took a firm hold, he found that he could actually look over the edge of the wall onto the loggia beneath. Already the battering ram was crashing against the door that led from the outer room onto the loggia, and it must have seemed to the two Baglioni that they were only a moment from death. Above all other voices, like a rising fountain above still water, came the maddened screaming of the voice of Mateo Marozzo, who was yelling:

"Down with the doors! Down with them! Oh, God, give my hands one grasp on his throat!"

Like a hunting dog, Marozzo had followed his enemy and was now on his traces. It was a foolish hand, Tizzo knew, that had spared Marozzo in the house of della Penna.

He threw down the crimson cloth which he had carried up with him. The reaching hand of Giovanpaolo caught it.

"Now, Beatrice!" called Giovanpaolo, and helped the girl upward.

Partly from his strength to lift her, partly climbing like a cat, she swarmed up the length of the cloth and over the edge of the roof.

"Up to the window!" commanded Tizzo.

She went panting past him, and by his body and his scabbard climbed to the window above.

Giovanpaolo was already following, and the task of Tizzo was a heavier one, now. He had twisted the end of the cloth about his right arm, which swung over the edge of the room; the grip of his left hand was fastened upon the end of the scabbard, which terminated in a small knob. Even so, the smooth metal made an evil hold; he had to bow his head and grind his teeth together in the last extremity of effort as he felt the full weight of

[144]

Giovanpaolo swing dangling from the cloth over the depth of the piazza.

There was one instant of that frightful strain. Then the powerful grasp of the knight was on the edge of the roof and he heaved himself onto the roof beside Tizzo.

"Marvels and miracles!" gasped Giovanpaolo. "How have you done this thing, Tizzo?"

"Swiftly! Swiftly!" urged Tizzo. "They are at our heels!"

He had snatched up the crimson cloth as he spoke, and at the same moment the doors which had held so stoutly to resist the batterings of the crowd, as though they had weakened the instant that the need of them had diminished, now were beaten down, and the pressure of men poured out instantly upon the loggia.

Tizzo, retreating through the window above, his whole body shaken and trembling from the effort which he had made, heard them shouting beneath them in despair and in wonder. It was the screeching of Mateo Marozzo that again drowned all other sound.

"He cannot have flown—three of them, they cannot have flown—but Tizzo has the wings of a devil. Look everywhere!— We shall find them—God cannot disappoint me again!"

In the shadows of the room above, Giovanpaolo was saying: "You are the general, brave Tizzo. Oh, my friend, you are the leader and I am the humble follower. Tell us which way we should move now—or have we only dodged death for an instant?"

"Up with me to the highest roof. There is still a way," said Tizzo.

And he guided them from the room down that upper corridor which he had passed through before, and below them the house seemed to rock with the turmoil of shouting. They climbed the stairs and issued by the dormer window onto the top roof, leveled for a garden.

The moon was down, the stars were out in clear multitudes, seeming to tremble above all the horrors of Perugia. But the three made only an instant of pause, then Tizzo led the way across the roof to the edge which was nearest to the neighboring ledge. He cast sword and ax before him, then leaped lightly across the ten-foot gap.

The girl turned back up the roof, ran forward, bounded high, and landed light as a cat on the safer side. Giovanpaolo's foot slipped as he made his leap. His feet, striking the very edge of the roof, gave him a precarious balance and he began to fall backward, striking wildly with his arms at the thin air. But the swift grip of Tizzo was instantly on him, and he was drawn forward into safety.

Through a trap door which was unlocked they passed from the roof down darkling stairs into a house of silence, into which only the vague uproar from the outside penetrated as from a distance.

"Are we safe here, Giovanpaolo?" asked Tizzo.

"This is the house of Carlo Barciglia," said Giovanpaolo. "And he is among the traitors. I saw his face. But he is at his hellish work in the house of Grifone and we may win through this place if we have fortune."

In fact, they met not a living soul. All the people, no doubt, had been drawn out into the piazza. Giovanpaolo led them straight down into the armory of the house, where they paused, not to equip themselves with armor, but to take three hooded cloaks which might cover their faces and their bodies from recognition. After that, they walked, by Tizzo's suggestion, straight out into the open street. They were not the only men who were masked on this night when few could tell who was a friend and who an enemy.

"In command at the gate of San Ercolano," said Tizzo, "there is the Baron Melrose, who is my friend. He would not have a hand in this work of murder, and for my sake he will pass us safely through, perhaps."

"Let us go there, then, in the name of God," said Giovanpaolo. "There is blood in the very air we breathe, inside Perugia."

When they came down to San Ercolano, they found a close group of a dozen or more men-at-arms on the ground, and others in command on the walls. The great iron chains had been drawn across the gate.

Their progress was challenged instantly by the crossing of a pair of huge halberds, those ponderous, two-handed axes with which horse and rider could be struck to the ground.

"Who goes there?" came the challenge.

"A friend of Baron Melrose," said Tizzo.

"I know the voice. Let them come to me," said the voice of Henry of Melrose, instantly. So they were passed into the room of the captain of the gate, where Melrose was walking up and down uneasily. He banished his soldiers from the room, as he grasped the hand of Tizzo.

"How have you escaped from the hands of Marozzo and the rest at the house of della Penna?" he demanded. "Show me your face, Tizzo. Are you hurt?"

"Not in the flesh," said Tizzo. "I am safe and sound."

And he threw back the hood to smile on the big Englishman.

"Good! Good!" said Melrose. "Tizzo, the sight of you with a whole skin lets me breathe again. I have been wondering how I could persuade them with cunning or with blows to let you escape, because you have made strong enemies in this town, my lad. Who are these with you?"

"My best of friends," said Tizzo. "And people who may be friends of yours on another day, sir."

"Will they?" said the baron. "I hear that there is wild work at the house of Grifone. I must see the faces of these two."

"It is not wise, my lord," urged Tizzo.

"Not wise? Are they a pair of bright angels who might dazzle me?" asked Melrose.

"I say, it is not wise. If there is friendship between us, for the sake of that let them pass through with me!"

"Why, my lad," said Melrose, "for all I know the king of the clan, the eagle of the sky, the lion of Perugia, Giovanpaolo himself might be one of them! My friends, unmask, if you please!"

Giovanpaolo turned his head slowly toward Tizzo. His hand made a slight motion toward his sword.

"No!" exclaimed Tizzo. "It is better to trust to him than to fight against him. Do as he commands! He has a heart greater than any in Italy!"

Giovanpaolo, slowly, raised the hood from his head; Beatrice flung back her own with a quick gesture.

But Melrose, dropping his head suddenly, stared at the floor.

"There is dust in my eyes, Tizzo," he said. "I cannot see. God

[147]

and my employers forgive me—but—battle is battle and murder is murder! The key to the small outer portal is lying on that table. Take it—go, all three of you. Quickly!"

There was not time even for thanks. The heavy key was fitted into the lock on the farther side of the gateroom; in a moment more they walked freely down the slope beyond the city wall.

CHAPTER

31

FAR beyond Perugia, three dark figures, small on the top of a great hill, looked back to the dim tremor of the lights of the city.

Giovanpaolo, dropping to his knees, began to pray, softly, aloud. He prayed for the souls of his father, his dead brother Semonetto, the warrior soul of Astorre.

And the girl and Tizzo dropped back until the voice was only a murmur in their ears.

It seemed as though all possibility of lamentation had gone from her. Her pale face, clear and cold as a stone, lifted slightly toward the dim light of the stars. And Tizzo, saying nothing, looked sometimes at the girl he loved and sometimes toward that sworn blood brother, Giovanpaolo.

He could not tell for which of them his heart ached most.

Giovanpaolo rose and came slowly on toward them, his head bowed. But he straightened himself with a sudden effort and said: "There is no time for grief. None at all. We shall be at the house of my uncle before morning. By midday we shall have a hundred lances with us. By night there will be an army. There is no time for grief."

"When I think of this night's work," said the girl in a trembling voice, "I could turn myself into a man and spend the rest of my life in armor, with a drawn sword."

"There will be swords enough," said Giovanpaolo. "And a melancholy work for them to do, because we must strike against our own kindred. Beatrice, except for Tizzo, the house of the Baglioni would have fallen indeed and the name would have been borne by traitors only."

They listened, and heard far away the rapid ringing of the bells of Perugia, all striking together to beat out the alarm.

It was easy enough to understand what the alarm bells meant. The traitors had paused in the midst of their murders to discover that Giovanpaolo had definitely escaped from the city. And therefore their work remained a headless task. It was all to be done again.

The bells were still ringing when the three turned their backs on the dim city and went steadily away across the darkness of the hills.

CHAPTER

32

It was a month later when Tizzo rode swiftly through the camp of Giovanpaolo and, coming to the tent of the commander, which was distinguished by the long pennon which flew from the peak, slipped out of the saddle and threw the reins toward one of the men-at-arms who stood guard at the entrance.

Entering the tent, Tizzo saw Giovanpaolo striding up and down, his head a little bent toward the depth of his thought. On the table lay a map. Pieces of armor were stacked on a folding chair. The whole tent was filled with confusion.

"Ah, Tizzo," said Giovanpaolo, hardly turning his fine head toward the interloper, "what is it now? More brawling? More tavern drinking? More duelling? You have put Gismondo of Urbino to bed for a month with one of your sword tricks; the Spaniard from Naples will never see out of both eyes again, they tell me; and Ugo of Camerino will be a lucky man if he ever recovers the use of his left arm."

"It was only the left arm," said Tizzo, seriously. "I knew that he was a fellow you put a value on, and that was why I did not teach his right arm the sort of manners it ought to know."

Giovanpaolo threw himself wearily back into a chair. He shook his head.

"Is the world always no more than a playground for you?" he asked, sadly. "Here we are shut out of Perugia, half of our friends killed, my own family slaughtered like sheep in the middle of the night, and the army which I am raising to retake the city already muttering and growling because I am slow in giving them pay. The men promised to me by the city of Florence have not appeared. All men begin to doubt my fortune. The sky turns black over me; and still you are dancing, drinking, laughing, fighting day and night without a care in the world."

"Look!" said Tizzo, and held out a rolled letter which Giovanpaolo pulled open and read aloud:

Friend and Fire-eater, My Tizzo:

I send you this letter by sure hand. I have already rewarded him, but give him plenty of money when he arrives in honor of a dead man. That is myself.

The days went very well immediately after the Great Betrayal. The wine ran in the gutters, so to speak; the people cheered the murderers of the Baglioni; the traitors sat high in the saddle and they remembered Henry of Melrose with a good many favors and quite a bit of money. I began to feel that I might spend a happy time here except for the stench of murder which rises in my heart when I think of the midnight work which has been done in these streets.

However, when I was about to skim the cream off my cup of fortune and go away with it I was suddenly haled before the chiefs of the Great Betrayal—before Jeronimo della Penna, I mean, and Carlo Barciglia. For Grifone Baglioni is no longer accounted anything. Except for him they never would have taken the place, of course, but since the Great Betrayal conscience has been eating his heart; he has turned yellow and is growing old. Every day he goes to the castle of his lady mother and begs her to let him enter and give him her blessing, and every day the Lady Atlanta bars her doors against him and sends him a curse as a traitor instead of a blessing as a son.

So I was before Jeronimo and Carlo alone, and the information against me was dug up by that double-tongued snake of darkness, that hell-hound of a Mateo Marozzo, who hates you so sweetly and who wears on his forehead the cross which you put there with the point of your dagger. If he remains long out of hell, the chief devil will die of yearning.

It is this Marozzo who discovered that on the night of the Great Betrayal it was through my gate that there passed the Lady Beatrice Baglioni, accompanied by the main head and brains of the Baglioni family, the famous Giovanpaolo, and that Firebrand, the hawk-brained wild man, Tizzo, who had snatched those two lives from the slaughter.

I damned and lied with a vengeance and offered to prove my innocence in single combat with Marozzo, but they have seen my sword-work and they shrank from that idea. In brief, out came two eyewitnesses and I was damned at once, and thrown into prison. Here Jeronimo della Penna is letting me lie while he revolves in his mind a punishment savage enough to be equal to my fault. After that, be sure, I shall die.

In dying, as I run my eyes down the years, I shall see no face more dear to me than that of my young companion who never showed his back to a friend. I shall think of you, Tizzo, as I die. Think of me also, a little, as you live.

Farewell,
HENRY OF MELROSE

[151]

CHAPTER

33

GIOVANPAOLO, when he had finished reading the letter, his voice dropping with an honest reverence as he pronounced the last words, remained for a time with his head bent.

"I know the brave Englishman," said he at last. "I know he has been a bulwark of the house of the Oddi. I have seen him in battle and anyone who has watched the work of his sword can remember him easily enough. I know that it was he who allowed us to pass out of the city on the night of the Betrayal. I would give all the jewels and the gold in this place and all I could send for in order to set him free. But that would not help him. Money will not buy a man out of the cruel hands of Jeronimo della Penna. And what can *you* do, or any other man? We can only pray that we may storm the city and set him free before Jeronimo makes up his mind what form of torment he will use on Melrose."

"I must go to him," answered Tizzo.

"Listen to me," urged Giovanpaolo. "How can one man help him?"

"The man who brought me the letter is an assistant jailer. I've bribed him with a fine sum of money. He is going to meet me in Perugia and admit me to the house of Jeronimo, where Melrose lies in one of the great cellars. He will furnish me with a file to cut through the manacles. After that, I must try to get Melrose away."

"How will you take him out of the city? Will you use wings?"

"Chance," said Tizzo. "I've worshiped her so long with dice, I've made so many sacrifices in her name, that she would not have the heart to refuse me a single request like this one."

"Tizzo—tell me in brief. What is Melrose to you? He is brave; he has an eye which is the same flame-blue as yours in a fight; he is true to his friends. I grant all that. But other men have the same qualities."

"Paolo," said Tizzo, "you and I have sworn to be true to one another. We have sworn to be blood brothers without the blood."

"That is right," nodded Giovanpaolo.

"Well, then," said Tizzo, "if I heard that you were lying in prison, expecting death, my heart would be stirred no more than when I hear that the Englishman is rotting in misery in the dungeon of della Penna."

Giovanpaolo, after this, merely made a mute gesture and argued no more.

"Beatrice is in the inner tent," he said. "You will want to say farewell to her?"

"No," answered Tizzo. "If I see her, I'll fall out of this resolution of mine and be in love with life again. Tell her so after I have gone."

"I shall tell her," said Giovanpaolo. "What is your plan?"

"Simply to enter the city and go to the house of a certain Alberto Marignello, in the little lane off the via dei Bardi. This Marignello is the fellow I have given the money to, the one with the keys to the cellars of della Penna. When I have the keys—why, you see that I'll not know the next step until I come to take it."

"Tizzo, you are a dead man!"

"I am," said Tizzo, cheerfully, "and that is why I have come to say farewell!"

He held out his hands, and Giovanpaolo, with a groan but with no further protest, held out his hands to make that silent farewell.

The green, the orange, the yellow and the crimson no longer flashed on the body of Tizzo when he came near Perugia in the twilight of that day. His skin had been darkened with the walnut stain which he had used on the night of the Great Betrayal, and his red hair, darkened also, tumbled unkempt about his face. His clothes were ragged; his back was bowed under a great fagot of olive wood to which was lashed a heavy woodsman's ax. In the full light of the day a curious eye might have been interested in the blue sheen of the blade of that ax, but in the half-light of the evening the glimmer of the pure Damascus steel could not be noticed.

When he came to the gate, a pair of fine young riders were being questioned by the captain on duty there, but none of the guards paid the slightest attention to that bowed form under the heavy load of wood. A young lad inside the gate bawled: "Look! Look at the donkey walking on two legs!"

In fact, hardly the poorest man in Perugia would have carried such a crushing burden of wood on his back into the town, but Tizzo, with a hanging head and a slight sway from side to side of his entire body, strode gradually up the steep slope of the street. He turned right and left again before he came to the wide façade of the great house in which lived Atlanta Baglioni, the mother of the traitor to his house, Grifone.

In the dusk, he came to the entrance of the courtyard, where the porter merely sang out: "What's this?"

"A broken back and a load of olive wood," said Tizzo. "Where shall I leave the stuff?"

He made as if to drop it to the pavement but the porter cursed him for a lout. "D'you wish to litter the street and give me extra work?" he demanded. "Get in through the court and I'll open the inner door."

He led the way, but stopped suddenly as he saw the form of a man kneeling on the farther side of the court under a shuttered window, crying out, not overloud: "Mother, whatever I have done, I have repented. If I have sinned against God, he will have his own vengeance. If I have sinned against men, my heart is already broken. But if you turn a deaf ear to me, the devils in hell are laughing!"

"So!" muttered the porter. "Always the same! Always the same! But she is the sort of pale steel that will not bend. This way, woodcutter."

He led through a doorway, but as he was about to close the

[154]

door, the man who cried out in the corner of the courtyard rose and rushed to enter behind the burden-bearer. A streak of light from a window flashed dimly across his face and Tizzo recognized the most handsome features of Perugia, the richest of her sons, the pride and the boast of all her youth, Grifone. He was a great deal altered. Even in that faint glimpse, Tizzo could see the pale, hollow face. Then the door slammed heavily and shut out the vision.

"So! So!" panted the porter. "God forgive him for his sins; God forgive my lady for shutting him away; and God forgive me that I have seen such things in my life!"

He showed Tizzo where to carry the wood into a storeroom, and locked the door behind him.

"And now for the payment!" said Tizzo, standing straight with a groan. "I have brought twenty backloads of that wood, now, and I need the money for it, friend."

He leaned on the handle of the ax and wiped sweat from his face.

"You want money? There is not a penny ever paid out in this household except by my lady," said the porter. "Do you want me to break in on her now?"

"Brother," said Tizzo, "there is neither flour nor oil in my house, to say nothing of wine, and I have to walk a league to come to my place."

"Have you carried that backload three miles?" asked the porter.

"Yes," said Tizzo, truthfully.

"Well," murmured the porter, "I shall see what can be done. It is very late, but the lady is kind as milk to every man except to her poor son."

He left Tizzo standing, leaning against the wall, and finally ran down some stairs and told Tizzo to follow him. "She will see you. But this is a strange thing—that she knows everything and yet she does not know of any twenty backloads of wood of the olive. Well, we shall see."

He took Tizzo up the stairs and brought him into a little square anteroom where a table was piled with neatly arranged papers of account.

A moment later the lady of the house entered. The Lady

Atlanta wore the black of deep mourning with double bands of blackness as though for two deaths. To be sure, her husband had been dead ever since the infancy of her son; she had never married in the interval because she had kept one memory sacred although her great wealth had tempted a number of famous suitors; and now it was plain that she mourned for Grifone, her son, as though he were dead also.

This darkness of the clothes made her face marble. Her brow was as clear as stone, her eyes were unmarked by time, and she wore that faint smile which Greek sculptors knew and loved. At first glance she seemed still in her twenties. In fact, she was not yet forty years of age.

She took her place at once behind the table, sitting straight in a backless chair and resting on the edge of the table a hand of wonderful youth and delicacy of outline.

"Your name?" she said.

"Andrea," said Tizzo, bowing until his shaggy hair almost touched the floor. "Andrea the son of Andrea the son of Andrea, the son of Luigi of the millside near the village of La Pietra."

"Andrea," said she, "you claim the payment for twenty back-loads of olive wood?"

"I do," said Tizzo, bowing again.

"I have no record of ordering this fuel, my poor friend," said the lady.

"I carry the order with me," said Tizzo.

"You carry it with you?"

"Yes, my lady."

"In writing?"

"In token," said Tizzo.

He shifted the ax which he still held and drew from his breast on a slender string something which he held in the hollow of his palm so that the porter could not see it but the lady could. What she saw was a broken ring.

She saw, also, the sudden flash of meaning in eyes too bright, too flame-blue for the darkness of the skin and the hair.

She saw this, and instantly looked down at the floor.

"Go to Fortinacci the steward," she said to the porter, "and ask him what he knows about this affair of Andrea the son of Andrea the son of Andrea. I will talk to Andrea in the meantime."

The porter disappeared, and Lady Atlanta rose at once. "What is the ring?" she asked.

Tizzo, with his grimy fingers, laid it at once in the white palm of her hand and she bent over it curiously. She started straight again, suddenly. There was a wide incredulity in her eyes as she said: "It is one half of a broken signet ring of Giovanpaolo Baglioni!"

"The other half," said Tizzo, "is worn about his neck."

"In sign of what?" she asked.

"In sign that we are sworn brothers," said Tizzo.

C H A P T E R

34

The Lady Atlanta, looking with her cold, steady eyes into the face of the stranger, said to him, suddenly: "You are the red-haired man, the Firebrand; you are that Tizzo—and yet you cannot be he! Hair may be stained and skin darkened, but Tizzo is a man who can cleave a thick jousting helmet with one stroke of his ax—"

Here her eye ran down along the arm and the hand of Tizzo to the blue, shimmering blade of his ax.

"Ah, it is true!" she murmured. She smiled with a radiance that made her young as a girl.

She hurried to the door and slid the bolt, whispering: "What is there that I may do? I know that you saved two sacred lives of my family. Now you are risking your head again by entering

Perugia. Tizzo, you had better walk into a flaming furnace than into this town!"

"Withdraw the bolt, madam," said Tizzo. "If you honor me with a private interview, even that is enough to make men look at me, and if they look at me twice, I shall be discovered."

"True!" she said, and drew out the bolt again, instantly. "But what is there that I can do, Tizzo? Tell me how I can aid you? Whatever purpose brought you to Perugia, I shall make it my purpose!"

"My purpose," said he, "is to rescue a friend from his prison in the cellars of della Penna."

"With how many men are you to attack the house?"

"With my two hands and this ax," he said, smiling. "It is not force that will save my friend. The only thing that will unlock the bolts of della Penna's house is chance and a little bribery. I am using both."

"Tizzo, the chance is dreadfully slight. And if they capture you, your head will be on a pike before morning!"

"The chance is very small," he admitted. "There is a better and a surer way of saving my friend: beating open the gates of Perugia and restoring the city to its rightful rulers."

"Tell me what way!" she demanded, eagerly.

"You have the means in your own hands. The agent is now in your courtyard calling out on your name and begging you to let him speak to you. Your son Grifone is trusted with half the charge of the walls. He could open the gates easily, and allow the soldiers of Giovanpaolo to enter the town."

"Since Judas," she said, "there never has been such a traitor as Grifone Baglioni!"

"He is your own son!" said Tizzo.

"I forswear my claim in him. He is a changeling. My true son was stolen out of my bed and a murderer's brat was placed on my breast."

"My lady, if ever the same blood showed in two faces, it is in you and his highness, Grifone."

"It cannot be," she said. "Or if I have had a share in the making of his body, I have had none in the forming of his heart. In his own house—at midnight—with his own hand he gave the signal

[158]

for the butchery—and he led the way—Ah, God, when I gave him birth, what a curse I brought upon my poor Perugia!"

"One word from you, and he would throw himself on the side of Giovanpaolo."

"Giovanpaolo would not have the traitor's aid—not for the price of two cities, each twice greater than Perugia."

"My lady, it is true that Giovanpaolo would never forgive him, but if Grifone will restore the Baglioni to their own, then a peace can be made between them. His highness, Grifone, can withdraw with all his possessions to another place. And time may partly close the breach between them."

"Death alone can close it!" said the Lady Atlanta.

"Madam, I beg you to think—it is in your power to restore the Baglioni to Perugia."

"It is the dearest wish of my soul, but shame would keep Grifone from lifting a hand to help the men he has wronged."

"Be sure that his heart is suffering. There is torture in his face. A word from him will make him repent everything and strive to make amends to all the people of his blood."

"Tizzo, I have sworn a great and sacred oath never to look on his face, never to speak to him, never to listen to his voice. If I hear him crying out under my window, I run to another room and stop my ears."

"An oath which is wrong should not be maintained. Every priest will grant you absolution for breaking it."

"I did not swear it with thin breath; I swore it with my heart and soul."

Tizzo, for a moment regarded the beauty, the terrible anger in her face. And he knew that persuasion would be impossible.

"Then I kiss your hand and leave you, my lady," he said.

She retained his hand in both of hers, the fierce passion dying gradually out of her eyes.

"But you, Tizzo," she said. "I know what you have done. I know by words, and also, I saw that great jousting helmet cloven to the bottom by your axstroke. There is not strength in your hands for such a feat and therefore it must be a strength in your heart. Trust me, that if I know any manner in which I may aid you and help you, I am at your service. There is money here

[159]

—or jewels which have a greater price—will you have them?"

She actually stripped the rich rings from her fingers. But Tizzo shook his head.

"There are men in this house whom I could trust to support you in anything."

"No, my lady," said Tizzo. "I have had enough money for my purpose. More would only be a weight in my pocket. And as for men, the thing I have to do is better and more easily managed by one hand than by twenty. Secrecy has to be the point of the sword for me now."

"Must I feel that my hands are empty to help you?" she exclaimed.

"No, my lady. I shall remember you when I come to the time of need, and that will make me stronger."

"You will go on this wild enterprise, Tizzo?"

"I must go, at once."

"Tell me what service I can do, other than this, for Giovanpaolo and his men?"

"Send to my friend, Antonio Bardi, and tell him that Giovanpaolo forgives the part he played in the Great Betrayal. At least, Bardi did no murder on that night."

"How can Giovanpaolo forgive a single soul who took part in the Great Betrayal?"

"Because he is as wise as he is brave. My lady, send for Bardi. Tell him he is forgiven if he wishes to strike a blow on our side. Send, also, for my foster father, Luigi Falcone. He has taken no stand on either side. But he will ride and fight for me. Those two men inside the city, if they will meet in your house and lay their plans together, may be strong enough to open Perugia to the attack of Giovanpaolo. Farewell!"

"Farewell, noble Tizzo!" said the Lady Atlanta. "If I were a man, I would go at your side, tonight!"

It was easy enough for Tizzo to get down the stairway and out into the empty courtyard, unobserved.

A thunderstorm was rolling over the city, lighting up its towers and mountain ranges of clouds with long ripplings of cataracting lightning. Brief, rattling showers raised a pungent odor of dust in the air, and scurried the people out of the streets, as

[160]

Tizzo turned away from the great, unhappy house of the Lady Atlanta.

He had never seen, he was sure, a lady so beautiful. Not the young and lovely wife of Grifone, even, was so like an immortal. Compared with such majesty and purity of features, the Lady Beatrice was a mere tomboy. She was a mere prettiness, in contrast. But then it was her spirit that set the hearts of men burning.

Thinking of her, Tizzo turned into the via dei Bardi and there forgot everything except his purpose. From the street of the Bardi, he turned into the alley that branched off from it, crooked and downhill as the course of a stream; and the lofty, irregular front of the houses might well have been a canyon which the running water had worked out of the living rock.

The house of Alberto Marignello had been well described to him. He found it almost at once and was about to cross the street toward it when a slender youth, wrapped in a cloak to defy the rain, said to him: "Tizzo, there have been many men there before you!"

He turned with a half groan of bewilderment and fear. "Beatrice," he whispered, "in the name of what god have you come to Perugia tonight?"

CHAPTER

35

SHE stood back with one elbow leaning against the wall, her hat pulled half down across her forehead, her legs crossed, her whole attitude one of super-boyish impudence and mirth. He had seen her so often in man's clothes, she was so certain to slip into them whenever there was an emergency of importance, that his quickest memory of her was not in dresses at all. She was saying: "I came to Perugia in the name of the great god of the fire, in the name of the Firebrand; I came for Tizzo. Does that answer please you, my most noble lord?"

"Beatrice, listen to me—"

"If you talk so earnestly, people will notice you. If they look at you twice, they'll soon have you clapped into a fire to burn in good earnest, Messer Firebrand."

"They will find you in the town. They will surely recognize you, Beatrice. And if they get their hands on you—"

"They don't murder women," said Beatrice. "Not even in Perugia."

"They'll do worse. They'll marry you to one of their brutal selves for the sake of your estate."

"And then comes noble Sir Tizzo and runs my false husband through the gizzard and makes me a widow today and a new wife tomorrow. You see, I risk very little. No matter what road the story starts away on, it will wind up with Beatrice and Tizzo hand in hand at the close."

"My God, how wild, how foolish, and how charming you are," said Tizzo. "Giovanpaolo should not have told you where I had gone."

"I pulled the story out of him like so many teeth. Tizzo, you would sneak away and let yourself be killed? Sneak away without a word of farewell to me?"

"I had not the courage to face you."

"When I knew you were gone, I was empty," she said. "I felt, suddenly, as though you had never kissed me, as though you had never said you loved me. I felt as though danger were another woman, and you had gone to her. So I had to come here and meet you in the street."

"You must go instantly from the city."

"With you, Tizzo, I would go anywhere."

"I cannot go with you farther than the walls."

"Then I shall not leave Perugia."

"Beatrice, I beg you—if you love me—"

"I only love the man who lets me share his dangers," she said.

"I will take you to the walls and see you safely away."

"I shall not go unless you come with me."

He groaned. And then he said: "The work which lies before me is something I cannot turn my back on."

"Your work is spoiled before it commenced," she said.

"Why?"

"I've lingered up and down this street, and I've seen half a dozen men enter that building."

"Why not? More than one family lives in it."

"Men in cloaks, with something under the cloaks."

"Bread from the baker, perhaps."

"Bread or steel ground sharp along two edges, more likely," she said.

"Marignello has been paid his price. He would not betray me."

"Perhaps he could get a greater price from della Penna."

"He would not dare to confess that he had been in touch with me."

[163]

"No? He would simply say that, from the first, he had been attempting to draw you into a trap."

"There is not that degree of guile in him."

"Tizzo, for all your cleverness—and I know you are not a fool —you continue to think that men are as honest as yourself. And that *is* a folly. Why, Tizzo, every man in Perugia knows that Mateo Marozzo, for instance, would pay all the gold in his treasury for the sake of one chance to drive a knife into your body!"

"Marozzo hates me. They all hate me, now. But I must count on Marignello. Without him, I have no hope. And that means that Melrose has to die without a hand lifted to save him."

"Henry of Melrose," she said, "has followed adventure all his life. He could never expect to die peacefully. Let him have the end that he has invited."

"I cannot, Beatrice."

"Will not, you should say."

"I love you, Beatrice; but even you hardly stir my blood and draw my soul from me so much as that wild Englishman."

"He taught you half a dozen tricks of fencing, and therefore you love him."

"There is something more than that," said Tizzo, frowning. "Long ago, when I saw him, suddenly I had to follow him. I left the inheritance of a great house and a huge fortune for the sake of tagging about the world at his heels."

"Perhaps he used a charm on you?"

Tizzo crossed himself and murmured: "God forbid! But I must go forward in this."

"You mean that you will surely enter that house?"

"Most surely I shall."

"Well, then, I shall show you one thing first," said the girl.

Before he could stop her, she was halfway across the street, and he saw her pass straight through the door of the tall house. As she opened the door, he had a glimpse of a dull light and suddenly reaching hands. He saw a flash of naked steel here and there in the background.

He ran like a deer to the rescue but the door slammed heavily; he arrived at it only in time to hear the clank of the heavy iron bolt rammed home into a stone socket.

To beat against the door with his ax would simply be a folly. He ran to the left into a meager alley hardly the width of a man's body and saw, high above his head, the glimmer of a light through a barred window.

Springing up as high as possible, he was barely able to hook the lower edge of the ax over the sill of the window. Then he drew himself up into the casement and curled into the embrasure. Through the bars of the window he found himself looking down into a large room with a fire flickering on a deep hearth and a mist of woodsmoke in the air. And in the midst of the room stood a full dozen of men clustered about the Lady Beatrice, holding her fast by the arms.

Alberto Marignello stood before her, his rather handsome but heavy face darkened by a scowl.

"Now, my lad," he was saying, "explain why you open the door of a place where you have never been seen before?"

"I come here because I bring a message."

"What sort of a message?"

"A brief one," said the girl.

"From whom?"

"From a man I met outside the gate of San Ercolano."

"Well, what sort of a man?"

"A young man with red hair."

"Ah, ha!" said Marignello. "Young—with red hair, and blue eyes that never stop shining?"

"Yes, that is he."

"You see?" said Marignello. "He has seen that Tizzo—that blue-eyed devil of a Tizzo! Well, and what message did he give you?"

"To come here and find a man called Alberto Marignello."

"That is my name."

"Well, then I'm to tell you that he cannot come tonight."

"Ah, he cannot come?"

"No."

"Will he come tomorrow?"

"Tomorrow after dark, if you will come out to the camp of Giovanpaolo and arrange a second meeting place."

"I go again into the jaws of the lion?" said Marignello. "I am not such a fool."

"That was the message. And then I come here," said Beatrice, angrily, "and you all leap at me like dogs at a bone."

A strangeness came into the mind of Tizzo. He half wanted to shout: "Fools! You have in your hands the greatest prize, bar one, that you could ask for. You have the sister of Giovanpaolo. With her in your hands, you are safe, and Giovanpaolo himself will not dare to attack the city—not if he had a million armed men behind him!"

And again, with his bare hands, he wanted to tear at the iron bars and wrench them from their stone sockets and plunge into the room.

Here a great booming of thunder began, one of those cataracting sounds which pour over heaven like a cart over a brazen bridge. Inserting the stout oaken haft of the ax between the bars, he bore down with all his strength. Something gave. It was not the stone socket, but the soft iron itself bent, and so was pulled loose. With his hand he was able to draw it away from the socket.

As the uproar of the thunder died down, one of the men said: "This story that the boy tells is all very smooth and well. But I wish to ask when he passed through the gate at San Ercolano?"

"Oh, half an hour ago," said the Lady Beatrice.

The fellow who had asked the question turned with a sudden grin on his companions. He threw out his hand to make an important gesture. Then he said: "It was less than a half hour ago that I passed near San Ercolano and found out that the gate had not been opened during the entire afternoon."

"The small portal in the gate was open, however," said Beatrice, and the heart of Tizzo stood still as he listened.

"The portal was not opened!" shouted the fellow who had last spoken. He had a broad, brutal face and Tizzo swore that he would never forget that countenance.

"The portal was not opened. The entire guard was taken from the gate at noon! At noon, mind you! And the boy lies!"

"Ah, ha," said Marignello. "Is that the way of it? Now, he looks capable of a good lie, when I look at him again. His face is a little too fine for those clothes. Give me your hand, boy!"

Beatrice held out her hand, and Marignello leaned over it. Suddenly he threw it to one side. He exclaimed: "It is soft as the

hand of a woman! This fellow never has done a stroke of work!
What has your labor been, eh?"

"I've been a tailor's apprentice," said Beatrice, instantly.

"Ha? So! Well that may be, too," said Marignello, half convinced by this remark.

"No tailor's apprentice ever stood so straight," said another.
"From sitting cross-legged, their shoulders begin to stoop before
they're twelve years old."

"Aye, and their chins stick out in front."

"Aye, and they squint!"

These remarks came in a general murmur. The thunder rolled
heavily again, and Tizzo used that noise to cover the wrenching
jerk with which he pried loose a second bar. Another pair, and
he would have opened a sufficient space to admit his body. After
that, if once he got down into that room with his ax—well, they
would have something to think about other than this "boy" they
were questioning.

"You are not a tailor's apprentice," said Marignello, pointing
to her hand. "See, there is no enlargement of the thumb and the
forefinger of the right hand, and the left forefinger is not stuck
full of the little scars of the needle point. Confess that you have
lied."

"I was ill for six months and the scars wore away from my skin,"
said Beatrice Baglioni.

"I never saw a tailor," said Marignello, "who dared to look
people straight in the eyes in the manner of this lad. He holds
up his chin in the manner of one who has told servants to come
and to go. Come—the signore will be here in a little while, and
then we may learn something more about this lad."

It was only another moment, in fact, when a knock came distinctly at the street door.

"Shall I open?" asked one of the men.

"No, not till I have spoken," said Marignello.

He approached the door and called out: "Who is there?"

The answer was indistinguishable to Tizzo, but Marignello
called again: "What word has passed between us?"

He paused for the answer and then said to the other: "This is right. He has named the word which he and I alone know. It is the signore."

He then unbarred the door and there entered a man in a scarlet cloak whose collar was wrapped up high about the head and face in order to shut off the rain.

He threw back this cloak and revealed himself in a fine doublet and costly hose that had a silken sheen. He had a colored handkerchief thrust inside his belt and carried a dagger as well as a sword. His soft hat was of blue velvet, and it was pulled low over his forehead. In spite of this, the silver gleam of a scar appeared just above the center of the forehead and looked like a streak of grease. Tizzo recognized his own handiwork. With the point of his dagger he had drawn a cross into the flesh of Mateo Marozzo, the point of the sharp steel shuddering against the bone. This man he had branded for life, and it was a deed which he looked back upon only with pleasure. He wished, now, that he had driven the dagger through the fellow's heart.

Marignello said: "We have caught a queer lad here, who says that he's a tailor's apprentice. But he hasn't that look. He says that he carries a message from Tizzo. Will your lordship look at him?"

Marozzo approached the Lady Beatrice and stared full in her face.

Then he said: "This is, in fact, a very queer—lad! Marignello, take yourself and your men away. Let me have plenty of time alone with this—lad. And I may make something of him!"

MARIGNELLO got quickly out of the room, the slamming of the door behind him and his companions being quite covered by an immense, crashing downpour of the rain. In that uproar, Tizzo managed to work the other bars from the sockets. He had plenty of room, now, to slip through the window, but his position was frightfully complicated. If he leaped down, the ten foot drop to the floor from that high casement probably would send him sprawling, and before he could rise the dagger of Marozzo would be in his back. He waited, the corners of his mouth jerking with eagerness.

He could hear Marozzo, now, saying: "Dangerous, beautiful— most beautiful, most dangerous, Lady Beatrice! Can I tell you how welcome you are to me?"

"My dear Mateo," said the girl, "I ought to be welcome to you. You can make a very neat sum of money out of me, I suppose."

"Money?" said Marozzo. "Do you think that we will sell you? No, sweetheart, you will never leave Perugia, and so long as you are inside the city the hands of Giovanpaolo are tied. He cannot strike at us for fear we may strike at you. You mean more than money to all of us. You mean life, Beatrice, life!"

He began to laugh, putting his face close to hers, jeering.

"And the handsome fellow with the red hair—the Firebrand— Tizzo—I suppose it was he who drew you into this crazy adventure, my lady? Your reputation—what is that to a man whose brain is all in a flame? Such a bright flame that the pretty little moths, the charming, delicate Beatrices, are always flying into the fire!"

"Mateo," she answered, "Tizzo has nothing to do with this."

"Certainly not. You didn't even know that he was expected here this evening? You were merely walking up the street by chance? You merely happened to walk through this door? Certainly Tizzo could have nothing to do with it!"

She took a deep, quick breath and looked fixedly at Marozzo.

"Mateo, you can make a fortune, a great fortune, if you'll see me out of the city."

"If an angel came down and offered me a throne in heaven for returning you to your brother, I would never do it!" said Marozzo.

"No," she said, slowly, "I think you mean that!"

"I mean it with all my heart. We are leaving the house now, my lady!"

"To cheat your friend Marignello of his share in the reward? There is as much fox as dog in you, Mateo," she said.

And Marozzo, overwhelmed with a sudden frenzy of hate, flicked the tips of his fingers across her face.

It was not thought that governed Tizzo. Far better for him to have slipped back down to the street and waited for Marozzo and his prize in the darkness of the narrow way. But he could not resist the lightning impulse which overcame him when he saw the girl struck. He slid through the window and dropped to the floor, and his foot, striking a wet spot on the tiles, shot him head-long on the slippery pavement.

He was already half twisting to his feet when he saw Marozzo running in at him with a leveled sword. An agony of quick fear had turned the face of Mateo white and pulled his mouth into a horrible grin; an agony of joy at this golden opportunity set his eyes blazing. He might have brought a dozen men swarming by a single cry, but that conflict of his emotions seemed to have throttled him. Or perhaps he saw, in this gleaming instant, a chance to accomplish a double deed—the capture of Lady Beatrice and the death of Tizzo. Such a thing would make him a hero forever among the powers who then ruled the city of Perugia. He would be, at once, among the great ones.

So he sprang at Tizzo, the sword shooting out before him for

[170]

the death stroke. It came with such speed that there was no avoiding it, but Beatrice caught at the backward flaring cloak of Marozzo with such strength that he was checked and jerked a little to the side. That gave Tizzo the fraction of a moment he needed for rising to his feet. The head of the ax, light as gilded paper in the practiced grasp of his hands, struck aside the next thrust. He was in no position to use the edge of the ax for a counterstroke. Instead, he drove the butt of the haft between the eyes of Marozzo and snatched the sword as it fell from the unnerved hand.

Marozzo fell in a heap, not utterly unconscious but still struggling to recover himself. To Tizzo the miracle was that a yell of alarm had not roused the house before this.

"Quick! Quick, Tizzo!" gasped Lady Beatrice, already at the street door.

"Go in the name of God," he commanded. "Go to the house of Lady Atlanta and she will shield you. I have one more thing to attempt here."

With a twist of cloth he was tying the hands of Marozzo behind his back. Then he drew the little poniard from the side of Marozzo and flashed it before his eyes.

"If you mark me again like a branded beast—" groaned Marozzo. "Kill me outright, Tizzo. Ah, God, to think that I had you so close to the point of my sword!"

"A greater miracle is going to happen," said Tizzo. "You will have a chance for your life if you listen to me! Beatrice, will you go? Will you go? Are you staying here to drive me mad? Slip away! Swift, to the house of the lady, and she will help you from the city."

The girl stepped to the table and sat down on the edge of it, swinging one small foot.

"I stay here," she said. "I haven't had so many chances of seeing you at work, Tizzo."

He glared at her, baffled.

"There is still danger!" he insisted. "There is a frightful danger —I beg you with the blood of my heart—go at once!"

"While you stay here?" said the girl. "No, I stay where you stay. Save your breath. You can't persuade me to leave you."

[171]

He glared at her once more, half enraged, half desperate. Then he turned back to Marozzo.

"Stand up!" he commanded, and Marozzo rose. His eyes saw one thing only, the deadly splinter of steel, the almost invisible needle point of the poniard which was at his breast.

"Step to the door," said Tizzo, and led his captive there.

He pulled that door a trifle ajar and ordered: "Call to Marignello and tell him to send all his companions away. Tell him you have learned something that is only for his ears and yours. In a hearty, happy voice, Marozzo, or by St. Stephen you'll have something sharper than arrows in your heart!"

"I'll be no tool of yours!" panted Marozzo. "Stab me, then; but I'll not do your work for you! The day is cursed that first saw you!"

"Ah, Mateo, do you invite me?" asked Tizzo through his teeth. "Don't you see, Marozzo, that wild horses are drawing me forward to your slaughter, you jackal? But do as I tell you and I give back your dirty life. You hear?"

In that moment of shame and surrender, Marozzo glanced toward the girl and found her hard, cruel eyes fixed upon him. His head dropped.

"Make up your mind," said Tizzo. "Will you call to Marignello? Heartily?"

"Yes," said Marozzo.

His head jerked back. His eyes were half closed, and suddenly he shouted to the full of his lungs: "Marignello! Help! Hel—"

The point of Tizzo's dagger could have stifled the first word of that cry, but he could not strike it into a defenseless throat. His whole heart yearned to kill the traitor, and still he could not use the edge of the dagger. Instead, he jerked it about and struck with the pommel once, twice, and again into the midst of that still beautiful face.

A smashed red ruin took the place of a face. Marozzo slid through the arms of Tizzo like a figure of sand and lay helpless on the floor.

"Tizzo, they are coming!" panted the girl.

"They are," he admitted. "But I can't leave. There's still a chance. I *must* get from Marignello the keys that he holds— Beatrice, for the last time—will you run for your life?"

A tumult of many footfalls came hurrying, and Tizzo barred the inner door against that influx.

"Signore Marozzo? Your highness?" Marignello was calling out anxiously as he came.

And then a light and silver sound of laughter chimed in the room, making Tizzo jerk his head suddenly about. It was the Lady Beatrice, with her head tilted back, now crying out: "Your highness—Signore Marozzo—how can I help laughing—"

The inner door was shaken.

"Your highness—did you call to me?"

"Yes, for wine," said Lady Beatrice. "I'll unbar the door for you, Marignello—"

She looked fixedly at Tizzo and walked up to the door. He, understanding suddenly, dragged the fallen body of Marozzo aside and placed himself where the door would cover him as it swung open.

There he waited. A crack of light struck in on him as he stood there while the door swung wide under the hands of the girl.

"Only you, Marignello," she said, still laughing. "There is a secret, here, and you are the only man his highness will admit to it. Step in!"

"A secret? I thought I heard a yell for help—" began Marignello, as he stepped through the door.

The girl shut and barred it instantly behind him.

"But where is Signore Marozzo—" began Marignello. It was only then that he saw the gleam of the poised ax in the hand of Tizzo. He made no effort to leap back. There was not a man in Perugia who did not know the singular and deadly magic which Tizzo could work with that weapon.

"Tie his hands," said Tizzo softly, to the girl.

It was done instantly.

"Is there a rear door out of the house?" whispered Tizzo to the stricken Marignello.

The eyes of the man dropped to the still figure of Marozzo on the floor.

"You still have a chance for life," promised Tizzo, "but only if you lend us your help."

"May I live? Oh, God, is it possible that you give me my life?"

[173]

breathed Marignello. "There is, my lord. There is a door at the back of the house."

"Then tell all those fellows of yours to leave the place by that door—to return here tomorrow at the same time. Sing out in a hearty voice. You hear me?"

Marignello nodded. His eyes blinked. Twice he moistened his lips and took deep breaths, before he called out in a ringing tone: "It's finished for tonight. Paolo—Guido—all of you out the back way; I have to confer here with his highness."

"This is all too damned strange," said a heavy, growling voice beyond the door.

Marignello looked down again at the limp figure, the blood-dripping face of Marozzo, and shuddered.

"Orders from his highness," he said. "We've found wonders in the boy—and tomorrow night, my lads! At the same hour. We'll have the trap and we'll have the Tizzo to catch in it, and double pay for all."

There was still a little murmuring, but presently the footfalls began to withdraw. The knees of Marignello were bending under his weight, and the cold burden of fear.

"Be brave, Marignello," said Tizzo. "I have made a promise. Fill your part of the bargain, and you shall live, I swear."

"God and your highness forgive me for treachery!" groaned Marignello. "But they offered me a fortune, a treasure of gold! They hate you so, and they fear you so, that they would buy your death with your own weight in gold. Yes, they would make a statue of you all in precious metals and set jewels in the head of it for eyes. They would give that away to make sure of your death!"

"I understand," said Tizzo.

The girl had gone to the street door and was listening, but the crashing of the rain muffled all other sounds outside the house. Small gusts of wind worked down the chimney and knocked puffs of smoke out into the room.

"But you have, somewhere in the house, keys that fit doors in the prison cellars of della Penna," said Tizzo. "You were not lying when you told me that you were a trusted man?"

"I was not, signore. No, no, I am a trusted man—and God forgive me for once betraying my trust! There are three sets of

[174]

the keys, one in the hands of his highness, Jeronimo della Penna, and the head jailer keeps one—he never leaves the house; and I have a smaller set."

"What will your smaller set open? The outer door of the cellars?"

"Yes, signore."

"Marignello, you will still be a treasure to me! Where are those keys?"

"They are at the keymaker's."

"Ha?"

"His highness, Jeronimo della Penna, ordered me to have my set copied."

Tizzo groaned, but the girl, turning from the door, said: "He lies, Tizzo."

"Why do you think so?"

"Three sets of keys to one dungeon—that is more than enough. If Jeronimo used all the wits he possesses, he would never have so many. Besides, would he trust such keys into common hands? Into the hands of a keymaker, who might make ten sets as easily as one?"

"True!" exclaimed Tizzo. He turned sharply on Marignello, who cowered as though he expected death to strike him that instant.

"You have lied, Marignello?" he demanded.

"Ah, my lord, consider! For these years I never have broken my trust to my master! How can I break it now?"

"You were bribed by Henry of Melrose."

"No, signore. I took his money, but then I carried the letter to my master. He read it through and told me to deliver it—and keep the bribe. You see, I tried to be honest."

"I think you have," said Tizzo, with a queer turning of his heart. "As well as you could, you've tried. You've tried to betray me and trap me—but I suppose that money can buy outright a conscience like yours. But now, Marignello, make up your mind. Will you give me the keys or will you not? Will you give them to me, or will you die here?"

"They are in that closed cupboard at the corner of the room," sighed Marignello.

Beatrice was instantly at the place, and when she had pulled the door open she drew out from one of the inner shelves a bunch of keys which were dark with rust in places but polished with use in others.

"Are these the ones, Marignello?" she asked.

"They are," said Marignello, sinking his head. "And I am a ruined man forever!"

"You have made a fortune out of your treachery," said Tizzo. "Why not leave Perugia, then, and spend your money in another place?"

"Because wine in other cities has no taste, and bread in another place will not fill the belly. Except in Perugia there is no good air for breathing; in other places, the men are fools and the women are foul," said Marignello, mournfully.

A deep sigh from Marozzo, at this moment, called attention back to him, and Beatrice stooped above his body.

"Now for the keys," said Tizzo. "One by one—slowly—here, I draw a diagram on the floor as you name me the rooms and the passages, one by one. Now, begin!"

C H A P T E R

37

THEY left Marozzo and Marignello lashed hand and foot, converted into two lifeless hulks which were rendered silent with strong gags. The cloak and the hat of Marignello were taken by Tizzo. That of Marozzo would shelter Beatrice from the rain. And now, with the ax under the folds of the cloak, Tizzo stood beside the girl in the street. The eaves above them shut away most of the rain, which rushed down just past their faces.

"You see that where I am going now, no one can go with me," said Tizzo. "I have to be as secret as a cat, as casual as a pack mule. If I tried to take you with me, I would be lost at once."

"I know it," said Beatrice. "But if you go, Tizzo, I shall never see you again!"

"The keys give me a good chance. The clothes of Marignello may help me more than everything else."

"Suppose that you even get to the Englishman and then find that already he has been torn and ruined by torture so that he can't follow you?"

Tizzo groaned.

"I must not find him that way!" he said.

Then he added: "You can go to one of three houses—that of Lady Atlanta, or to my foster father, Luigi Falcone, or to the place of Antonio Bardi. Which one will you choose?"

"Lady Atlanta."

"Farewell, Beatrice."

"Tizzo, say something now for me to remember through the years when I think of you going into the rattrap."

He laughed a little. Soft-footed thunder ran down the farther sky. Lightning slid along a crack of brightness.

"You'll remember that I drank too much wine, loved dice and fighting. Remember, too, that I loved my friends and one exquisite lady—one that could be more troublesome than smoke in the eyes, more delightful than a warm fire in December."

He could see that her eyes were closed as she leaned back against the wall.

"Now go before I begin to weep," she said.

He turned and hurried up the street.

He had with him the ax muffled under the cloak, the broad, strong dagger of Marignello, and a file made of the most perfect steel, three cornered, ready to eat through other metal like fire through wood. Also, he had keys and a plan of the cellars of della Penna. These items were all advantages. Against him he had the hands of a strongly occupied house where one word of alarm would bring a score of well-armed men.

Was that why he was singing under his breath when he looked up at the gloomy façade of the house of della Penna?

He passed the main entrance, with its lanterns lighted, the horses waiting saddled in the street; for now that Jeronimo della Penna was the chief lord of Perugia, he had to have horses in readiness night and day.

Around the corner he came on a small portal which was sunk into the wall, a little round-topped doorway. Into the lock of this he fitted the largest of his keys, and felt the wards moving instantly, silently under the pressure.

That success was to him prophetic of victory all the way through. It seemed a sufficient proof that Marignello had not lied. He pushed the door open, and found himself in a little semicircular guardroom where a man in breastplate and morion was rising and picking up an unsheathed sword. He gave one glance at the weapon and at the little gray pointed beard of the guard. Then he walked by, making his step longer, heavier, more lumbering to match the gait of Marignello.

"Well, Marignello," said the guard, "this is before your time, isn't it?"

Tizzo went silently on.

Behind him he heard a muttering voice say: "Surly, voiceless, low-hearted dog!"

But Tizzo, turning a bend of the corridor, left the thought of the guard behind him. He had passed through the second stage of success and now he could swear that all would go well. A great premonition of victory accompanied him.

The stairs, exactly as Marignello had charted them, opened to the right of the hall. In a niche in the wall were placed three or four small lanterns, and one of these he took with him to light his way. The dull illumination showed him the descending stages as the stairway passed over laid stone and then was cut into the living rock. A singular odor filled the air. Gray slime covered the damp corners.

Down for two stories he passed into the bowels of the earth before he came to another hall somewhat narrower than the ones above it.

The third door on the right was his destination. When he came to it he waited for an instant, his ear pressed to the iron-bound door, his heart beating wildly. It would be worth everything to shine his lantern into the blue eyes of the Englishman and see his face change when he recognized his friend. All danger was worth while in the light of that moment of recognition.

He tried the prescribed key. It worked, but not so easily, the rusted lock groaning a little under the weight of his effort. At last the door sagged inward; he took a sudden, long step inside and pressed the door shut behind him. Then he raised the lantern high.

What he saw was emptiness. There was not a soul in the cell. A flat bit of moldering straw in a corner might have served as a bed at one time. That was the only sign.

He looked up despairingly at the glimmer of sweat on the ceiling of the rock. He saw the innumerable chisel strokes with which the tomb had been carved in the rock. He would need a patience as great as that if he were to find the Englishman in another part of this underground world which generations had enlarged, patiently, to provide storerooms and prisons for the lordly family which lived in the upper regions of light and air.

He sat down, like a prisoner himself, on the pallet of straw, and tried to remember. As he had charted the plan of the underground rooms at the direction of Marignello, so now he redrew the plan in his mind, bit by bit, carefully. This flight of chambers, all small, ran from side to side of the cellar. Above were slightly larger rooms. In the lowest level of all there was only the torture chamber, fittingly placed at the foot of the entire structure so that the frightful sounds from it might not rise to the upper levels, poisoning the souls of all who heard.

Had Marignello simply lied—speaking truth until he came to the last and most important step of all? Did the scoundrel really have in him one strong devotion—to his trust in the house of della Penna?

If so, it was a miracle; for one evil corrupts the entire soul.

With the lantern, Tizzo examined the heavy iron bracket and ring which were fastened at the foot of one side of the wall, opposite the door. The ring was completely covered with rust, but when he examined the inside of it, he found that the rust powdered and flaked away. He stared at the floor. There was already a very thin deposit of the same iron dust on the floor, enough to stain the tips of his fingers red.

No, Marignello had not lied entirely. Into that ring, very recently, fetters had been locked and by their chafing had loosened the rust.

Perhaps Henry of Melrose already was dead. Perhaps his body had been taken from the cell and buried. If not to a grave, to what place would he be removed?

Yes, living, they might take him to another room—the torture chamber underneath!

Tizzo was up, instantly, and in the corridor outside. Something gray and dim streaked across his feet. He heard the incredibly light scampering of a rat, saw the gleam of the long, naked tail, heard a faint squeak that made his flesh crawl.

There was no air for breathing. Fear like a vampire sucked the life from him. He would have given a year of life for the sake of ten deep breaths of the outer night.

At the bottom of the steps there was no corridor, only a brief anteroom, so to speak, and then a very powerful door, crossed and recrossed with such iron bars that it could have endured the battering of a ram designed to tear down a wall.

The key for this door had not been named by Marignello, but there were only three that could possibly fit the yawning mouth of the lock. It was the third of these that, actually, turned the bolt and slid it with a slight rumbling noise. The hinges of the door did not creak, however. For whatever hellish purposes, this room was used and opened at not too infrequent intervals.

Gradually, he pushed the door open and stepped inside.

What he saw was such a quantity of gear hanging from the ceiling, such a litter dripping down the walls, such complicated machines standing on the floor, that it looked like the interior of some important manufacturer's shop—some place, say, where iron is formed to make singular weapons or tools of trade. But those machines were not designed for the working of wood or of iron; they were framed to work torment into the human flesh, and the ingenuity of a thousand devils could not have done more.

Wherever the swift eye of Tizzo glanced, he saw monstrosities that sickened him. A pair of huge metal boots, he knew at once, were used to encase legs, while various turnscrews and wheels attached to the boots indicated the pressures which could be applied. On the wall, a great cross of iron was equipped with three terrible screws so that the victims could be crucified alive. The rack, with its double wheels at either end and all its strong tackle, looked like a carriage turned upside down, and of course it occupied the place of honor, being an instrument on which all sorts of tunes of agony could be improvised. Then there was the wheel which could turn a man head down or else spin him into a nausea. There was the hurdle for the water torture; there was tackle for hoisting men by the wrists or the thumbs into the air and leaving them suspended. There were iron weights, hammers, picks, saws with frightful teeth that reminded Tizzo of the story of the poor man who, in this prison, had a span sawed off his right arm every day until the arm was gone to the shoulder before he was willing to confess where he had buried his treasure.

But the eyes of Tizzo fled from these horrors, and the light of his lantern now showed him, stretched on a heap of straw that was gray with time, a fine figure of a man who now lifted his head and allowed Tizzo to see the resolute face and the intensely blue eyes of Henry, baron of Melrose.

CHAPTER

38

Tizzo, with the door of the torture chamber closed, standing then above the Englishman, found the face of his friend in a sea of wavering light, because the lantern was being held in an uncertain hand.

[181]

Melrose, making a great effort, raised himself to a sitting posture. He was chained at the wrists, at the ankles, with a connecting chain which ran from the hands to the feet and thence to a great ring which was attached to a bolt that sank into the stone wall.

"Ah, Tizzo," said Melrose, "have you changed sides, made peace with your enemies, and made yourself snug in Perugia again?"

"I am here in Perugia again, my lord," said Tizzo. "But only to take you away with me."

The baron closed his eyes and nodded his head with a strange smile.

"Ah, is that it?" he said. "Here in Perugia? And to take me away?"

Tizzo threw back the cloak. He leaned the great woodsman's ax against the wall and showed the file.

"This is the way to cut the Gordian knot," he said.

Melrose opened his eyes, looked at the file, and shook his grizzled head.

"It won't do, Tizzo," he said. "You're going to walk me out of the prison. Isn't that the thought?"

"And why not?" said Tizzo.

"Can you find a way back for yourself?"

"I think so."

"Then find it now, and use it."

"What?"

"I shall not go with you."

"My lord?"

"Damn my lord," said the Englishman. "What made you come here in the first place?"

"You taught me what to do when a friend is in trouble," said Tizzo.

"In what way?"

"I have not forgotten the day you entered Perugia and risked your head in order to set mine in freedom."

"Ah, I remember something about that," said Melrose. "And that good fellow, that Giovanpaolo, not only set you free but refused to take my life in payment for yours, though he knew that

[182]

I was a lifelong servant of the Oddi, whom he has reason to hate."

"Giovanpaolo is my sworn brother," said Tizzo. "And chiefly because of what he did that day. If there were a way for him to break into Perugia suddenly, I should not have had to slip into the town by stealth. We should have bought you by our work in battle, my lord."

"Perhaps you would," said Melrose. "But I rather think that Jeronimo della Penna would have used an extra five minutes to run down into his cellar, when he saw the day—or the night— was lost. He would have used that time to come down and put a knife into me. The bottles of wine in his cellar, Tizzo, are not half so dear to him as all the revenge which he opens, like a sweet perfume, when he sees me."

"Why does he hate you, my lord? Because Giovanpaolo slipped through the gate you were guarding?"

"And the Lady Beatrice—and you. Mostly because of you, Tizzo. The fact is that he hates you a little more than he hates the rest of the world because, as he says, you cheated him. You pretended to be on his side."

Tizzo dropped to one knee and began to use the file on the heavy manacles that linked the wrists of the prisoner together.

"It is no use, Tizzo," said the prisoner.

"No use?" exclaimed Tizzo, looking up in astonishment.

"Not in the least. Do as I tell you. Leave the prison at once."

"Why is there no use in setting your hands free?"

"Because, my lad, even after they are free, I shall not be able to use them."

"I don't understand," said Tizzo, staring down at the deep, silver-shining trench which the file already had cut into the comparatively soft iron.

"Why, Tizzo, it means that I have paid a visit to the lady, yonder."

"What lady?"

"It has a good many names. Some people call it the engine of grace. Others call it the rack."

And Tizzo, groaning aloud, said: "God, God! Why have I come a day too late?"

[183]

"The rascal Marignello required time as well as money," said the prisoner. "But a day ago you would not have found me here. I was in a cell on the tier above. This morning della Penna decided to begin spinning out my death in a long, thin thread. He stood over me during the torment. He kept feeling the hardness of my shoulders and thighs as the strain of the rack grew greater. He kept telling them to go more slowly, more tenderly. Tenderly was the word he used, laughing. He laughed, and told them to use me more tenderly. Stretch the beef today and cut it up tomorrow. He stood over me with the rod of iron, ready to tap some of my bones and break them, but that was a temptation he resisted. Tomorrow he will break an arm. The next day a leg. Then another arm. Then a few ribs. What, Tizzo? Would a connoisseur swallow off his wine? No, he would taste it slowly, rolling the drops over his tongue and up against his palate."

"God curse and strike him!" said Tizzo.

"Not God. *You* must strike him," said the baron. "I tell you, Tizzo, that I could not walk from the prison, even with all the doors thrown open. I could hardly crawl or writhe along like a snake. A snail would be faster than I. You are not a mule to carry me hence. Therefore, escape, yourself, as you may. And afterwards, if Giovanpaolo takes the city, strike no blow except at Jeronimo della Penna. Strike only for his head. Beat him down. And for every stroke that maims him, that slays him by degrees, cry my name. Cry 'Melrose!' while you enjoy the killing of him. That will be a comfort to my soul, no matter how deep in hell I am hidden away. I shall hear every word you utter. I shall taste every drop of his blood. I shall laugh at hellfire as della Penna dies."

"I shall kill him afterwards," said Tizzo. "God knows that I shall kill him, but now there is only one task."

He gripped the wrist irons and began to file at them, furiously.

And the noise was like that of the singing of a mosquito in the torture chamber.

"Take care of what you do!" said Melrose. "If you throw yourself away, I am cheated of my revenge. Listen to me, Tizzo. If I even dream that revenge will fill its belly with the life of della Penna, I can endure everything. For every pang he gives me, I

[184]

can laugh loud and long, because I shall promise myself that he will die by worse pains afterward. And, being a coward, he will taste every agony thrice over. My death will only enrich me, if I can hope that he will die afterward, and by your hand, my noble friend."

Tizzo said nothing. He merely set his teeth, and the file turned the iron of the manacles hot as it bit into the metal.

"Tizzo!" exclaimed Melrose. "If ever we fought together, and if ever I taught you the innermost secrets of my swordcraft, I beseech you, leave me—save your life—do not cast yourself away in trying to help a hopeless wreck from the reef. I shall only sink, myself, and draw you down after me."

"The courtyard of Marozzo," said Tizzo, "and my own life bleeding away, and Marozzo ordering more of his men to fight with me, and then the entrance of Astorre and Giovanpaolo, with you—you who had given up your life in order to pay down a price that would ransom me. God! Do you think I have forgotten?"

"Ah, you remember that?" said Melrose.

"Aye. I remember."

"And another thing?"

"When I first saw you," said Tizzo, "I knew, suddenly, that I had met the man I wished to follow around the world."

"Like a young, impressionable, silly fool," said the Englishman. "I have received nothing from the world but blows and I have paid my reckoning in the same coin."

Then he added: "Tizzo, I ask one boon of you."

"I shall not grant it," said Tizzo.

He asked, in his turn: "But tell me what angel drew you on, my lord? What made you, in the first place, risk your life in order to save mine?"

"An imp of the perverse, it seems," said Melrose, "that must have told me that if I risked my life in the first place I then should have the privilege of drawing the two of us down into perdition, as I am drawing us now. Do you hear me?"

"Rather," said Tizzo, "an angel of heaven who told you that death is an easy thing, when there are two friends to endure it."

"Friends?" said the baron, loudly and suddenly. "Well, call it that—"

But as he said this, there was a dim sound of steps in the corridor outside, and then a wrangling of iron at the door to the torture chamber.

"They have come to take me to the finish," said Melrose. "Jeronimo could not wait any longer. His appetite was greater than his patience. But, ah, God, that he should find two morsels to swallow instead of one!"

CHAPTER

39

Tizzo, fingering his ax, looked desperately toward the door. The quick, soft voice of Melrose stopped him.

"No, no! Tizzo, you may strike down one or two but the mob will kill you. They'll worry you to death. You are trapped. But no man is dead to hope while there is still breath in him. Do you hear? Out with the lantern. Roll in under the old straw, here. They shall not find you, if God is willing!"

The key was already grating in the lock when Tizzo, letting the commands of the baron take the place of his own thought, blew out the lantern and slid into the straw. There he lay flat, turning his face so that it dropped on the cold side of his ax.

Above him, he heard certain rustlings, and felt the straw being straightened by the manacled hands of the baron. Then a crushing weight fell on him, as Melrose must have straightened out and laid his body directly down across the hidden bulk of Tizzo.

The door had flung open and a faint gust of the stale air blew even through the straw to the nostrils of Tizzo, casting up dust that gave him an agonizing desire to sneeze.

But footfalls were pouring into the room. And he heard the deadly jangling of naked steel, and the queer humming, muffled noise of blades against scabbards.

Then Jeronimo della Penna cried out: "Look everywhere. If he was not above, he may be here!"

It was the voice of Marozzo that broke in: "He *must* be here because he goes to his work as straight as a ferret to blood—a ferret to the throat of a rabbit. Look well. I, from my own purse —a hundred florins of gold—do you hear, men? No, five hundred florins to the first fellow with sharp eyes who comes on the traces of the devil!"

To this Marignello's voice added: "He will not be here, my masters. I said nothing of the baron being here. I *knew* nothing of his being here. He was brought in here after I left the cellars."

Della Penna said: "Your work was worthless, Marignello. Your thoughts are worthless, also. By God, I have a thought to try you on the same rack that tried Melrose."

He added, loudly: "To your work! Look everywhere!"

It was hard for Tizzo to breathe, there was such a pressure upon his body. And then there came to him a queer reaction— that it was better to burst upright before their eyes, ax in hand, and strike right and left, dying like a man. It was better to do that than to lie here and be discovered like a crawling rat.

"Everywhere! He may hide himself in a beam of light!" said Marozzo.

The voice of Marozzo was recognizable, but this enunciation was much stifled. Plainly his mouth had been smashed and per- haps many of his teeth knocked in by the battering which Tizzo had given him.

Men were trampling all about the room, knocking against metal, bumping the walls.

Something whispered through the straw and grinded against the stone not an inch from his face.

"No use thrusting your sword into that bed," commanded della Penna. "Do you think that anything could be hidden under the. bulk of Melrose without being stifled?"

And della Penna laughed as he spoke.

After a moment that half-muffled voice of Marozzo said: "Is there any possible way by which he might have escaped from the house after he found that the cell of Melrose was empty?"

"No," said della Penna, "unless he went up the stairs and into the house itself. That could not be."

"Why not?"

"Because there are servants everywhere."

"Jeronimo, in God's name remember that we are talking of a man who could hide himself in the shadow of a cat, if he wished to do so."

"How could he escape through the front door, which is always guarded. In these days, I have a dozen men-at-arms at that door."

"Numbers mean sleepy eyes," said Marozzo. "What of the window?"

"None except those twenty feet from the pavement outside."

"Ha! He could run down the perpendicular side of a wall!"

"Are you going to call him half fly and half cat?"

"And mostly devil!" cried Marozzo. "He is not here. Jeronimo, leave this place. Spread the alarm. Let the town be raised. God knows, if we can catch him, we have at a stroke secured half the strength of Giovanpaolo."

"You may be right," said della Penna.

He commanded someone to go at once and have an alarm rung, a word carried about the town to all the gates that Tizzo, not for the first time, had slunk inside the gates of Perugia. There was a rich reward on his head.

Then della Penna's voice sounded close by.

"Ah, Melrose," he said. "How is it with you?"

"Better, my lord," said Henry of Melrose. "I breathe the air and still can taste it. It is better than wine."

"Well, strangling might be a good end for you. I don't know. How do your joints feel, Melrose?"

"They ache with sympathy for you."

"For me?"

"Certainly, Jeronimo."

"I don't understand you—but then, I never could understand any man from the beef-eating English."

"Why, my lord, you are searching for Tizzo, are you not?" asked Melrose.

"What of it?"

"Nothing. It is merely a token."

"A token of what?"

"That you have named the wasp who will sting you to death."

"Damn you!" snarled della Penna, and Tizzo heard the sound of a blow that re-echoed through his brain. Had della Penna struck that chained and helpless man?

"Well and knightly done," said Melrose. "Your servants watch you, Jeronimo. They learn how men of noble birth should treat one another."

"I have a mind to give you another taste of the rack at this moment," declared della Penna.

"Give me enough tastes of it, close enough together, and soon I shall have a mouthful."

"Do you hear him?" said della Penna. "He means that if I give him enough of it I shall soon have him dead. D'you know, Melrose, that if you were of a little different pattern, I would like to have you around me. But since I can't buy you, I shall have to bury you."

"It is one of the pities of the wars," answered Melrose. "We are not able to love the sort of poison that might physic us."

"Good again," laughed della Penna. "I shall return to you again tomorrow, and the rack may even sharpen your wit a little more. Come, my lads. Out of this, and run through the house. Search in every corner. Remember, he can make himself as small as a rat."

Then he added: "Put irons on Marignello. I shall have some use for the rack with him, tomorrow, also."

CHAPTER

40

THE door closed, the lock grated.

"The way is open, Tizzo," said the baron softly.

Tizzo wriggled into the open and began to blow out air through his nose, and to wipe the chaff and dust from his hair, from his face, from his eyes. He dusted himself all over.

"Neat as a cat," said the baron. "Was it hard on you, Tizzo?"

"There are thirty excess pounds of you, my lord," said Tizzo, "and I felt the weight of all of them. However, I can breathe again now. I swear to God that for a moment I was about to leap out and try for the head of della Penna with my ax."

"Wrong, Tizzo," said the baron. "Consider what a masterpiece he is, what a perfect semblance, picture, statue, harmony of evil! There is a man without charity or kindness, without decency or gentleness, without courtesy or heart, courage or warmth. A mere brain. A fox. A cold fire. Where will you find him again? Where is there his like? Merely to be killed by such a man is to be remembered by history. To be listed among his victims saves a man from oblivion. No, no, Tizzo, thank God that your eyes have seen such a prodigy."

"He is a prodigy," said Tizzo, "and I pray that I may have the prodigious pleasure of killing him."

He resumed his work with his file, and in two strokes of it cut through one of the manacle irons. With the edge of the ax he pried the bracelet wide open at that mouth and let the hand of the Englishman escape.

He fell to work on the other handiron when the baron said: "Hush! Do you hear it?"

Tizzo, listening for a moment, started violently.

"They are coming again!" he muttered.

"No. They are walking on guard outside the door. You have startled them, Tizzo, and now they are worried. They fear that you and the devil may come romping, hand in hand, down those stairs, yonder, ready to beat open the door and fly away with me in a cloud of red smoke. They have, in fact, corked the bottle; and inside that bottle you are to die!"

"True!" said Tizzo.

He stood up and stared at the door.

"Tell me, now," asked Melrose. "This is the end. There is no possible escape. Day and night that door will be guarded. And this means that you must surely die. So tell me now how great is your regret that you have come here for a foreigner, a mere Englishman from the barbarous north?"

Tizzo said: "Are you tempting me to use some fine words? Well, my lord, I'll only say that so long as I die in company, with a friend, I cannot ask any more of my life."

"What is better than a friend?" asked Melrose.

"A blood relation, but I have none."

"Are you sure?"

"My mother is dead, my lord, as I think I told you. There was never a father to me."

"Do you remember your mother, Tizzo?"

"I was a very young child when she died."

"Shall I describe her?"

"You, my lord?"

"A tall, slender girl. Brown-eyed, Tizzo. The grace of a wild deer and the step of a faun. A sweet smile and a gentle heart. A face as calm as prayer. Laughter as bright as the first spring day. And a faith that would have stirred a god and shamed a devil."

"Did you know her?"

"Do I speak as though I were ignorant, Tizzo?"

"No, my lord."

"Shall I tell you more about her?"

"Every word is like a life to me!"

"She was a girl so good that she could not expect villainy in others."

"I have seen such people," said Tizzo.

"There are tears in your eyes, Tizzo."

"Well, let them fall, also," said Tizzo. "I am not ashamed to weep for her. I would have died for her, if God had granted me that much grace."

"Instead of which, she died for you."

"Is that true?"

"Yes. You being born out of wedlock, the hate and the scorn of others killed her quickly."

Tizzo covered his face. Then he said: "If I could find the demi-devil, the villain who betrayed her—"

"What would you do?"

"He would be my father," said Tizzo. "I could only—I could only—curse him and leave him!"

"Aye, perhaps."

"Did you know him?"

"I knew him very well."

"Tell me of him, then."

"That knowledge would only poison your last moments. Tizzo, you are about to die! You should be on your knees, praying."

"I was never a praying fellow," said Tizzo. "I would rather listen to a story, even if it is about a villain."

The baron shook his gray head, without smiling.

"This Englishman—" he began.

"Ah, it was an Englishman?" exclaimed Tizzo.

"Yes. I told you that he was my friend."

"Am I half English?" murmured Tizzo, looking down at himself in wonder.

"Aye. Half at least."

"That is where I caught the red hair?"

"Your mother's hair was black as the wing of a raven."

"Dear God, if I had only known her!"

"But shall I tell you more about your father?"

"Yes. I almost half forgive him if he was a true friend of yours."

"I said he was a friend, but very often he was a bad companion."

[192]

"Ah?"

"I mean, Tizzo, that there was no constancy to him."

"That is a bad vice," said Tizzo, gravely.

"It is," said the baron. "That fellow would sometimes be serious and sometimes laughing. Out of his laughter he might fall to brawling, and out of his seriousness he might fall to laughing. I never could tell what he would do next."

"A wild, evil man?" said Tizzo.

"A dancing, drinking, dicing, fighting man," said the baron.

"For all of those sins, God forgive me!" said Tizzo, sadly. "Now I know from whom I inherit them. Was he cruel?"

"In battle? Yes. Otherwise, no, I should say not. Merciful enough."

"Charitable?"

"In this way—that he found it hard to refuse a request. If he won a man's money, he was apt to give half of it back if the fellow laughed at the loss and showed himself a good fellow."

"I like that," said Tizzo, adding up the points. "Yes, I like that a great deal. And brave?" he asked, catching his breath a little in a dreadful doubt.

"Brave? Men called him brave," said the baron. "That is to say, this Englishman I tell you of was a fellow who loved danger as some men love a partner at a dance. He was accustomed to brawling. Sword-shine was more often in his eyes than daylight. He was used to danger, and therefore he loved it for the sake of old neighborliness."

"Ah?" said Tizzo, smiling suddenly. "I wish that I could have seen him! What was his blood?"

"He was of an old and noble name."

Tizzo braced back his shoulders and frowned.

"Good, also!" he said.

Then he asked: "And my mother—did he love her?"

"So much, Tizzo, that when he heard of her death he fell on the ground and beat his head against it. He was half mad for many days."

"Was he? Was he in fact?" said Tizzo. "Ah, God, who is to judge the sins of others—who that is as sinful as myself? He was

[193]

young; she was young; they loved one another. And if they missed the priest—"

"True," said the baron.

"A brave, kind, wild man," said Tizzo.

"I would not praise him too highly. He knew no books. Nothing but battle. I have seen him as savage as a mad dog, as headlong as a fighting stallion, as drunk as a fool, and as cruel as a tiger."

"What shall I think of him?" said Tizzo. "What did *you* think of him?"

"I have prayed God to forgive his sins. He is still alive."

"Alive! In the name of Heaven, tell me his name!"

"It will give a point to your hatred of him."

"I cannot hate my flesh and blood," said Tizzo. "Tell me his name!"

"His name," said the baron, "is Henry, baron of Melrose."

CHAPTER

41

THE diamond-hard edges of the file, in the meantime, had freed the other arm of the prisoner, had liberated one leg, and now, as Tizzo listened to the last revelation, the last manacle fell from the baron. He was again master of his limbs—with the slight strength that remained to him. And Tizzo, grasping the hands of his father, stared wildly into his face. Then, throwing back his head, he cried, shutting his teeth to keep back the noise of his joy, "God made the blood in me speak when I first saw you!"

"A dog of a lying servant that I sent into the village those years ago, swore when he returned that both the mother and the child were dead," said Melrose. "And then I beat my head and groaned a while and said a prayer for two dead souls. But this long time afterward the wretched scoundrel confessed that he had found the mother dead, indeed, but the child was living. Why had he not told me about it? Because he did not wish to have me chained in one spot to support a son. He wished to be a free traveler and therefore he would have me free also. The villain confessed all this on his deathbed. I rushed back to the town. But how could I find my son? My own hair was red as fire when I was your age. The dying rat of a servant had told me that my dead boy had hair the color of mine, and I trusted that this was the truth. But there was more than one redheaded lad in the town. Which, therefore, was the one of my blood? Why, the first that would cross swords with me and stand to me like a man! Ha, Tizzo! In that little test I nearly had my throat cut by the damned trickery and cunning of your swordplay. I never before had met a man with the heart of a knight in armor and the feet of a dancing boy!"

"But how could you make sure that I was he?" asked Tizzo, anxiously.

"By the cry of my blood to you, lad! And then, also, I've been back to the village twice. I have been able to trace the Firebrand to the little redheaded foundling. Mother of Heaven, to think that I have missed these years with you! But, ah, Tizzo, do you forgive me for my greatest sin of all?"

"What shall I do except pray with you for the sake of her soul?" asked Tizzo.

Here, as they stared at one another with rejoiced faces, they heard the deadly noise of the big key grating in the lock. Tizzo had barely time to blow out his lantern and thrust it away under the straw. There was no time at all for his own body to be pushed into the bedding out of sight. The waver and throw of the lantern light already was shimmering across the room when he fled to the shadow cast by the bulky rack. There he crouched, hearing at the door the voice of Jeronimo della Penna saying, "Come in, my friends. You will have a chance to do something more than stand guard now. You will be able to play a little game which will warm your blood for the rest of the night."

Della Penna, followed by the three guards who had been posted outside the door, crossed the floor of the torture chamber. On the way, the master paused in front of what seemed a suit of complete armor.

"This," said della Penna, "this, now, might be the trick which would serve for the end of the game."

He pulled at the shoulder of the armor and it opened wide, showing to the peering eyes of Tizzo a hollow interior set over thickly with needle-sharp bits of steel, projecting inwards.

"But not tonight," said della Penna. "Not while there is still so much pain to be drawn out of his tendons and joints. My Lady, the Rack, has not finished with him.

"Ah, my lord," he said, "you are now feeling much recovered, eh? I've come to tell you that the cunning rat, Tizzo, has escaped from the house; but because that is a cruel disappointment, I know you will want to make us some amends. You and the rack, eh?"

The long face of della Penna lengthened still more with his laughter. Then, breaking off into a snarl, he commanded, "Pick him up and stretch him on the wheel!"

Two of the men-at-arms instantly laid hold on the prisoner. And Tizzo, saying three brief words of a prayer, could not help casting one yearning glance toward the open door that might mean liberty. Then he freshened his grip on the handle of the ax and slipped from the side of the rack, stealing forward.

There was a great outcry from two voices, at the same moment.

"Look, your highness! The irons are gone from his hands and ankles!"

"They are, by Heaven!" exclaimed della Penna.

"Witchcraft!" exclaimed one of the men.

"You fool!" shouted della Penna. "Look to yourselves. The witch that did this work is still in the room—a witch that carries the name of Tizzo!"

He drew his sword as he spoke and turned sharply around. The men-at-arms, less ready in their heavy armor, swung about also, hardly in time to meet the rush of Tizzo. For his softly shod feet made no noise on the stones. He came like a shadow at them.

Della Penna, seeing that rushing figure, groaned with terror and sprang back behind his armored men. The foremost of them, swaying up his massive halberd, thrust full at Tizzo with the lance point at the end of the weapon. Tizzo wasted no time in parrying that stroke. A swerve of his body allowed the thrust to waste itself close to his side; then the ax in his hand clanged against the morion of the halberdier.

If that stroke had landed truly it would have ended the life of the soldier; even the glancing force dropped him with a crash, face down and senseless.

A sword gleamed at the throat of Tizzo—della Penna thrusting from between the shelter of his two remaining men-at-arms. A sidestep made that sword point reach empty air, only. The swinging blade of the ax met a downright sword stroke and the brittle steel shivered to pieces. A backward leap foiled the third man-at-arms as he shouted, "Before God, this is no man, but a dancing shadow!"

That same shadow leaped in again; the ax swayed and rang on the helmet, a brief, dull, horrible chopping sound, and the wide blade clove straight down through the skull.

The third warrior, with the mere stump of his sword in hand, turned with a yell of horror and fled. Jeronimo della Penna, unweighted by steel, was racing for the door far before his companion. And as far as that door the vengeance of Tizzo pursued him. Then Tizzo turned back to see that the baron of Melrose had forced himself to his feet, where he stood swaying, helpless, then making vague steps like the movements of a man half senseless with wine.

Steel rang on stone along the outer passage as one of the fugitives cast away a weapon to lighten his flight. The yelling voices that called for help grew dim around the corners of the corridors.

Tizzo cast one glance at the dead and the senseless forms on the floor. Then he rushed to Melrose and drew one of the big arms over his shoulder.

That towering bulk of manhood which he had always admired so greatly was now a curse to them both; it was an unwieldy mass barely able to move at all and far too ponderous for Tizzo to carry to any distance. He could only help Melrose forward from the torture chamber.

"Go, Tizzo!" pleaded the father. "You see that I cannot be saved. They are raising the house. Every murdering rat of them will come running and swarming on you, in a moment. Save yourself. For my sake. The name of Melrose must not die from the face of the earth. Tizzo—I command you—you have done enough. No son in the world could do more. Now fly—fly! Use those devilish dancing feet of yours! Do you hear? I give you the blessing of my heart. I command you to go!"

"Hush," said Tizzo. "If my name is Melrose, my blood is Melrose. Will you have me turn from my own blood? Save your breath for the labor. And if we die, you can strike one blow for us both—"

So, panting, he supported the staggering weight of his father up the outer steps, groaning and cursing the slime that made the stones slippery.

It was a terrible labor. The very brain of Tizzo reeled with the might of the effort as he put his shoulder into the weight of the great, helpless body and so bore it upward. The stairs had no ending. The turns of them would never cease.

And the knees of Tizzo had turned to water before he reached the level of the floor above. It was then that they heard clearly the sounds of the gathering storm overhead.

CHAPTER

42

Doors seemed to be opening and shutting, letting out the noises of armored, trampling feet, the familiar dry clashing of steel against stone; voices shouted, far and near; there were so many elements of sound that the whole made a sort of humming roar. There must have been, literally, scores of men running toward the point of danger; and now the tumult opened with thundering violence on the staircase above. Like a flood of water, that throng was descending to sweep away the lives of those two fugitives.

Tizzo, gasping with an effort, hurried the big, shambling form down the corridor to that very cell which he had entered before. He had not locked the door. A mere thrust of the hand opened it now, and they entered as many dancing lights began to strike through the darkness.

There, leaning against the wall, half spent already, Tizzo said, "They will go past us. They will go down to the lowest level. They will not leave the torture chamber till they have searched it. And you and I still have a ghost of a chance."

"A weak ghost, Tizzo. My lad, I plead for the line of Melrose. Go on—save yourself—"

"You say the words, but your heart is not in them," said Tizzo.

"It is true," admitted the Englishman, suddenly. "If you left me, I should know that there was little of my blood in your body. What is death, when two men face it, true to each other?"

"It is nothing. It is a song!" cried Tizzo.

"But, ah, if I could raise my arms to strike one blow in the battle! It is the punishment of Heaven for all my sins—to stand like a sleeping fool while my son fights for my life."

"You have fought in your turn for mine," said Tizzo.

"Lord God, Almighty Father," groaned the Englishman, "forgive my sins and let my hand hold a sword for ten seconds only. Kill me, then. Stamp on me like a poor beast. But let me die fighting!"

The tumult that descended the stairs had now rushed completely past the door of the cell where Tizzo and his father were sheltered for the moment. That door Tizzo now flung open and supported Melrose into the corridor.

Over the level, the returning strength of Melrose enabled him to walk with less and less resistance, but as they struggled up the stairs again he was almost a dead weight on his son. Too furious a hurry would melt the strength out of Tizzo as a hot fire burns wax. He had to take a pace and hold to it, stubbornly; and yet, beneath him, he began to hear the echoes of a wild outcry.

Anger has a sound like despair when it comes shouting from many throats. Those men of della Penna, their master at their head, had reached the torture chamber far beneath by this time, and their yelling was from purest rage, of course. Yet it seemed to Tizzo like the lamenting of the eternally damned.

Now for one blast of the great new giant—gunpowder—to crumble together the walls of the prison and drop headlong masses of stone on the heads of all those manhunters!

Melrose, panting, struggling, nevertheless still whispered his prayer, "Almighty God, I do not ask for the power to swing a sword. Let me only have the strength to draw a dagger and use it. A single blow—one gesture of glory is all that I ask for—one drop out of the infinite sea of Your mercy!"

They had, in fact, reached the highest level of the cellar, and before them there was a straight way toward the outer door; but Melrose was almost too exhausted by pain and the frightful effort of moving his witless limbs to stand erect any longer. Both he and Tizzo reeled from side to side as they moved down the hallway.

And still the prayer, in a new form, was issuing from the lips of

[200]

Melrose. "Glorious God, I ask not to strike with any weapon, but with my bare hands let me grasp one villain by the throat before the steel is struck into me from every side. Let them hew me to pieces—or let them keep and burn me inch by inch afterwards. But let me strike one blow before I die—"

That panting, broken whisper continued, drowned from the hearing of Tizzo because the rout of the pursuers was spreading back again through the upper stairways.

He could hear the wild voice of della Penna screaming, "They are here! Two grown men cannot hide in a rathole—but look in every corner. If we lose them, I shall go mad—mad—mad! If you fail to take them—every man of you look to himself. Swiftly, swiftly! Be everywhere with wide eyes. Your swords ready. Take them alive if you can, but even dead they will be beautiful pictures to me!"

That screeching voice of rage sent small shudders down the back of Tizzo as he worked his way down the hall. Then he heard running feet approaching from the rear.

They were coming very quickly. But here, thank God, was the outer door. One warder remained there at his post with the same partisan which Tizzo had seen in the grasp of the jailer before.

The approaching rush of many feet had put the jailer on his guard. He stood now with the great weapon held at the ready, that is, slung sidelong across his body, the head gleaming above his left shoulder. It was an engine designed to strike down horse and man. It made the infantryman the peer of the mounted warrior. And now, into the view of the sentry there came the vision of the great, staggering, wavering gray-headed man, and beside him the tense, lithe figure of Tizzo.

He stared and elevated his halberd for the stroke when Tizzo, with a cry, ran straight in on him, his smaller and more active ax poised to strike.

It was not for nothing that he had crossed with the best of the swaggering young blades of the town, and that he had performed such feats with the ax that every clod in Perugia knew of the strokes of Tizzo. The halberdier, the moment his eyes made sure of Tizzo, the moment he saw that famous ax at a balance in his hands, cried out: "Mercy, in the name of God!" and fled slinking along the wall with his halberd flung down upon the ground.

Tizzo let him go. He was no lover of bloodshed even in the midst of battle. The game was the thing, not the slaughter which delighted some. A moment later he was throwing back the bolt of the portal, thrusting the door wide.

But when he looked back he could see Melrose staggering, almost pitching to the floor with every short forward step he took, and behind him danger came pouring up the corridor like the shout of battle up a throat. He saw them coming, the glitter of the weapons in the tossing lantern light, then the wild faces; and always the shouting roared louder and louder.

He leaped to Melrose and supported him outside the door. To be in the open was at least some comfort. The taste of the sweet night air was a blessing and a mercy. And a changing wind had knocked the rain clouds out of the sky and blown up over the black towers of the city the golden beauty of a summer moon.

"Open air—the moon—the bright face of the Almighty God!" gasped the Englishman. "Now I can die content. Tizzo—for the last time, go—save yourself!"

As he spoke, it became impossible for Tizzo to save himself. Out of the portal of the cellar rooms, like a great smoke from a small mouth, came sweeping the men of della Penna—half-dressed servants who had been called up in the middle of the night unexpectedly, and the men-at-arms who had been on duty. Others in greater numbers were running from the interior of the house. The whole garrison was pouring through toward the street, but in the first whirling batch there were a dozen assailants who hurled themselves upon Tizzo.

His father, staggering back from this attack, had been brought to a pause by a sharp angle of the wall which protected their backs against assault but which also would make it more difficult for them to escape in any direction except straight to the front.

And straight in front lay the thronging swords of the enemy.

Tizzo, flashing back and forth in front of Melrose, like a panther in defense of some old lion, made the swinging arcs of the ax gleam with incredible lightness, incredible force. The cleaving power of that weapon was far greater than that of any sword.

Where it struck solidly, it left more hideous wounds, also; and in the cunning grasp of Tizzo it did not possess the usual disadvantage of being a weapon of offense only. The dance of it in his hands swept aside the striking of many swords: his light advances staggered the crowded ranks of the enemy.

A man in full armor, the young nephew of the master, Marco della Penna by name, was directing that attack. He had in fact been in charge of the guarding of the house of his uncle during the emergency of this time of danger. He, now, seeing before him two of the greatest enemies of his house and above all the notorious red head of Tizzo, came striding through the crowd of his men like a giant with the plume blown high on his helmet and the great two-handed sword poised for a blow.

He shouted out to the others to join him, and the battle would be ended in an instant. But the rest held back an instant to see their mail-clad champion dispose of this dancing wisp of a Tizzo. And Tizzo, as he flashed back and forth in front of his father, panted forth a wild sort of laughter that was half a song. When that lofty champion came striding, Tizzo sprang a step to meet him, turned the swordstroke with an incredibly deft counter, and then hit right upward with the reverse of the swing of his ax. Under the arm, where the steel joints of the armor were multiplied and the steel itself was thin, Tizzo struck; and the ax crunched through the iron as through brittle wood, clove the flesh, crushed through the shoulder bone.

Marco della Penna, feeling himself so struck, so maimed and ruined for life that he never again could wield a weapon, dropped his sword and tried to break in with his dagger at Tizzo. But a hammerstroke from the back of the ax stopped his frightful screaming and laid him senseless.

Here there was a mere instant of pause, partly because a man of such importance had fallen, and partly because reinforcements were certainly coming at once out of the house. There was no occasion, it seemed, for men to put themselves in further danger from that uncanny, blue-bladed ax. Besides, Baron Henry of Melrose had leaned, weak as he was, and picked up the great fallen sword of della Penna. This he now managed to poise above his head, given strength and control of his body by the battle heat that was in him.

"Melrose! Melrose!" he thundered, and made the men of della Penna shrink a step farther back.

At the same instant there came a most astonishing change. For the battle cry of the Englishman was echoed by a shrill cry, "Melrose! Melrose! A rescue! Melrose!"

And over the paved street rattled the hoofs of several horses. Right at the crowd came a single rider, young, slender, shouting the battle cry of the baron; and Tizzo recognized the voice of the Lady Beatrice. Her horse, and those she led, were trained battle chargers. They did not hesitate to strike into the crowd, rearing, smashing out with their hoofs, and the della Penna men did not abide that charge.

Straight into the baron pushed the girl. He grappled at the horn of a saddle with his hands; the strength of Tizzo heaved him up until he was suddenly straddling the back of a horse, grasping at the familiar reins. Effort that should have killed another man in his condition seemed merely to have warmed his blood and brain.

"A Melrose! Melrose!" he shouted again, and vainly tried to sway the big two-handed sword again.

There was no need for more fighting. The men of della Penna had a chance to see, now, the slightness of the rescue party and they were running back to the attack, but the street was open and the three rushed away up it, leaving only yells of furious despair behind; and through that outcry, Tizzo recognized the voice of Jeronimo della Penna himself.

Disappointed malice would surely burn the heart of the man to a cinder.

CHAPTER

43

Tizzo stepped to the bed and drew the curtain.

Antonio Bardi slept there in the midst of a troubled dream, one clenched hand thrown above his head. He had changed since the night when he joined the traitors at the Great Betrayal which had slain so many of the Baglioni. He looked older. His face was thin and even in sleep expressed a settled unhappiness.

"Antonio!" murmured Tizzo.

Young Bardi was wakened suddenly even by that quiet voice. He sat up with a start, snatching a dagger from under the sheet.

"Wait for me, comrades—" he called out.

Then, recovering from his dream, he stared at Tizzo. The dagger dropped from his grip—slowly he stretched out both his hands.

"Tizzo, it has been my prayer that you would come to me, ever since the news came that you, madman that you are, had entered the city."

He rose, flinging a thin robe about him, thrusting his feet into slippers. Joy made him young again, as he saw his friend. He ran to the doors of the room and bolted them.

"How is it with you, brother?" he asked Tizzo, but then he answered his own question, saying: "But I see that you are well and I know that you are happy. You are in the enemy's country. Every breath you take is drawn in danger. Every minute may be your last. And therefore you are happier than kings."

"And you, Antonio?" asked Tizzo.

Bardi sighed. "Do you remember how you found me in this house not so many weeks ago?" he asked. "Do you remember that I was dying of the plague, Tizzo, and that a casket of the family jewels had been spilled out half on the table and half on the floor? Wealth would not help me, then, because famine and the plague were eating me like two wolves. And then you came to save me—you, a stranger, when no man of my own blood dared to enter the house on account of the poison in the air. Well, Tizzo, there is a poison in the air now. It kills me as surely as the plague. It is the poison of treason. And I am the traitor!"

He threw up his clenched fists.

"But the cold-blooded devil, della Penna, knows that my heart is not with him. He watches me day and night. He fears that at any moment I may gather all the wealth I can carry and with it slip away to join the army of Giovanpaolo."

"No, brother," said Tizzo. "You have a harder part than that. You must stay inside the city."

"I? Why do you say that, Tizzo? I tell you, I could make my peace with Giovanpaolo for all the troubles that have passed between us."

"You could," said Tizzo, "but if you try to escape, you'll find it a hard thing to take away even your own body, to say nothing of anything else. Besides, you can help Giovanpaolo more by remaining inside the town. Have you heard from one or two people this same night?"

"Why do you ask?" said Bardi.

He peered with a worn and anxious face at his friend.

"A great lady, for one," said Tizzo.

Bardi, starting, seemed about to check himself and then answered frankly: "I have seen her, Tizzo."

"And a man with her, perhaps—a man who has been very close to me?"

"Luigi Falcone. Yes. I have seen them both. Was your hand behind that, also?"

"This is the point: Can I return to Giovanpaolo and tell him that he has strong friends inside the city?"

"It would be truer to say that his strong friends in the city wish that they were outside, and riding in his ranks."

"You must see, Antonio, that one friend inside the city could be worth more than five hundred men-at-arms in his ranks. He has not strength enough to storm Perugia. It stands on its hill like an iron fist raised. There are more armed men inside it than Giovanpaolo can collect. And Jeronimo della Penna is watching over the town like a cat over a dish of milk. The chains are fastened across the streets every night. The walls are manned. The gates are guarded. Della Penna handles everything as though Perugia were besieged by a great army. And how can we break in against such precautions? Only through friends inside the town. We have those friends—you, Falcone, the Lady Atlanta. Working together, you can win some control over one of the gates. By bribery or by personal influence you may seduce some of the guards. Then, from the top of your house, fly a flag of some sort. Several flags, if you wish. But a red one among the rest. The direction toward which it points will indicate to us which of the city gates you have mastered. And when you fly the flag, we shall know that on that same night you expect us."

"Aye," said Antonio Bardi. "It is dangerous work, but it could be done. I am suspected; so is Falcone. All who have been your friends are hated now like so many poisoned wells inside Perugia. But we—and the Lady, who has the courage of a man—may be able to do these things."

"You *must*, Antonio."

"We *shall*, then," said Bardi.

A rumor of noise broke upward through the house; there was a sudden tapping at the door of Bardi's room.

"Hide, Tizzo!" breathed Antonio Bardi. "There is no servant I can trust. They are all in the pay of the devil, della Penna!"

Tizzo, casting one glance at the window through which he had entered, nevertheless stepped back behind the high tapestries which draped the bed. He heard the bolts of the door slide, then a breathless voice exclaiming: "Signore, they have come! The men of—"

The tramping of armored men followed; then the voice of Mateo Marozzo was sounding through the room.

"I greet you, Bardi, in the name of Jeronimo della Penna, to know where you have hidden away the traitor, Tizzo!"

The flesh of Tizzo congealed as he listened.

Then he heard Bardi answering, calmly: "Since the night when the Baglioni were expelled, you should know that there is no friendship between Tizzo and me. He is a sword in the hand of Giovanpaolo, and that sword is pointed at my throat, along with all the rest of the danger which the Baglioni are gathering, for the attack on the city. What sort of nonsense is this, Marozzo, to come with armed men into my house at night and ask for Tizzo? Even if he were a hawk, he would not dare to fly over the walls of Perugia!" Then he added: "What's happened? Where has there been fighting? Or has a horse kicked you in the face, Marozzo?"

"The damned villain, the murdering Tizzo has been at me by treachery and trickery!" exclaimed Marozzo. "But the end of him has come. He will never leave Perugia alive! They are doubling the guard on the walls, and he is caught like a bird in a net. He and the English Melrose!"

"Melrose lies in the dungeon of della Penna," said Bardi. "Do you have to man the walls to keep him from escaping? Aren't there irons to load him with?"

"He was loaded with iron," said Marozzo, "but the fiend, the wizard Tizzo entered the prison and cut the irons from the body of Melrose."

"Impossible!" cried Bardi.

"You say impossible—I say impossible—but the thing is done! Melrose has been taken from the torture chamber at the bottom of the prison. Taken away by one man, even though his great bulk was so wrenched by the rack that he had hardly the strength to stand up. Carried away by that lean ferret, that Tizzo—God, I go mad when I think of it! They are gone! They are gone! Bardi, if you give them shelter your head will fall the next day."

"I know Melrose," said Bardi. "Not even a giant could have dragged his helpless bulk up the long stairs of della Penna's cellars."

"Not a giant, but a Tizzo could manage the thing. It has been done. And the work is signed by the true signature of Tizzo. With his shoulder shorn almost from his body, young della Penna lies under the care of the doctors, ruined for life. He must exist with one arm all his days."

"I listen to you," said Bardi, "but still I cannot believe you."

[208]

"Bardi," said Marozzo, "the thing I have told you is entirely true. I have seen the blood that Tizzo spilled and the irons through which he cut. He is adrift in Perugia. He cannot have left the city so soon. And now the walls are well manned. He is likely as not to come at last to your house for shelter. Listen to me, Bardi! With him there is Melrose—a helpless mass of flesh, unable to stir without assistance. With him there is also a greater prize than all else—dressed as a slip of a boy—the Lady Beatrice Baglioni!"

"God rains miracles on Perugia tonight!" said Bardi. "The Lady Beatrice, inside the walls of Perugia, Marozzo, you are mad!"

"So I thought when I saw her," said Marozzo. "But I with my own eyes have seen her this night, and talked with her. I *am* out of my wits when I think of it. Yes, she is here, drawn by her crazy passion for Tizzo which would make her run through flames. Bardi, if they come to your house, you will become the first man, the favored citizen of Perugia if you turn them over, at once, to della Penna."

"The Lady Beatrice!" exclaimed the stunned voice of Bardi.

"Farewell," said Marozzo. "Remember that all suspicions against you will be allayed if you can make the trap which catches Tizzo."

MAROZZO had departed when Tizzo issued from behind the bed.

Bardi, suddenly holding out his hand, grasped that of Tizzo strongly.

"There is such a flame of high heart in you," said Bardi, "that you could turn a cat into a lion! But is the rest true? Melrose—have you used witchcraft to steal him from the prison of della Penna, from which no man ever has escaped?"

"No witchcraft, Antonio. Only a stolen pack of keys, a sharp file, and that ax of mine with the good blue Damascus steel in the head of it! All of these things—and then Lady Beatrice in the last moment bringing up horses like a cavalry charge to give us wings for our escape and scatter della Penna's men. Now you know the entire story."

"I hear the miracle told in simple words, but a miracle it still remains. Where are they now?"

"Waiting for me in the dark throat of a little alley, not far from here."

"The Lady Beatrice!" murmured Bardi, staring. "And you left them there?"

"There was one thing more important than their safety. The retaking of Perugia. I had to find the key that would open one of the gates of the city to us. And I have found it, Antonio. You are the man!"

"I am—I shall do it! God stands on your side, Tizzo. Otherwise it could not be that you would pass through such dangers unhurt!

But you and the Lady Beatrice, and Melrose—how will you leave the town?"

"I have no idea," confessed Tizzo. "We have made two steps toward safety. What the third one will be, I cannot tell."

"I shall go with you," said Bardi. "The moment I am dressed, I shall go without, whatever comes of the adventure—"

"You will stay here," commanded Tizzo. "Antonio, if you love me, remain here to play your part well. The other task is entirely mine. See Falcone and the Lady Atlanta again. Concert your measures. Spend money like water if you must; it will all come back to you. And let me go alone."

"How will you leave the house?"

"By the window that gave me entrance."

"Not even a cat could climb that sheer wall."

"Not a cat, but a Tizzo can do it."

Bardi, approaching the window, stared down at the profound darkness. There was only a faint, starlit glimmer of the wet pavement beneath. He drew back with a shudder.

"And yet your eyes are laughing at the danger!" breathed Bardi. "What breed of man are you, Tizzo? Give me your hand. Farewell!"

But hardly a moment later Tizzo, at the bottom of the great wall, picked up the woodsman's ax which he had left there and went swiftly toward the little dark-throated alley where he had left Melrose and the girl.

Two steps from the entrance he called, softly, and the thinnest of whistles answered him. He had heard that signal before, from Lady Beatrice, and he recognized it now; that was why he was half-laughing with joy as he went forward.

The girl said: "All well, Tizzo?"

"Aye, all well," he answered. "All well till daylight."

He could make out the big outline of his father, stretched on the wet pavement at full length. The girl had made of her cloak a pillow on which the head of the Englishman rested.

"And you, sir?" asked Tizzo, on his knees beside the baron.

"Every moment better," said the baron. "My legs and arms are still half asleep, but the life is coming back into them. Before noon tomorrow I shall be able to wear full armor and leap onto my horse again without touching the stirrups. But still even to sit up is a little hard. Tell me what you have done. You could not scale that wall after all, could you?"

"Easily," said Tizzo. "I have seen Antonio Bardi, plotted with him the opening of Perugia, and heard the voice of Marozzo announcing that a double guard is on the walls. Perugia buzzes like a hornet's nest. It is known everywhere that you have escaped, that Lady Beatrice is inside the walls, and that I am here, also. We have from now until daylight to devise a means of getting out of Perugia. As soon as the sun is up, we shall be found, even if we squeeze ourselves into a rathole."

It was much later when Tizzo looked up and saw the pale blue-green invading the sky and making the stars a trifle dim.

"Day is almost here," he said, "and we are no nearer the solution."

"True," said Melrose. "But the glory is, Tizzo, that when we are found, I shall be able to swing a sword and die like a man. Strength has come back to me!"

The girl stirred a little. She, abandoning the problem to the two men, had been sound asleep, her head on the shoulder of Tizzo. Now she yawned and stretched, then rose, settled her hat on her head, and looked about her.

"What have you decided, my masters?" she asked.

"We have decided that Perugia is as good a place as the next one to die in," said Tizzo.

"We could try to get over the wall at some low place," said the girl.

"The walls have a double guard," said Tizzo. "We might begin to climb down, but we'd be full of crossbow quarrels before ever we got to the bottom of the great walls."

"Can we bribe the guard at a gate?"

"I've thought of that. But nothing we can offer will be worth a tithe of the immense reward that Jeronimo della Penna will give for our capture."

"That is true, of course," said the girl.

She began to walk up and down, whistling very softly.

Then she said: "Tizzo, if I cannot follow you, you must follow me."

[212]

"How?" he asked.

"In silence and with a little hope," she answered. "Come! Let us go!"

CHAPTER

45

ALFREDO, the son of Lorenzo, got to the stable shed, fed his mules, harnessed them, watered them, and at last led them out to hitch them to the vast two-wheeled cart whose creakings and squeakings could be heard almost through Perugia. The cart was heaped with a load of rubbish of all sorts, collected in the latter half of the preceding day.

But as he brought the mules out, pulling their stubborn heads along with a powerful hand, he saw three figures, dim in the half-light of the dawn, standing in his yard. One, the largest by far of the three, leaned against the wall, as though very weary. Another remained near the big man, wrapped in a cloak.

The third, a mere strip of a boy, advanced toward him, saying: "Well met, Alfredo!"

Alfredo picked a good thick club off the top of the loaded cart.

"Before daylight there are no good meetings," he said. "Who are you?"

"A friend," said the stripling.

"You lie," said Alfredo. "I have no friends except the gray mule, there. He would do something for me in a time of trouble, I think."

"Nevertheless, I am a friend," said the youth.

"Prove it," said the carter.

"One day the carriage of a noble passed and thrust your cart off the road. The cart was broken in the ditch. The next day I brought you money to buy a new one."

"May all the highblood in Perugia be damned!" said the carter. "The Baglioni first, because they are the leeches, the bloodsuckers, who grow rich on the labor of the poor men. Their taxes eat the marrow out of my bones. But a curse on all men who drive in swift carriages, drawn by galloping, blooded horses; a curse, and a double curse on them all. Now, as for this story you tell me, you have heard of the thing, but the truth is it was the noble Lady Beatrice herself who brought me the money the next day— the queen of heaven bring her happiness in return for it!—and as for you, you are a liar."

"I have told a few lies in my time," said the girl, "but I am the Lady Beatrice.

"And this is the Englishman who escaped from the prison of Jeronimo della Penna. This is the baron of Melrose."

"This mule next to you—that seems a mule," said the carter, "is really the winged horse of the poet. Do you think I am a half-wit, my lad? Come, Come! Trouble me no more."

"And this," said the girl, "is Tizzo."

The carter, stunned, continued to stare at her for a long time. "Let me see you," he said. "It is true that you are a woman. Yes. No man ever had legs as sleek and small about the knees as those. But the Lady Beatrice—she would never be fool enough to come here to me for help. And—if that is the great Tizzo, the Firebrand —here—here—look here! This is the thick top of a jousting helmet; yonder is my own ax.

"Let him try to split this fragment, if he is the man with the magic in his hands!"

He put a round bit of arched steel on the ground as he spoke but Tizzo, stepping forward, produced his own ax from beneath his cloak.

"If that is honest steel," he said, "I shall give you the proof you ask, friend."

With that, he flourished the ax through two brief circles, and then struck a flashing blow. The whole head of the ax sank into the ground; the steel helmet top was shorn straight in two.

Alfredo the carter actually dropped to his knees, and, picking up the two fragments of the steel, stared from one hand to the other.

At last he looked up with a groan of wonder.

"No other man in Perugia could do such an enchantment!" he exclaimed. "And it is true that you are Tizzo! And if that is true, all the rest—and—God the Father, this is the Lady Beatrice!"

He rose slowly to his feet.

"My Lady," he said, "ten thousand people are searching for the three of you. Half of Perugia will be given to the man who discovers you. What made you come to me?"

"Because you carry a load of rubbish out of the town every morning. And this morning you shall carry the three of us in the rest of the worthless stuff."

It was not hard to arrange the hiding place. It was done by removing part of the rubbish from the cart and then constructing a little shelter with the use of two hurdles and some crosspieces. Into this stifling hut the three crept, crushed close together, and over the hurdles the carter heaped enough to restore the appearance of the load. After that, Tizzo could hear him calling out to his mules. The cart started with a lurch.

The wheels were so big that the cart kept jerking from side to side as the wagon passed down the slope of a street over the big cobbles. The carter, walking beside it, kept calling out to the mules. The piece of wood which he used as a brake screamed continually through the friction.

After a time the cart stopped. There was the familiar, telltale clinking of steel as armored men moved near.

"I'm Alfredo, son of Lorenzo," called the carter. "And here's the load of rubbish that I'm taking into the country this morning."

"You won't take it this morning," said a commanding voice. "Haul it back to your house. There are orders that nothing, not even a mouse, is to dare to leave Perugia today."

"Consider, my captain," said Alfredo, "that if I turn back, I must haul the weight up the hill. And have pity on my poor mules and myself."

"Consider you, fellow?" said the captain. "Would I be such a fool as to consider you when I have myself to consider? Shall I put my head under a sword for the sake of a carter? No, I still have wits left to me."

"Let me at least leave the cart here near the gate. Then I can haul it out tomorrow. But to pull the load back up the hill—"

"Shall I leave the street blocked near the gate? Do as you're ordered and get the stuff away from here!"

"Well," said the carter, "I call you to witness that I have tried to do as his highness commanded me, but the captain of the gate has prevented me."

"What highness?" asked the captain.

"Jeronimo della Penna. He swore to harry the skin off my body with whips unless I had finished clearing his courtyard of rubbish today," replied the carter.

"Ah?" said the captain. "Are you working for Jeronimo della Penna? Did he tell you to do that?"

"Della Penna is not having any building work done in his court-yard—none that I know of," said another voice.

"Not in the courtyard," said Alfredo. "The work is being done inside the house, but the rubbish of the old walls is heaped in the second courtyard."

At this, there was a small laugh. The captain said: "Well, get on your way! If della Penna has given you commands, I suppose they must be executed. Otherwise whips will take the skin off *my* body. And that's a tune with different words to it. Get on with you!"

The cart started forward with another lurch. Again the brake started screaming, but it was a delightful music in the ears of Tizzo. Presently the bumps grew less hard and regular. The wheels were continually rising and descending, making the entire cart rock like a small boat going over waves, so Tizzo could guess that they were voyaging over the ruts and the bumps of the long white road that led among the hills toward the town of Perugia.

For a long time that journey continued before the cart halted

[216]

again, and the voice of Alfredo called: "Your highnesses, we are around the shoulder of a hill, and the sight of Perugia is shut off from us. Shall I empty the rubbish here?"

"Yes, empty it here," said Tizzo.

And presently the stuff was being raked away and poured noisily down to the ground beside the road. At last, the three could issue, brushing the dust from their clothes, coughing the dust from their lungs.

CHAPTER

46

Tizzo was standing in the fine quarters of Giovanpaolo, who had taken over the villa of a rich merchant.

He on one side of the table, big Henry of Melrose on the other, attacked a great roast of veal with their knives and fingers and drank plentifully of good red wine. Lady Beatrice, still in her boyish costume, walked up and down the room eating, with all the hungry abandon of a true boy, some bits of cold chicken and stopping at the table to sip wine. While Giovanpaolo, work thrust aside for the moment, enriched his eyes with the picture before him.

There was another member of the group, for a short time, and that was the carter, Alfredo, son of Lorenzo. He, dusty cap in hand, blinked his one eye at Giovanpaolo and was unable to name the reward he expected. He could only say: "Another pair of mules would be a blessing to the four who now work for me, your highness!"

"You shall have ten pairs of mules," said Giovanpaolo.

"No, in the name of God!" cried Alfredo. "For where should I put ten pairs in my shed?"

"You shall have larger quarters!" exclaimed Giovanpaolo.

Alfredo shook his head, saying: "Too big a bite of good fortune may choke me. Let me swallow happiness morsel by morsel, my lord. But when Perugia is retaken—"

"Are you sure that we shall retake it, Alfredo?" asked Giovanpaolo.

"The wisdom of your lordship will surround it," said Alfredo, "and the fire of Tizzo will burn a way through the gates. Oh, yes, Perugia will be yours again, and soon! But when it is taken, if I could have the honor of running at the side of Tizzo and watching the ax of his honor at work on the heads of traitors, I would have something that would keep me in talk whenever I sat down to a cup of wine, so long as I live."

"You shall not run beside me; you shall ride on the finest warhorse in the camp. What else will you have, Alfredo?" said Tizzo.

"Leave to go away for a little while and catch my breath," said Alfredo.

"So!" said Giovanpaolo, when the carter had gone. "I felt like a one-armed man—I felt like poor young della Penna, Tizzo, when you were gone from me. But why did *you* go, Beatrice?"

"Because," said the girl, "I had to see Tizzo again if only to tell him that his brain is as wild and as dizzy as the color of his hair."

"She had to come," said Tizzo, "in order to show me the trap I was entering, and spring it by throwing herself into danger; she had to come in order to save my father and myself in the first great moment of danger; she had to come in order with her fine wit to have us both carried safely again out of the town."

"My lord of Melrose," said Giovanpaolo, "now that you have come to us, you will always be welcome. Your strength will make itself felt when we storm the city. But tell me only one thing: Why did you let Tizzo go this long time without telling him that he is your flesh and blood?"

"Because like a fool I thought that the time had not yet come," said the Englishman. "What had the boy got from me? A chance to win hard knocks in the world, only! But I hoped that before long I would be able to give him a house and lands and fine horses and a whole armory of axes and swords and spears and everything else that he prizes most in the world. When I could, one day, take him into that paradise and say: 'Tizzo, all this is yours; it is your father who gives it!' Then, when I could do that, I felt that he might incline to forgive me. But, as I said before, I was a fool."

"Nothing is folly that has a glorious ending," answered Giovanpaolo. "When you have eaten, Tizzo, tell me what you have done."

"No, Giovanpaolo. I'll simply tell you what to do. Have your scouts, every day, sharpen their eyes when they ride toward Perugia, and above all, let them look toward the tower of the house of Antonio Bardi. For, one day, many flags will appear on that house, and one of them will be red. In whatever direction that red flag is placed, be sure that the same night the gate toward which it is set will be in the hands of our friends and will be opened. The Lady Atlanta, Luigi Falcone, Bardi, have all been drawn into a pact. They will act for you."

"Have you done that?" cried Giovanpaolo. "Then, if only the time comes before the lord of Camerino has advanced his men to the rescue of the town, we have still one chance in three of conquering Perugia!"

The lord of Camerino, in fact, did not advance suddenly to the relief of the city of Perugia. He was gathering a strong force, and it was plain that his thought was actually to meet Giovanpaolo in the field and beat him out of it with sheer numbers. Merely to throw his forces into the city was not to his taste.

And so a few days intervened which were a priceless gift to Henry of Melrose, among the rest. For, every day, he was twenty hours in bed, and four hours on horseback or exercising gingerly with weapons, feeling his way back to a strength which grew momently. And this same leisure time was used by young Tizzo in adoring his Lady Beatrice, in drinking wine with boon companions—for the entire camp was his companion—in playing dice, in riding races against the other youngsters on their finest horses, in fencing, wrestling, running, leaping, practicing with his great blue-bladed ax, in twanging a harp and composing songs to his own music, in the reading of a curious old Greek manuscript which Giovanpaolo, knowing his taste, had presented to him, in thumbing out little models of clay—for one day he swore that he would be a sculptor like that great broken-nosed genius, Michelangelo—in sleeping, eating, laughing, laboring, and filling every day to the brim with his abundant activities. For every moment his flame-blue eyes were open, they were employed with the first object or the first thought that came his way.

Lady Beatrice said to him: "Do you love me, Tizzo?"

He answered: "Love you? No! Love is no word for it. I love your beauty and hate your smallness; I worship your dignity and despise your arrogance; I adore and I detest you. I revere and I scorn you. If you were an inch taller I should spend all my days on my knees giving up offerings to your beauty. If you were a shade more gentle, I should perish from the greatness of my devotion. If you had not the claws of a cat as well as the velvet grace of one, I should die, instantly, because my heart would burst with joy. Therefore, never change, Beatrice!"

"If there were ten of me," said the Lady Beatrice, "I might be enough to keep a tenth part of your thoughts for the tenth part of a year. But as it is, you must be off every moment to some other diversion. Where are you going now, you dizzy-wit?"

"I must keep an appointment, my love," said Tizzo. "Beatrice, I must go at once to see Giovanpaolo. He wishes to speak with me on a matter of the greatest importance, an affair of the attack, and I am late for the appointment already!"

He rose at once and went to find the quarters of his friend.

He found there, not only Giovanpaolo, but also his father, and the leaders of the host, who quickly gave him place until he was close to Giovanpaolo.

And Giovanpaolo said to him, with a smile: "What have I interrupted? Hawking, hunting, fencing, jousting, racing, drinking, gambling, story-telling, idling, or merely silly talk?"

"I have been doing all those things," answered Tizzo, gloomily. "And I was thinking, on my way here, that a man who serves the great is never his own master."

"That is true," answered Giovanpaolo. "And whenever you are the true master, God help those who are your enemies—or your servants, perhaps. They will be rich today and beggared tomorrow. But, to the point. We have had scouts out toward Perugia all this time, and at last one has returned with a sweating horse to say that flags fly from the tower of the house of Antonio Bardi, and one of those flags is red, and lies in the direction of the gate of San Pietro."

"Then the city is ours!" cried Tizzo, in a fervor.

"True, Tizzo, true," said Giovanpaolo, "if we may take the gate of San Pietro and so master a friendly ward and the lower city. But still the main city will be lost to us, and in the higher city is all the strength and the force of Perugia."

"We may take the gate of San Pietro," said Tizzo, "and then we must rush on to the next gate into the city."

"That is the 'Two Gates,'" said Giovanpaolo.

"Which admits us into the higher city?" asked Tizzo.

"It admits us to that place," answered Giovanpaolo. "And the question that now rides with us is this: Shall we—"

"We shall strike in with lance and sword and ax," said Tizzo, "and God show Himself for the right!"

"Well said," answered Giovanpaolo. "And who shall say where the favor of God lies, even the holiest hermit? Without that favor, we shall never win. The city is high, the walls are strong, and there are many valiant and strong men inside the citadel."

"Which means," said Tizzo, "that a small party must press up close to the gate and win that of San Pietro, then rush forward and gain the gate to the higher city."

"At night?" asked Giovanpaolo.

"At night, the owl in every man awakens," said Tizzo, "but at noonday the owl sleeps. At noon we shall approach the city. Such a small number that we shall seem to be friends at that hour of the day."

"No, no. Night, night is the only time!" said Giovanpaolo. "Night is the only chance for small numbers against great."

"Night which confuses the defendants confuses the assailants also," said Tizzo.

"And in the daytime, we have a chance to recognize our friends, hate our enemies, and strike all the harder."

[221]

"But the first men in the gate are bound to be slain," said Giovanpaolo. "Who would lead such a forlorn attempt?"

"You speak to the leader," said Tizzo. "That is I!"

CHAPTER

47

Tizzo armed himself; that is to say, he stood as a passive figure while three valets busied themselves in adjusting his armor.

They put upon him the cuirass, which covered both the breast and the back. Epaulières guarded his shoulders, brassards covered his arms. There were elbow-guards and coverings for the inside of the elbow joints, without which a side slash or an upstroke might disable the stoutest knight. The avant-bras guarded the lower arms. But first, of course there was a sort of steel mail nightshirt, which guarded the body under the cuirass and might turn the point of the deadliest crossbow bolt. Then there were the cuissarts to guard the leg to the knee, the kneeguards, the legpieces, and laminated coverings for the feet. The gauntlets, newly invented for Charles VII of France, were pieces of iron sewed upon strong leather gloves, and when all of this paraphernalia had been donned, Tizzo put on the great war helmet, with its visor, and its beaver, pierced with breathing holes.

When he was fully armed, he picked up his ax and walked a few paces, making strokes and parries here and there, after which he had various bits of the armor loosened to give him a freer action.

At last he was ready to start on his dangerous journey. His lance was given into his hand, and the battle ax which really was simply a woodsman's ax was hung at his saddle bow. His sword was belted about him with strong chain. The spurs were fixed on his heels. His poniard, so useful for stabbing through the bars or the breathing holes in the helmet of a fallen enemy, was put into the scabbard over his right hip. And now, at last, he was ready for war. He was so armored that only the mightiest blow could crush in or cut through his steel plate. His whole body was clothed with a weight which was yet so subtly and cunningly hinged and laminated that he was able to move every limb with the most perfect freedom.

To Tizzo it was above all more important because he carried with him as a favorite weapon the blue-bladed ax. He now could trust to the armor to cause counterblows to glide from his body while with vast two-handed blows which he had learned from the foresters, he could wreak destruction to this side and to that.

In this party that gathered about him there were fifteen men in complete armor, and on horseback; there were also ten men armed with the harquebus. This more or less recent invention was a long tube of steel which shot out a great leaden bullet, and though the gun was slow to load and had to be balanced on a tall supporting staff, and though its range was not great, it was known that the bullets would pierce through the stoutest armor that ever was made to cover the breast of the most famous knight in the world. Thus a commoner, in a fortnight, could master an art which might bring down the greatest baron in the land. Farther north, in the realm of England, they still used the long bows whose arrows had pierced the steel plate of the knights of France at Crécy as though the metal were silk, but in the southland gunpowder was taken to more kindly.

There were twenty and five in the company which Tizzo led against the great and famous city of Perugia, perched on its height. Since Etruscan time, it had been a known place. Now a score and more of fighters advanced against it!

Tizzo had said to the Lady Beatrice: "Do you love me?"
And she had answered: "In part, yes. But I am afraid to love

[223]

you, Tizzo. You are here today, and dead tomorrow. How long will you live, Tizzo?"

"As long as my luck," said Tizzo. "My happiness is that you will not die grieving for me."

"I'd rather die fighting beside you," said the girl.

"You speak words, but no answer," said Tizzo.

"Tizzo," said the girl, "to be frank, do you love me half as much as you love the naked face of danger?"

"No," he said, "not half so much."

"If you did," she answered, "I should despise you. Spur forward. God help you. Ah, that I were a man to be able to see how you enter into this action."

Giovanpaolo said, briefly, in making his farewell: "My army will follow you, coming up as close as the shelter of the hills warrants it. But the first and the main brunt falls upon you. Remember only this—that glory is not given to those who fall in vain!"

These things Tizzo was thinking of as he approached the walls of Perugia, content in two things. The first was that his party was so small that the watchers from the walls of the city could have no idea that this was an attacking force.

The second comfort was the nature of the men he had with him.

That Amadeo, the Corsican, was the sort who would die to prove himself a more honorable man with the sword than with the dice. There was the bulk of the carter, Alfredo, looking very vast inside a suit of complete armor and carrying at the bow of his saddle a huge spiked battle mace, the only weapon which, he said, he was sure that he could manage. But best of all, at the side of Tizzo rode a knight famous through six kingdoms and the empire—Henry of Melrose, the Englishman.

He, as he rode, could not help singing, and when Tizzo asked him what the song might mean, he only laughed aloud.

"We Englishmen," he said, "have to sing of love when we are about to die!"

"I would rather sing of wine," said Tizzo, tersely, and led his men on toward the great gate of San Pietro.

There were men on the walls above. There were men on the ground beneath. There were more men inside the gateway, when

Tizzo arrived. A touch of the spurs sent forward his fine Barb mare, the gift of Giovanpaolo himself.

"Who goes?" called the languid voice of the captain of the gate.

"Friends of Jeronimo della Penna," answered Tizzo.

A wild yell was his response.

"It is Tizzo! Close the gate! Close the gate!"

Several men with staves thrust the gate shut. The galloping horse of Tizzo arrived too late. But at the last moment he heard a voice cry: "The lock will not turn! It has been fouled!"

Truly, Antonio Bardi and Luigi Falcone had not been false to their word! The spiked breast plate of Tizzo's Barb struck against the gate. It thrust open.

Spears pushed out at him; he waved them aside with a swift motion of his ax. A halberd descended, and glanced with stunning force from his helmet. He pressed on through the widening gap of the gate, while a wild cry went up from the men on the ground, from the men on the great wall above.

"Strike! Strike! Strike!" cried Tizzo, and as his mare cleared the lips of the gate, he set the example with the swinging of his ax.

They had swarmed out to meet him and they showed the valor that was worthy of a good cause. He saw a footman actually hurl himself at the knees of the mare and try to gather them inside his grasp.

The ax of Tizzo split the helmet and the skull of the man like cheese. The mare pushed on.

Then a bristling forest of spears lodged against the armored breast of Tizzo. He tried vainly to beat those thrusting points aside, when on either side of him rushed two mounted forms. The one was Henry of Melrose. The other was the carter. The Englishman swung a long, two-handed sword. The carter was wielding that mace which bristled with stout steel points.

"Melrose! A Melrose! A Melrose!" yelled the Englishman.

And the Italian shouted: "Tizzo! Tizzo! Tizzo! A firebrand! Sparks in your eyes and smoke in your brain! Traitors and dogs! This from the hand of a true man—and this—and this!"

With every phrase, he rose in his stirrups and discharged a

blow. His riding was not of the most graceful, but his handwork was wonderful. The labor of his years had hardened his muscles. His terrible blows smashed strong helmets like paper, and the long, two-handed sword of Henry of Melrose, his favorite weapon, shore through the hafts of spears or halberds with his parries, and then clove the wielders to the life with terrible strokes.

The cunning of thirty years of battle lived in his hands.

So the brunt of the battle was rushed away from Tizzo, and he was given a clean passage. He could even afford one turn of his head, to see a new rider at the foot of his little squadron, a mere lad, as it appeared, clad in gaudy armor, swinging a one-handed sword of the lightest fashion, and crying out in a voice which carried with it a certain sweetness that was familiar to the ears of Tizzo.

He knew the cry. It was the wild-headed, the flame-hearted, the glorious Beatrice who, once more, had followed him into the very lion's jaws of danger!

And he, half-exultant, half-groaning, spurred on the Barb mare and, with a sweep of his battle ax, glanced the keen blade from the helmet of the captain of the gate and drove it sheer down through the shoulder of the man, mortally wounding him.

They had won the gate of San Pietro. But there still remained before them a veritable wilderness of danger. How long would it take the forefront of the charging host of Giovanpaolo to reach the gate and assist his vanguard?

Tizzo, looking back, saw a stream of dust pour around the shoulder of a hill, beyond the gate, and through that dust fluttered pennons, and the flashing of armor.

They were coming as fast as true heart and strong horses would bear them. In the meantime, from the top of the wall, rocks and immense javelins began to descend as the wall guard joined in the battle. To remain near would be death, one by one, to all the band which Tizzo led. But forward?

He could hardly tell what lay forward. There was the inner gate, to be sure, which communicated with the heart of the higher city. They could not hope to win this, but they could at least make a thrust in that direction.

That was why, rising in his stirrups, he shouted: "Forward all! The higher gate! The 'double gate'! Ride! Ride!"

And in a small but savage tide his followers, every one, rushed behind him along the way which he showed.

Here, to the left and to the right, men were running to meet this mysterious and insane attack in the middle of the noonday. Above him, the bells of the town had just begun to beat out the wild alarm. But Tizzo led the charge straight up toward the higher gate, where the wall arose like the sheer face of a mountain, bristling with armed men.

A troop had issued from that gate. Tizzo, with the carter on his left hand and Baron Henry of Melrose on his right, smote that troop before it could form, struck it as a sledge hammer strikes a brittle stone, and smashed it. The recoiling troopers poured back through the higher gate. And with them rushed Tizzo and his companions!

CHAPTER

48

COULD twenty-five men win the double gates of Perugia? No, not at midnight, not at dawn. But in the sleepy hour of the noonday, when all Italy disposes itself for sleep—yes, that was a different matter. Men, still yawning, rose, heard the alarm bells, the shouting and the clashing in the streets, and rushed forth with bewildered minds. And before them were the weapons of the small, determined group.

They had, actually, with one rush cleared both the outer and the inner gate. But here all progress ceased. The inner guards were now at work and they came strongly on. These were the chosen men of Jeronimo della Penna, and they fought like heroes, as Tizzo soon learned.

Here was no chance to fell a few with blows and drive the rest by fear. In those days, the men of Perugia were the most desired mercenary warriors in all of Italy, and now the men of the town lived up to their reputation nobly. Shoulder to shoulder, hand to hand, they pressed in with their shields raised, their swords always thrusting like the bright tongues of snakes. Fools cut and carve; wise men use the point.

And the charge of Tizzo was wasted, foiled, beaten back, back toward the jaws of the gate. A little more and they would be thrust out through the gates, and then all the thunder of hoofs down the street, as the forefront of Giovanpaolo's riders approached, would be in vain.

Tizzo, striking with all the force he could lend to his terrible ax, was seconded by the full press of all his men, and still they had to give back, though the street began to run blood before them.

It was then that a voice shouted suddenly: "Melrose! A Melrose! Tizzo! Tizzo! Tizzo!" and there was a sudden thrust of armored knights from the dim mouth of an alley.

"Tizzo! Melrose!" they shouted, and at the same time they were crying: "Bardi! Bardi! Falcone! Falcone!"

Those battle cries were enough to tell Tizzo what was happening. His foster father and his sworn friend, Bardi, had collected some of their chosen retainers at this critical point, and now they were driving in to make a diversion in his favor.

That charge struck the enemy, staggered it, thrust it aside, and here beside Tizzo a visor raised and he saw the sweating face, and the bald forehead of his foster father, Falcone.

"Ha, Tizzo!" cried the knight. "Now to the real glory!"

A rush of pikemen poured down the street, men running shoulder to shoulder, the forward ranks bent over so that three rows of bristling spears stuck out in front. And this wave of fighters struck Tizzo and his friends. They hewed vainly at the spear-points. A forest seemed falling upon them. The horse of Falcone went down, and he himself and the brave carter struggled on foot, quickly borne down, when a great shouting came thronging through the gate for which they fought.

"Baglioni! Baglioni!" roared the newcomers.

It was Giovanpaolo in the forefront of his charge. They rode down those stout pikemen. They scattered the valiant men-at-arms. But there and then the keynote of the battle was established. For no man asked for quarter. Dismounted knights fought with the truncheons of their spears, with their swords, till these were broken, with their poniards, with their hands and teeth.

No swift movement could be expected. Here on one side fought the men of Giovanpaolo to regain the possessions of a lifetime. On the other side struggled those who had seized the goods of the banished men. To be defeated was to pass into exile again, and to be captured was to be slain without mercy later. Therefore, every step of the fight was marked with slaughter.

That first thrust of the men of Giovanpaolo brought their famous leader right up to the side of Tizzo, where he shouted: "Well done, my miracle. Ah, Tizzo, with one more like you, I could conquer the world! Forward, forward! Always forward! But these dogs still are biting when they die!" Indeed, they were still biting.

And then the advance struck the chains.

All forward movement stopped at once. From side to side in the streets were stretched great bars of iron, padlocked at the sides and jointed with heavy iron. Raised as high as the breast of a horse, they halted the animals. No beast could leap that height, uphill and onto the pikes that bristled in opposition.

So the advance was checked; and in the meantime the forces of Jeronimo della Penna, gathering force and confidence, with harquebus and with crossbow began to pour in a terrible fire from every raised place. A bullet which missed here was sure to strike there. The caroming lead left devastation behind it. One ball of lead drove through three armored bodies and a cry went up: "We are against a fall! It is murder, not battle!"

A wild panic was beginning, and if it gained head would wash the forces of Giovanpaolo out of Perugia—out of Perugia, and forever.

Then a voice called to Tizzo: "My lord! Tizzo! Here is a way through the barriers! I hold the anvil, and you strike, Tizzo!"

That was the shout from the husky throat of Alfredo, the carter, as he thrust under a joint of the chain a great wooden block, such as might have once been the joist of the awning of a shop. It lifted the joint of the chain and Tizzo, without a word, seeing his chance, swayed in the saddle, spurred the Barb mare forward, and smote with the full force of leaping horse, swaying body, and driving ax.

The stout iron was shorn in twain. The chain of iron bars fell, clashing, and at once the riders of Giovanpaolo rushed forward up the street. The harquebusiers, grown confident, thrusting the muzzles of their guns closer and closer to the target, were taken by surprise and died almost to a man, and in a moment.

Those of the party of della Penna who filled the street were numerous enough to have beaten back the charge of Giovanpaolo, but the breaking of the chains seemed to dismay their spirits.

They fled as far as the next chain and there they rallied once again.

"Tizzo! Tizzo!" went up a shout from the army of the invaders. "Tizzo, where is your ax? Open the way for us."

And again the blue-bladed ax of Tizzo glanced through the noonday sun, and the chain was shorn through at the jointing.

As it fell, Tizzo cried out: "Ah, blessed be the Saracen who forged you, noble steel! Blessed the ore that yielded you like a mother to the world, and the wise brains that gave you lore. Forward, my braves! Forward, forward! Strike and slay!"

And at that moment a hurly burly of charging cavalry rushed down the street and encountered them. There was the cry for Jeronimo della Penna. There was the screeching voice of della Penna himself. That charge beat the Barb mare of Tizzo to its knees.

It was not so much a man as a horse that had brought Tizzo almost to the ground; for in the forefront of the defenders of Perugia rode a fellow in beautiful Milanese armor on a gray stallion so beautiful that Tizzo never had seen the like of it even in the stables of Grifonetto. Perfectly trained, the great charger made short curvets every time his rider raised the sword arm, and so gave a terrible added momentum to the descending force of the blow. Besides, with his steel-shod hoofs he worked like two good fighting men to make a way for his master.

A crossbowman who pressed up beside Tizzo, seeing the havoc the warhorse worked, called to him: "Watch this quarrel from my arblast, my lord, Tizzo, and you will see the gray horse strike its last blow!"

And Tizzo had answered: "Let the horse be! He who kills the good gray horse has done a murder!"

A moment later, he could repent what he had said, for in the next surge of the fight his own companions were borne back for a moment and the gray monster swept down on him. It reared and one striking forehoof glanced from the armored head of the Barb mare, flinging her down on her knees.

With that same fall, the guard of Tizzo was thrown wide and the descending stroke of the swordsman fell full on his helmet. That well-fashioned, exquisitely tempered steel turned the sword. It fell with a blunted edge on his shoulder plate, but the blow had been enough to daze him.

Other strokes came from right and left. A footman, springing through the press when he saw his opportunity, cut off the retreat of the rider by driving his dagger three times into the breast of the Barb before she could rise again.

Tizzo, springing clear of the stirrups as the mare fell dead, struck the heel of his ax into the face of the murderer. The visor was smashed by the blow. Blood spurted forcefully out from the breathing holes of the helmet as the man fell on his back.

But the danger had thickened around Tizzo suddenly. The men of Jeronimo della Penna, having gained a little ground in that forward surge, closed about Tizzo, shouting: "We have him! Strike! Strike! Tizzo is ours!"

"Yield!" shouted the knight on the gray horse. "Yield yourself prisoner to me, rescue or no rescue!" It was the voice of Marozzo.

Tizzo, for answer, aimed a blow that made the fellow reel in his saddle. But as he fought, Tizzo knew that only the excellence of his armor was saving his life. Immense strokes rang against it.

In a moment he would be overwhelmed. And, in the distance, he could hear the agonized cry of Giovanpaolo and see the frantic efforts of that great fighter to rescue a friend.

Help came in another way. A horseman in gilded armor, a slight figure, managed to leap his mount to the side of Tizzo with a spare charger on the rein.

"Here, Tizzo!" cried the voice of Beatrice.

Tizzo leaped into the saddle through a shower of blows and, swaying his ax from that vantage point, saw the girl pitch forward on the bow of her saddle, stunned by many strokes. Either her helmet had been insecurely put on, or else the blows had snapped the fastenings, for now the helmet was knocked from her head. Beneath it there was no coif of chain mail belonging to the hauberk which most fighters wore for a greater security. She had avoided that crushing weight; and now her head was naked; her hair flowed free.

Tizzo, groaning, drove his new horse between her and the press of danger, but not before he heard the shout of Marozzo: "It is the Lady Beatrice. A thousand, two thousand ducats to the man who takes her alive!" And a moment later, as Tizzo sweated and fought, he heard the same voice yelling: "After her! After her! Giovanni—Tadeo—Marco! With me and after her!"

Tizzo, looking askance, saw that the girl had forced her horse through the mouth of a narrow alley and was fleeing at full speed; but after her ran the great gray stallion of Marozzo like a greyhound after a rabbit.

Then a wave of hard-fighting men swept up to him from behind —a wave whose steel forefront was composed of Luigi Falcone, the sword of Lord Melrose, Giovanpaolo himself, and that terrible, long-striding carter.

He gave them no thanks for saving his life. And through a gap behind their advance, he drove his horse presently down the side alley.

CHAPTER

49

SHE would flee where? All through Perugia the tumult was not spread. Here and there men would be arming and issuing from their houses singly or in groups. But the major portion of the fighting citizens must be gathered about the focus of uproar where the forces of Giovanpaolo had burst through the gates of the town. In all the rest of the city, where would Beatrice find a harborage?

He remembered then the Lady Atlanta. Her charity was greater than the sea; her kindness was without limit except to traitors. And Beatrice, riding for her life, surely would remember this friend.

Tizzo drove his horse at frantic speed straight for the palace of the Lady Atlanta.

There were, as he had expected, small, hurrying groups of men-at-arms proceeding toward the battle. As they saw the fugitive, they cried out to stop him and asked which way the fighting inclined. But Tizzo gave them no answer. They might as well have been howling dogs.

Twice his horse skidded at paved turns and was almost down. But at last he had reached the entrance to the courtyard of the famous house and found inside it half a dozen men in full armor who were beating with maces and axes at the main door of the house. And inside the house the shrill voices of frightened women ran up and down the stairs as they fled for safety and found no place to go.

Tizzo, lifting himself in the stirrups, shouted: "Baglioni! At them, men! No quarter! Baglioni! Baglioni!"

He turned in his saddle as though waving a charge to follow him, then spurred straight across the courtyard. They did not wait for him. A last shower of blows burst in the entrance door, but three of the men-at-arms who had followed Marozzo scattered to this side and that, yelling as though hot steel were already in them.

Mateo Marozzo himself, with only two companions, pushed through the opened doorway and there turned. They could see, now, that there was but a single rider coming at them, and Marozzo knew that single horseman very well indeed.

"It is Tizzo!" he yelled to his companions. "We are three and he is only one. Call back the others. Living or dead—two—three—four thousand ducats! Five thousand ducats! In the name of God, strike hard—be valiant—"

To try to push through that doorway on foot seemed a madness. Tizzo did not attempt it. His spurs bit cruelly deep into the tender flanks of his horse as he hurled it straight toward the threshold. Like a true warhorse, taught to charge even at a stone wall, it leaped the lower steps in splendid style, and, striking the smooth, polished tiles inside the great doorway, skidded and was flung from its feet. But the swinging ax of Tizzo, before the horse fell, had cloven through the helmet of one of those defenders.

As the charger crashed against the wall and dropped with a broken neck, Tizzo leaped clear of the fall and then he saw the man he had struck to the brain make a stumbling run with his armored, empty hands extended. Right against the tall curtains of red velvet that cloaked a side doorway the man plunged and when he fell the curtains came with his fall. That was not all that was involved. For when the outer door was closed, the inner hall was dusky dim even in the middle of the day. Four graceful lamps of silver hung by silver chains from wall brackets about which the looped cords of the curtains were also fitted. They were deep lamps of an Arabic pattern and filled full every day with a scented oil whose burning carried a gentle fragrance up the main stairway and through all the rooms of the great house. These lamps were torn down, brackets and all, by the fall of the man-at-arms who lay across the open threshold, now, with the velvet heaped in great folds about and above him. The spilled oil was instantly ignited; the flames leaped wildly and made the shadow of Tizzo spring and dance before him like a dark giant as he attacked Marozzo and the other.

Mateo Marozzo, halting with his companion at the first broad landing, shouted: "Stand with me, Tadeo! Two to one and the slope to climb is good odds even against a devil like Tizzo. Stand fast and strike hard!"

And a wild glory came up in Tizzo, so that he danced rather than ran up the steps. Out of his throat rang the words of the song of the grape harvest.

> September, golden with stain of the sun;
> September, crimson with blood of the grape;
> Under my feet the juices run
> And into my soul the joys escape!

And he shouted, as he reached them: "Oh, Mateo, now we should have music for this dance! Sing, dog! Sing!"

Tadeo was a good, stout fighter, and now he made a sweeping stroke with his two-handed sword that could have cleft the head of Tizzo from his shoulders as neatly as a flower is snipped from the throat of its stalk. But Tizzo dipped his head under the blow and struck from beneath, upward.

The ax, well-aimed, snapped the rivets at the base of the cuirass and with its flawless edge slashed through the chain mail of the hauberk beneath; only the bone of the ribs stayed the stroke, and a great, red gush of blood poured out from the wound.

The man gave back.

"Forward, Tadeo!" yelled Marozzo. "Forward! Forward! Brother, we strike and conquer together!"

Shouting out this, he turned and fled with all his might up the stairs.

But Tadeo, ignorant of this desertion, deeply wounded and tormented with pain, drove bravely in at Tizzo again.

"Your master has left you!" cried Tizzo. "Give back, Tadeo! Save yourself, man! The traitor has taken to his heels."

Tadeo did not seem to hear. Groaning, he flung himself at Tizzo and struck again, mightily, with the long sword.

The ax swung in a lightning arc. The blade of the great two-handed sword snapped like glass—and Tadeo, throwing aside the useless weapon, snatched out a poniard and grappled Tizzo in mighty arms.

They fell together and rolled over and over to the bottom of the stairs, the clashing armor making an immense uproar. Only the confusion of that fall prevented Tadeo from driving his poniard through the breathing holes of Tizzo's helmet. But as they reached the level of the floor at the foot of the steps, Tizzo's own dagger found the rent in the side armor which his ax already had made. Through that he stabbed twice and again, deep into the vitals.

Tadeo fell prone. With his last of life, he dug his poniard blindly into the tiles of the floor.

A roar of fire was in the ears of Tizzo; thick, rolling clouds of smoke billowed up the stairway. For the flaming curtains had kindled the woodwork of the lower hall. It was still possible to leap across the threshold to the safety of the courtyard beyond, but the fire had licked its way to the ceiling. It had run up the carved wood at the sides of the stairs. The whole house was being given to the flames!

But Tizzo turned and sprang back up the stairs.

Somewhere in that house was Mateo Marozzo searching for the Lady Beatrice. And even the noble dignity of Lady Atlanta would be unable to shield her young friend.

On the upper level Tizzo ran into a great, empty hall where smoke was already circling before the painted faces on the frescoed walls. The roar of the fire was increasing momently behind him.

A locked door on his right he burst open with a hammerstroke from the back of the ax, and as the door sprung wide, he heard a wild screaming of many women.

There they were, heaped together like sheep afraid of the cold —or the wolf. He saw their hands held up and their faces distorted by screaming as though murderers were already dragging them by the hair of the head.

But neither the Lady Atlanta nor Beatrice was among them. Either would have stood like a proud tower among all these cowards.

He rushed from that room, through the length of the hall again, shouting: "Beatrice! Beatrice! Beatrice! It is Il Tizzo! Beatrice, in the name of God—"

He seemed to hear voices, but as he came to a halt, listening, he knew that it was merely the distant screeching of the serving women.

Another locked doorway barred his way. His ax beat it open and he sprang into a bedroom in wild disarray. The curtains had been half ripped from the great four-poster bed. A tapestry sagged from the wall in deep folds, making a forest scene tumble topsy turvy as though waves from a green sea were breaking over the woodland scene.

And still there was no sign or sound to lead him.

He held up both hands. From the ax in one of them, warm blood trickled down over his right arm. He prayed aloud, panting out the words like a sobbing child: "Kind St. Christopher, noble patron of the unhappy, sweet St. Christopher, the guard of the traveler, show me the way to my lady, and I vow on your shrine two candlesticks of massy gold, set around with pearls, and on the altar I shall spread—"

But here he saw a flight of winding steps which rose from a corner of the room and his prayer was interrupted.

Up those stairs he ran, till the winding of them had him dizzy, and past one narrow tower room, and then past another, until he came to the wildest sight his eyes would ever see.

For there on the open loggia at the summit of the tower stood Mateo Marozzo in broken, stained armor, sword in hand, and in the corner of the loggia, facing him, was the noble Lady Atlanta, with her white nun's face and her cowl of black; and behind her on the loggia railing, dizzily poised against a background of narrow towers and the sun-flooded sky, stood Lady Beatrice. The loosened hair blew over her shoulders; the sun burned on her gilded armor.

If a thousand words had been spoken, they would not have told Tizzo more than this silent picture.

"Mateo!" he shouted.

His voice staggered Marozzo as though it were a stabbing point of steel. Then, whirling, Marozzo sprang at him with such a screech of hysterical fear that even Tizzo was daunted.

That was why the swordstroke of Marozzo glanced from his

helmet and drove him back half a step. And Mateo Marozzo, springing past, was already at the head of the winding stairs.

There Tizzo overtook him. The blade of his ax split the steel helmet like a block of wood. And as he stood back, he could hear the body falling with a loose, pausing, clashing uproar down the stairs.

"The house is burning!" he shouted to Lady Atlanta. "Drag your screaming women fools to put out the flames. Beatrice, I come again, quickly. Stay here in quiet. . . . Beautiful Beatrice, I adore you! Farewell!"

CHAPTER

50

THEY were gone from the courtyard, all the men and the horses. And Tizzo, running fast, left the smoking house of Lady Atlanta without another thought. Now that the beast Marozzo was dead, Atlanta would know how to bring her screeching household back to its senses. They had at least a fair chance of saving the house. And the uproar of the battle called Tizzo like the sound of a thousand trumpets. Angels could not have made a music that would have been sweeter to his ears.

A wounded man propped against a wall, groaning and dying, was nothing to Tizzo. What mattered was the well-harnessed warhorse that stood beside the stranger—a Barb mare like Tizzo's own. Instantly in the saddle of it, Tizzo drove at a gallop for the fight.

It had hardly moved from the spot where he left it. In that narrow-fronted melee, arms were already terribly wearied from constant striking. And from the nearest side alley, Tizzo burst into the throng shouting: "Baglioni! Tizzo for Baglioni! Melrose and Baglioni! Tizzo for Baglioni!"

He saw mighty workmen in the front rank, his father, Giovanpaolo, Falcone and others, but no voice was more welcome to his ears than the roar of Alfredo the carter. It was he who brought up the block at once, and the blue-bladed ax of Tizzo cleft the chains of that barrier.

The stream of the assailants instantly surged well forward.

A shrill screaming trailed through the air. Women were seen by Tizzo leaning out of windows, screeching prayers to one side and benedictions upon the other. He could not tell whether he were blessed or cursed, so he laughed as he spurred the Barb mare forward.

That terrible ax which was tempered to cleave all day like clay the hard olive wood, now struck right and left and with every lifting of it, the blood ran down the handle of the weapon. Blood bathed Tizzo himself, turned the brightness of his armor dim, drooped the plume of his helmet. But still his battle cry was as savage as at first:

"Melrose! Melrose! Baglioni! Tizzo to the rescue! Melrose! Melrose!"

The strange sounding name of the Englishman beat now into the ears of many who were not long to live. For the pressure of the inward stream was far greater than those who stood in defense could endure.

It was the failure of the chains that broke their spirits. On those great linked iron bars they had depended to prevent any action of mounted men in the streets of the town, and yet in spite of this impediment, the men of Giovanpaolo had pressed forward. And when new chains were encountered, before the men of Jeronimo della Penna could rally in force, the blue-bladed ax of Tizzo had cloven the iron of the joint and caused the chain to drop.

It was that strange ax in the hands of Tizzo that caused the panic to start, that shower of terrible ax blows, and the laughter of the man who wielded the weapon.

[239]

But that was not all. As he laughed, he was also cursing.

There pushed forward at his side the great bulk of the invincible carter with his mace and the huge form of the Englishman, ever wielding the great, two-handed sword.

They would hear him say: "Now for you, you fine knight of the red plume! Have at you! Melrose! Baglioni! Tizzo! Tizzo!"

Those last words seemed to strike a dreadful hypnosis through the limbs of the listeners. And then the terrible ax swayed, flashed, fell, was newly bathed in crimson, and the hoofs of the fierce Barb mare trampled another fallen form.

There were men—horrible to tell—who cried out for mercy, when they heard the cry of "Tizzo! Tizzo!" But the relentless ax soared and fell, unheeding.

Then a slight form bore up behind him and the voice of the Lady Beatrice called: "Are you man or devil? Tizzo, in the devil's name, since you care nothing for that of the Lord, show mercy!"

After that, the terrible ax forebore some of those who screamed out in surrender.

For the battle was no longer a battle. It was rout.

The labor of mounting the steep streets had ended. There was level going across the top of the town, and here the assailants were able to make a faster progress, until they came into the piazza before the cathedral.

Ten times, at least, rushing forward with a hungry purpose, Tizzo had made at the form of a knight armed cap-a-pie who continually shouted: "Della Penna! Della Penna! To me, brave hearts, good friends! Della Penna!"

And always he was shut away by a press of many men and hard blows.

It was as they entered the piazza that he saw a man who was armored with nothing whatever, and who carried a sword which he never raised, and the face of the man was the drawn, pale caricature of the features of the chief of traitors, Grifone Baglioni.

Tizzo was close enough to see Giovanpaolo spur toward this man and then halt his horse, shouting: "Is it you—you—"

Then he cried out: "Go your way—I shall not cover my hands with the blood of our house, as you have done! I shall not strike at you, Grifone!"

And he swerved his furious horse away from that target.

But Tizzo, crying out: "Let him stand! No man touch him!" found that his voice was wasted. For savage swords raised, and Grifone, expert swordsman that he was, never raised blade to defend his life. He fell under twenty strokes, and the wash of the battle poured over him.

This Tizzo saw askance, and giving up his struggle to reach the spot, as he saw the traitor fall, pushed fiercely onward toward the figure with the white plume above the helmet about whom men were constantly rallying.

"Della Penna!" was the cry that bubbled from the lips of the warriors who thronged about that tall form on the great black horse.

And Tizzo rushed the swift Barb mare toward the figure, shouting: "Melrose! Melrose! Tizzo! Tizzo!"

And he saw the man of the white plume snatch a lance from the hand of a man beside him, a great lance with a hooded hand-hold. Then, bowed above the long spear, della Penna rushed back to meet that implacable pursuer.

To Tizzo, it was like the first movement of a dance. He waited till the last instant, then with an upward stroke of the ax head, he knocked the lance aside and, with a half-swing of the ax, brought it sheer down on the crest of the knight. That blade was sadly battered and blunted by the cleaving of solid armor. But the true Damascus steel had kept its temper; and as a hatchet cleaves the block of wood, so that stroke cleft the helmet of della Penna.

He did not live to cry out once more. His body, lurching side-wise from the saddle, seemed reaching for the ground to break the force of his fall. And then the armored body crashed on the stones of the pavement loudly enough to be heard above the battle.

It was the final stroke.

There broke out, after it, a wild uproar of fear. No one remained to reward valor, and therefore all men fled. Moreover, the height of the town had been taken. As for the men who had supported the traitors, they took to their horses and poured out of Perugia as from a spot afflicted by the plague, and yet most of them had thought to spend the rest of their lives in the place as lords of the multitude.

So the fall of della Penna unnerved his followers. And the men of Giovanpaolo rushed hard on their traces.

It was said that fugitives from the battle were slain as far as ten miles on the other side of the city. And this was true.

It was said that a certain number closed themselves into the cathedral and were there cut down by the inbreaking forces of Giovanpaolo. But this was false. For the garrison of the cathedral surrendered when Giovanpaolo, unwilling to cover the floor of the house of God with blood, permitted the men inside to depart in peace.

But Perugia, down to the farther ward, was conquered and pacified all on one night, and blood ran on every street of the town.

CHAPTER

51

THERE was a scene which Tizzo did not see, but which remains to this day famous through all of Italy.

For the Lady Atlanta, with four of her maidens as a train, advanced through the bloodstained streets of Perugia as far as the main piazza where the cathedral still stands. There she walked among the dead until she came to a place where a man lifted up his unarmored hand.

And that was Grifone.

Some say that they said a great many things. Some say that it was a scene sufficient to cover many pages of a record. But what actually happened was as follows:

The Lady Atlanta, dropping on her knees, caught the hand of her dying son and called out to him. What he said in answer was: "Bartolomeo! Guido! Give me my armor! I must go out and fight gentlemen as though they were dogs!"

At this Lady Atlanta said to him: "It is I, my son! It is your mother, and therefore speak to me."

But Grifone said: "I am already in hell. She would not speak to me. It is some lying devil!"

In spite of what is written in other places, this is all that Lady Atlanta spoke to her son, and those were the words which he answered.

Afterwards, her women lifted the dead body and carried it away. There were a number of men who would have been glad to strike a weapon into the dead body of the chief traitor, who allowed the noblest of his kindred to be killed by treason on the night of the Great Betrayal, but the fact is that all men drew aside when they saw the black-robed figure of Lady Atlanta carrying her son from his dying place.

There were not many, however, who commented on the fact that he abandoned his house and rushed out into the street without armor, or that he failed to lift his famous sword in defense of his head. This, however, was the truth.

What between the taking and the retaking of the city of Perugia, there was hardly a house in the town which had not been plundered at least once. Therefore, very few of the citizens had a reason to rejoice. But it must be said that one of the most cheerful voices that was raised inside the town, on days that followed, was that of Alfredo, the son of Lorenzo, who appeared at his old task, except that he now had under him three four-mule teams, each pulling a high-wheeled cart, each cart driven by a special driver. The one-eyed man remained at his house unhappily roving up and down all day and regretting the vanished times of his hard work, but all his neighbors looked up to him as to a mountain.

In those days, there were many changes.

[243]

Great men were pulled down. Many heads of traitors fell on the block. And new men were made rich and famous.

Luigi Falcone gained a name as a great soldier instead of the repute of a scholar, only, and Henry of Melrose was given the rental of so many houses that he was made rich to the end of his days.

But Tizzo was not there. He was gone.

When men asked what had been done to reward the man who had prepared the way for the recapture of Perugia and who in person had formed the sharp edge of the entering wedge, they were told that he had disappeared.

And this was true. For all of the men who loved him, and they were many, were unable to find any trace of him until several days after the fall of the town.

It was at that time that the Lady Beatrice entered the room of her brother, now sole lord of Perugia, and threw a letter down on the table.

"News from whom?" asked Giovanpaolo.

"From the devil, I think!" said the girl.

She flung herself down on a chair and the tears began to run down her face as her famous brother began to read aloud, slowly:

Beatrice, blessed among women, my beloved, and most worthy of all loving, my glorious lady, my bravest and best of women, sweetest and dearest, a word from one who loves you to distraction, who dies for the lack of you, whose breath is not drawn because you are not near him, who cannot eat or drink without having the taste of his food and his wine filled by the thought of you,

My noble Beatrice,

Why am I not there in Perugia to share in your high joy? Why am I not there to grasp the hand of my father and my foster father and to make us lifelong friends?

Why am I not there to take you to the altar of our everlasting happiness?

Alas, Beatrice, in the battle I saw a scoundrel of a traitor who was mounted on a great gray stallion.

I saw him, and my eyes would not believe, and I chased him, and he fled.

For two days he fled.

But tomorrow I shall find him, without a doubt. I shall return riding the great horse perhaps long before this letter reaches you.

And in the meantime, my heart yearns for you.

I curse the villain who rode a horse so mighty that I could not help but pursue him.

Farewell.

I love you, my heart breaks for you, my blood runs cold in longing for you.

Farewell again. Keep my memory near your heart. Remember me to the great hero, to my father, and to Luigi Falcone. And to Antonio Bardi.

God, how much of my heart remains behind me in Perugia! But the gray horse I must have, and will have, and shall have.

Farewell again,
TIZZO